THE ROSIE BLACK CHRONICLES

GENESIS

THE ROSIE BLACK CHRONICLES

GENESIS

LARA MORGAN

WALKER BOOKS
AND SUBSIDIARIES
LONDON • BOSTON • SYDNEY • AUCKLAND

First published in 2010
by Walker Books Australia Pty Ltd
Locked Bag 22, Newtown
NSW 2042 Australia
www.walkerbooks.com.au

The moral rights of the author and illustrator have been asserted.

Text © 2010 Lara Dodd

All rights reserved. No part of this publication may be reproduced, stored in a retrieval system, or transmitted in any form or by any means – electronic, mechanical, photocopying, recording or otherwise – without the prior written permission of the publisher.

National Library of Australia Cataloguing-in-Publication entry:

Morgan, Lara.
Genesis / Lara Morgan.
ISBN: 978 1 921529 39 9 (pbk.)
Series: Morgan, Lara. Rosie black chronicles; bk. 1.
For secondary school age.

A823.4

Cover image © Shutterstock.com/aggressor
Typeset in Adobe Garamond
Printed and bound in Australia by Griffin Press

10 9 8 7 6 5 4 3 2

For Amanda, my friend

CHAPTER 1

Rosie shone her torch down among the scattered bricks. The light picked over dust and thick spider webs, and slid down into a deep fissure in the tunnel wall. She leaned forward to peer into it, then let out an exclamation that echoed in the darkness.

"What is it?" Juli said.

"There's something in here."

Rosie bent over and reached down into the gap. Her fingers brushed past cobwebs then touched something hard. It felt like a box. She grasped it and pulled, waggling it from side to side until it came free.

"Ew." Juli recoiled at the thick dust and the spider webs clinging to Rosie's arm.

"It's only dirt." Rosie held up her find. It was

definitely a box, slightly larger than her hand and with a raised design of some kind on the lid.

"Hold this." She thrust her torch at Juli who shone the beam of light down onto the box. Rosie rubbed at the dirt covering the lid, but not enough came off for her to make out the design on top.

"I wonder what's in it," Juli said. "Maybe it was buried before the Melt."

"I don't think it's been here that long."

"It's dirty enough." Juli clamped the torch under one armpit and shrugged her pack off. "We should clean it up so we can see what it is." She pulled a water bottle from her pack and flipped open the lid.

"Wait, what're you doing?" Rosie grabbed her hand.

"What? Oh, yeah." Juli looked embarrassed. "I forgot it wasn't a refill."

"You mean this isn't even recyc? It's pure?" Rosie couldn't believe Juli had been about to tip out a bottle of spring water that cost more than her shirt.

Juli made a face and snapped the lid back on. "Sorry, that's my vacuum suckage brain. You better have this." She shoved the bottle into the pack Rosie was carrying and grinned at her. "Come on, let's blast out of here. This place is creeping me out. Also, I'm starving."

Rosie rolled her eyes and took her torch back from her. For a skinny person, Juli was hungry a lot. "Okay.

We can wash the box in the river."

They climbed up and out of the tunnel, both of them squinting as they emerged. The afternoon was hot, sunlight a glare against the ruined buildings surrounding them. On her left a patch of cracked asphalt had salt-twisted trees growing up through it like weeds and on her right the rusting carcass of what might have been a car lay half buried under a wall. Rosie knew they shouldn't be here. The Old City was a narrow strip of mud and broken buildings alongside the river and was full of obvious and hidden dangers. It was outlawed, not even the gangs came here. The last time she'd come she'd almost been tagged by a Senate surveillance copter on her way out – not to mention there was always the risk of running into a Feral – but it was worth it. Some of the stuff she'd found here had bought enough food for a week.

"We should be able to get down to the water over there." She pointed towards an opening between some trees and a dilapidated building on the riverbank.

Juli squinted. "You sure that wall is all right? It's really leaning."

"We just came out of a half-collapsed tunnel and you're worried about that?"

"Better safe than squished."

Rosie dumped her pack on the ground. "Come on,

it's been there hundreds of years. I don't think it's going to fall down right this second."

"Suppose not." Juli sounded doubtful but followed as Rosie pushed through the clumps of knee-high salt reed to the water's edge.

Far out in the middle of the river and further west towards the sea, the tips of a few old skyscrapers rose above the swirling current, and King's Island, the tall stone memorial to the city that had once been, was a dark spike against the slowly dropping sun. In stark contrast upriver were the glimmering towers and buzzing shuttle lines of Newperth. The city was high-density, geothermal-powered shiny brightness – well, Central was, anyway. Outside Central things were less shiny and more prone to murk and power outages, but from where Rosie crouched, it was the apartment towers of the wealthy that stood out, the reflective UV shields shimmering in rainbow hues. Beyond them was the enormous monolith of plasglass and biostone that was the Orbitcorp complex where her aunt worked. Orbitcorp had its own spaceport, right in the middle of Newperth. Even now she could see the faint trail of ultra-heated vapour extending up into the atmosphere from one of the transports. She wondered if Aunt Essie knew anyone on it.

"Mars to Rosie." Juli squatted beside her. "The tide will be in soon if you don't hurry."

"Yeah, okay. I'm doing it." Rosie sluiced warm river water across her find, rubbing at the mud.

A dark blue, round-edged box made of lightweight metal emerged. There were four silver buttons, each the size of a fingernail, on the front, and stamped into the centre of the lid was the raised design of a half-sun with the rearing figure of a horse and rider rising above it.

"What is it?" Juli traced the sun with her finger.

"Don't know." Rosie frowned. There was something familiar about it, but she couldn't quite grasp where she'd seen it. She tipped the box upside down, searching for a handle or opening mechanism of some kind, but there were no indents, no keypads or slots, only the silver buttons. She turned the box over again and something clinked inside. They looked at each other. Juli's eyes widened. "I wonder—"

She didn't get to finish as a branch cracked behind them and someone said, "What are you two doing here?"

They scrambled to their feet and turned around, Rosie hiding the box behind her back.

A boy with dark hair twisted into a mass of dreadlocks was watching them. Rosie's insides lurched as she guessed he had to be a Feral. He was about her age, or a little older, it was hard to tell. He wore a pair of filthy jeans with holes in the knees and a stained beige T-shirt over a spare muscular frame. He had a small, slightly flat nose and blue eyes, a colour so bright and clear they seemed odd in his dark dirty face. He was good-looking, in a grubby, bad boy sort of way. If you liked that type.

He also had a knife slung around his waist in a fabric sheath. He stood with his weight resting on one hip, snapping a twig between his fingers.

Rosie tried to appear confident, despite her thudding heart. "We're just looking around," she said. "We were about to leave."

"That your boat I saw, is it?" The Feral's gaze was sceptical.

"No, it's mine," Juli said, "and you can't have it."

The Feral smirked at her. "How are you going to stop me?"

Rosie sent her a furious look and shook her head as Juli opened her mouth to retort. She shut it again and the Feral smirked some more.

"What've you got there?" He nodded at the arm Rosie was hiding behind her back.

"Nothing," she said quickly.

He raised his eyebrows. "I'm not stupid, you know."

"Really, it's nothing," Juli cut in, "but I've got some food and fresh water in my pack. You can have that."

Crap. Rosie almost groaned aloud. Why did she have to say that?

The Feral's smirk disappeared. "I don't need your charity." He snapped the rest of the twig, tossing it away, and Rosie felt real fear constrict her throat.

"Wait." She held out her free hand. "It's not charity, really. That's not what she meant. Take the pack — we just want to go home."

"Too late now," he replied and began to walk towards them, his hand on his knife.

CHAPTER 2

Juli gripped Rosie's arm and Rosie looked around desperately for some kind of weapon, but the only thing she had was the box in her hand. Maybe she could hit him with that. Their backs were to the river; there was nowhere to go. She tightened her grip. The Feral came closer.

"Please," Juli whimpered. "Please don't."

The only thing between them and him was Juli's pack, which she'd dropped on the ground.

The Feral glowered at them, then grinned and snatched up the pack. "Thanks for the present." He laughed and jogged away, disappearing beyond the buildings.

For a moment neither of them said anything. They

just stood there, staring after him. Rosie felt alternately stupid, relieved and annoyed.

Juli let out a long breath and released her death grip on Rosie's arm. "Was he a Feral?"

"Pretty sure." Rosie glanced at the river. "The tide's coming in, we should go. I've got to get home before my dad or he'll lose it – again." She walked back to where she'd left her pack.

"You know," Juli followed her, "he was scary, but also kind of cute."

"Are you serious? He stole your bag." Rosie picked up hers then swore.

"What's wrong?"

"He went through my stuff." The water and an old cup she'd found earlier were gone. Great. Rosie shoved the box in her pack and flung the bag on her shoulders. No extra credit for vegetables this week then.

"My boat!" Juli cried. "He's probably gone to get it."

Rosie swung to face her. Why hadn't she thought of that? "Come on, let's go." She ran towards the trees.

They jogged along a mud track past the derelict buildings then struck out into the undergrowth before winding back again towards the river. They'd left Juli's boat on a bank anchored to an old metal pole and Rosie was relieved to see it still there, bobbing up and down in about half a metre of water.

They waded through the silt and clambered in. Rosie dumped her pack in the watertight luggage hold under the solar panels, while Juli flicked a switch on the console. The engine burred into life. A curve of transparent pyloflex rose up around them to form a hermetically sealed bubble and a soft hiss sounded as purified air started to cycle.

"Ready?" Juli said.

"Go." Rosie deactivated the anchor as Juli pushed the throttle forward. The boat slipped out into the current and sped up, a wake flowing like muddy silk behind them as they buzzed along, staying close to the bank.

"That was lucky," Juli said. "Mum would have killed me if I'd lost the boat. Wonder why the Feral didn't take it."

"Probably couldn't bypass your secure starter," Rosie said.

The boat gathered speed and the overgrown walls and remnants of the Old City disappeared behind them. The wide expanse of water glimmered in the rays of the setting sun, stretching to the north bank three kilometres away. Ahead of them, Newperth sprawled along the river edge and back towards the hills. The towers of Central glinted, catching the sun's last light, while on the waterfront the shanty dwellings looked as flimsy as cardboard backed by the squat squares of the Banks' housing complexes.

Rosie squinted at another boat cruising along in the centre of the river and felt a tremor of unease. She picked up a pair of sights and peered at the larger vessel, then swore softly as she recognised it.

"What is it?" Juli said.

"The south ferry."

"Already?"

Rosie's guts were tight; her dad would be on it. "Can this go any faster?" she said.

"Yeah, but I'll have to take us closer to the current in the middle, there's less drag there, but there's also more chance of hitting logs and stuff."

"This has anti-collision, doesn't it?"

"Yeah, but ..." Juli sounded reluctant.

"Please." Rosie felt bad about pressuring her, but she didn't want to see that look on her dad's face again. "My dad's really strict. He'll go streamlined if I'm late."

"Okay," Juli said. "I guess I am an awesome driver." She smiled and steered the boat further out from the bank, revving the throttle.

"Thanks." Rosie put the sights down and watched the ferry move slowly upriver, away from the energy plant where it had picked up its human cargo. She didn't want to think about what might happen if her dad got home first.

They picked up speed and the hull started to jump

then smack back down in the water, pushing up a mist of spray, but it wasn't enough. The ferry was bigger and faster.

"It's catching up," Rosie said.

"I'm trying," Juli glanced at her, "but I don't think we're going to beat it."

Rosie stood next to Juli, hanging onto the low console.

"Sorry," Juli said. "Maybe you can tell him you were at the library in Central or something."

Rosie shook her head. It didn't matter what she said – late was late. No excuse was ever enough any more – not since Mum died.

They were coming to the bend in the river that swung up and around towards the Banks jetty. The ferry was level with them now, and a minute later it was past, the waves from its wash making the boat rock.

"I'll let you out at the floating markets," Juli said. "If you run, you might make it."

Rosie didn't say anything. She wouldn't make it; there wasn't enough time. She watched the ferry docking, the water churning and the engine chugging as it turned and bumped against the jetty. A small crowd of people was waiting on the jetty: wives meeting husbands, with children behind them; street vendors selling noodles in watery soup. Recyc water, of course. The knot in Rosie's stomach tightened and she turned away as Juli slowed the boat to enter the narrow channels of the floating market.

The market was a collection of interconnected floating jetties and shacks that stretched out into the river and was the selling hub for the poor. The mass of wooden huts and planks housed generations of families who had arrived from all over after the Melt. A few vendors called out to them as they passed, shouting the prices of noodles, dried seaweed or chillies. Curious children stared at them from behind the strips of cloth used as doors, and gaunt-faced people paddled canoes made from discarded containers up and down the narrow canals.

The people who lived here were poorer even than her – but not by much, she thought, not by much.

Juli guided the boat to the left to let a canoe slip past. "Where do you want to get out?"

"Just here." Rosie pointed to a jetty where a seaweed vendor was setting up shop. Juli turned the boat across the channel and headed up the canal.

The sun was lower and the light starting to turn pink as they bumped up alongside the jetty. Juli opened the bubble and grimaced as the stench of something rotting hit them.

"What is that?" She held a hand over her nose.

"Drying weed," Rosie said, trying to breathe only through her mouth. It wasn't an unusual smell in the

Banks. "It a geno breed that's got protein in it," she said. "It's what they sell around here."

"Remind me not to tell my parents to eat out here," Juli said. "Hey, you've got the box, haven't you?" As Rosie nodded, she added, "Do you want to come over tomorrow and open it at my house?"

Rosie hesitated. She had wanted to find out what was in it on her own, but how could she say no?

"Sure. I'll come over tomorrow morning, after Dad goes to work. Is that all right?"

"Total super!" Juli smiled. "I live in Central East, Darling Grove, number six. Just type my last name into the security pad."

"Okay." Rosie stepped onto the jetty.

"Wait." Juli pulled a blue plas disc from her pocket. "Take this – you won't have to pay for the shuttle."

It was a transport token for all city transport and the blue meant it was valid for a month. Tokens were expensive. More than her dad could afford. "That's okay – I can pay for it."

"Don't be moony, Rosie, take it." Juli thrust it at her. "I'll say I lost it if Mum asks. Go on."

Reluctantly, Rosie took the token, putting it in her pocket. "Thanks."

Juli gave her a smile. "You better hurry if you want to make it home before your dad."

"Yeah. I'll see you tomorrow."

"Bye." Juli was already backing the boat up and Rosie stood for a moment watching, wanting to jump back in. She knew it was too late. Dad would get home before her, but the longer she took, the worse it would be. With a last wave at Juli, she gripped the straps of her pack and ran up the jetty, the weight of the box bumping against her back.

CHAPTER 3

It was dark by the time she made it home and Rosie opened the door carefully. There were no lights on. A dull bass thump of music came from next door and the sounds of families getting ready for dinner echoed through the rest of the apartment building: doors banged and children shouted, but inside her apartment it was silent.

She walked inside and closed the door, pressing the light panel. Dim yellow light flickered on, buzzing and erratic.

Her dad was sitting on the couch, his thin frame hunched over, staring at their old photo album. The digital stills created an eerie blue glow across his face.

"Dad?" Her voice sounded small and wavering.

He didn't seem to hear her. "Dad, I'm home."

He looked up and it seemed he was coming back from somewhere very far away, but then his gaze focused and he was up and off the couch and coming towards her, hands reaching.

"Rosie, where have you been?"

She couldn't help cringing back as he gripped her arm.

"Nowhere, just out with a friend. It's school holidays, remember?"

"Holidays?" He frowned. There were dark circles under his eyes and she could smell something sour on his breath. "But it's late, Rosie … I didn't know where you were. Something could have happened."

"Nothing happened, Dad. I'm fine."

He hugged her tightly, pressing her face against his rough shirt. "There are people out there, bad people … What if something happened to you? What would I do? You must, must," he squeezed her tighter with each word, "come home earlier."

"Yeah, all right." He was suffocating her. She pushed away and headed for her room.

"Rosie …" His voice was pleading and it made her feel tired and hollow, but she didn't turn around.

"I'll be out in a minute, Dad." She kept moving towards her bedroom, trying not to see the images of her mother in the open album.

"Rosie..."

Why did he always have to do this? She pushed open the door of her room and slammed it shut behind her, removing her pack and sliding down the door to the floor.

Her chest was tight and she sat for a while staring at the dirty rug. The room was so small, her feet were jammed up against the legs of her bed. The grit from the floor stuck to her palms. It was hot and stuffy and she pulled her long-sleeved shirt off so she wore just a singlet.

She heard him walk across the floor, the squeak of couch springs, then silence. He was looking at the album again. Tears pricked at her eyes and she rubbed at them with the heel of her hand. *There's no use crying, Rosie Black.* Her mum's voice was in her head like it often was when she was upset. *Tears don't fix anything.* But what did? Staring at pictures didn't bring people back either.

Rosie had never seen her mum cry, not even at the end when the MalX had taken so much of her. It had been like looking at a ghost, a pale wraith of what she used to be. Except for her eyes — you could still see her in them, right to the end. That was the cruel thing about the MalX: it ravaged the body but left the mind intact — unless you could afford cortivide, the drug that separated the pain from the mind. But they hadn't had enough credit for that.

Concentrate on something else, she told herself. She removed the box from her pack and put it on her lap. Rosie ran her fingers over the design on the lid, tracing the lines coming out from the half-sun. Where had she seen the design before? She got up and pulled a battered reader off the shelf above her bed then searched the list of contents. There. *Space Explorations: Cosmic Companies.* She selected the code and a second later the revolving emblem of Orbitcorp, a blue planet struck across with a glittering trail of space dust, appeared on the screen. She scanned all the different companies owned by them: Geogalactic Rovers, Martian Gear Inc, Southern Skies Robotics and so many more. But none of them had an emblem anything like the one on the box.

Her stomach growled but she ignored it. Eating would mean she'd have to face her dad again. She'd wait. He'd get tired soon, and then she could go cook some rice or something. For a moment she had a painful vision of her mother in the kitchen, humming like she used to, with long brown hair, just like Rosie's own, clipped up, and messy curls floating down around her face as she made dinner. She'd always managed to get them vegetables once or twice a week.

No, don't think about it.

Rosie looked back down at the box. What was that logo? She tapped her fingers on the lid. Perhaps Aunt

Essie could help. She slipped her hand down between the bed and the wall to her secret hiding place and pulled out the palm-size com her aunt had given her.

The small screen flickered into life as she typed in the code for her aunt.

Aunt Essie was her father's younger sister. She had short spiky hair, wore tight pants and swore a lot. She didn't visit very often, just birthdays and some weekends, but she paid for Rosie to go to school at Central and she'd given her the com not long after her mum died. Call me whenever you need to, she'd said. One day Rosie hoped she might be able to pay her back.

Keeping an ear out for her dad, Rosie switched the com to silent and watched the bouncing triangle on the screen as the signal was transmitted.

The triangle changed to a star then faded to be replaced by a circling image of planets. A line of text popped up.

Hey, how are you?

Rosie smiled. Aunt Essie must be on the space station. If she was at home, she'd have been able to see her.

Hi, Rosie typed back. *You in space?*

Yep. What's up? You okay?

Rosie thought about telling her about Dad and the album again, but decided against it.

I'm okay but have a question. You might be able to help.

Boy trouble?

As if. Since Rosie had beaten the most popular boy in her class on the flight simulator, most of the others had treated her like a Feral – fringed her out. Apparently, girls weren't supposed to be better pilots than boys.

Just a project I'm working on, she typed.

During the hols?

Just something to keep busy, she hedged. *I'm checking out all the interstellar travel companies and stuff, for future reference. When are you coming home? Can I look through your research files?*

Sure. Not even in the Academy yet and you're looking for a job!

Rosie smiled. *Thanks*, she typed. *When are you back?*

Back ES Tue. Meet me at Orbitcorp 0900. You can stay the night – I'll square it with your dad.

Earth side, Rosie deciphered, and Tuesday was two days away. Maybe she could get there early and see the shuttle land. She'd seen it come in twice before but never got tired of it. She was about to type *okay* into the com when there was a soft knock at her door.

"Rosie?" Her dad called through the thin barrier. "I made dinner. Come get it before it's cold."

She stilled in surprise. He hardly ever cooked. This could be good or it could be painful.

"Um, I'll be out in a second." She finished typing and signed off, then hid the com and the box between the bed and the wall. The last time her dad had made dinner he'd broken down halfway through eating it. The sight of the few vegetables Rosie had managed to get for them had done him in. Seeing him cry was awful.

Rosie got off her bed. She smoothed her hair down then opened the door. He wasn't hovering. He was setting the table. In the middle was a bowl, steam curling out of it. He looked up from putting plates of rice down and she saw he'd washed his face and brushed his hair – even shaved.

"It's your favourite," he said. "Soy chilli."

Rosie went to the table and sat down. "Smells good." She tried to sound neutral, casual, as if this was normal stuff they did every day.

He smiled, a small fragile smile, and sat opposite her. She caught a whiff of cheap aftershave. Something caught in her chest, a grabbing tightness that moved up her throat as it sparked a memory she wasn't ready for. What Dad was like before. The forgotten sound of him laughing. She clenched her hands in her lap.

"I even got some carrots," he said. "Fellow at work traded some for–" His words faltered as he saw her face. "Anyway, have some – it's not bad. I think."

She spooned some chilli onto her plate.

"So did you do anything today?" he said. "Go anywhere?"

"Um, yeah, you know, just out, with a friend."

"A friend?"

"Yeah, Juli, from school."

"Great. That's great." His tone was too bright. "Are you going out tomorrow?"

She felt the tightness in her throat get worse and struggled to swallow a mouthful of chilli. "I'm going over to her house."

"Great." He nodded and moved his spoon around in his bowl. "And where does she live?"

"Central East."

He raised an eyebrow. "Moving uptown." His tone was still bright but his hand shook as he let go of the spoon.

"Uh-huh." Rosie felt what appetite she had slip away. He was trying too hard and it hurt to watch. The emptiness of the missing person in their lives hung between them like smoke that wouldn't clear. She took a breath, not knowing what to say. "Dad–"

"Rosie," he rushed in before her. "I'm sorry about earlier. I was ... having a bad moment." He leaned forward slightly. "But I'm okay now. Well, I'm ... look, it's hard. Your mother–" He stopped. "I'm trying, it's just–"

"I know, Dad," Rosie said quickly. "It's fine."

"No, it's not, it's really not." He seemed so sad and the wedge in her chest expanded. "I'm sorry," he said. "I know I'm not ... doing so well, that I need to do better for both of us. She would have ..." His mouth became pinched and he shook his head. "I will do better, love." He made a small gesture with his hand, like he was brushing something off the table. "One day at a time, eh?" He was pleading with her to understand. She nodded and tried to smile.

Pip leaned back against the wall, watching the man he called "boss". He didn't like the Central types, especially not this one with his clean soap smell and superior look. It reminded him too much of how *feral* a Feral he'd become. If he had the choice, he wouldn't be here, but choice didn't come into it.

He held out a dirty hand. "You got something for me, boss? I've been scouting the fringe all week."

"And yet you've brought me nothing."

"Couldn't boss, nothing to scope. Senate's been quiet this week. No noise on the radar, you know what I mean."

"There's always something." The man shot a quick

glance back towards the street.

Pip watched him, waiting. Most liked it when he called them "boss", made them feel important – sad king of their sad little heap – but not this one. He lived so far under the radar, a deep space probe would have trouble marking him. He didn't want to be called anything. No name, no trace. Pip suspected the name he'd given him – Riley – was fake.

"I could scope the fringes of Central," he said. "Hack into the Senate net ..."

"Hack?" Riley narrowed his eyes. "How? Where would you get the tech for it?"

Stupid! He could have punched himself. Think smarter. "Steal it." He crossed his arms, casual. "It's what I'm good at."

"Not as good as you think."

The man's gaze relaxed a bit and Pip hid his annoyance. The bites on his ankles itched but he quelled the urge to rub at them.

"I did steal something today, a bag from a couple of girls nosing around the Old City."

Riley was instantly alert. "Why didn't you say so?'

Pip shrugged. "Wasn't anything in it but girly crap. But they did have something else, something they must've found."

"And that was?"

"Not sure." Pip was intrigued to see him so interested. "I only got a glimpse, maybe a box. I couldn't tell for sure."

"You should have taken it from them."

"Might have been more trouble than it's worth," Pip said. "The girl pretended she didn't have it and didn't appear too eager to give it up. And I don't like getting rough with girls."

Riley was silent for a moment, thinking. "It could be nothing, but I still need to know what it is. Did you find anything in the bag, any ident cards, an address?"

"Nope, but they did have a boat. I checked it out — didn't take it 'cos it would've been a hassle to offload, but I remember the dock ident." He looked meaningfully at Riley's pockets.

Riley said nothing and just as Pip was starting to think he'd made a mess of it, he pulled a one hundred credit slip from his pocket and held it out to him. "All right, what is it?" Pip pocketed the credit and gave him the ident number then watched while Riley used his com to track it.

"It's an East-side family," he said. "Darling Grove."

"You want me to head out that way?"

"Yes. Have you got the com I gave you?"

Pip pulled it from his back pocket and showed it to him.

"Good," Riley said. "I'll send you the address and you go tomorrow morning. Keep your com open so I can contact you with further instructions."

"No worries, boss. I'll talk to you tomorrow."

Pip waited in the alley until the man had been gone for a good two minutes before he ventured out. He sidled down the waterfront, keeping close to the buildings and on the edge of the crowds coming in and out of the game hubs and bars. It was more crowded than usual tonight. One of the gangs was having some kind of party at one of the bar-cum-brothels and every wannabe was out to impress. Enhanced holo tatts and over-stimmed muscles was the look most men and women were parading tonight, and Pip kept well clear of them. Even an accidental bump was enough to send any one of them into show-off mode and turn him into a bloodied pulp.

He wasn't going to wait until tomorrow to find out more about those girls. He had his own methods, his own contacts that could help him. And he quite clearly remembered what the girl holding the box had looked like. He could tap into the Grid and see what he could find, maybe even track her down. He wanted to have as much information as he could before he talked to the boss again. Nothing killed a profitable relationship faster than useless information and he had more riding on this than just pocketing extra credit. Being a Feral forever was not part of his life plan.

Making for a break in the human traffic, Pip negotiated his way across the road, between the bio bikes and souped-up transports, and headed towards the shuttle stop.

CHAPTER 4

Rosie sat on the seat furthest from anyone else in the shuttle, the box in the pack on her lap. The air was cool but stale, and the shuttle cruised with a quiet hum along its track suspended above the streets. No one spoke. Rosie stared out the window as the crammed housing blocks of the Banks gave way to the wider streets of Central.

She hadn't slept much the night before and her eyes felt dry and itchy. Nightmares. She still got them every so often. Last night's had been particularly bad. Her mum, her skin covered in a red rash and peeling with MalX sickness, was reaching out to her and crying for her to help, to end her suffering. Her dad had even been in the dream this time, infected as well. He'd been holding her down, his skin grey and red, peeling off against her as she tried to get away from him to help her mum. She'd woken crying and exhausted.

She rubbed her eyes and stared as a block of apartments with a beautiful curved roof blinked past. The MalX hadn't only taken her mum, it had taken her dad away as well. At least the person he used to be. Sometimes when she looked at him she glimpsed an emptiness behind his eyes, as if there was nothing left inside and he was holding on by strength of will alone. A will that was failing. It frightened her.

She curled her hands around her pack. Damn the MalX, why was there no cure? Why hadn't the United Earth Commission done something when the disease first started spreading down from the southern Asiatic States? All they did was spray the mosquito breeding areas – as if that really helped. She'd heard some places near the equator had been evacuated and even some areas of the American Republic had it now.

Next stop: Central East. A pleasant female voice came over the speakers. *Please alight here for Central East.*

The shuttle zipped past the dark glazed windows of an office building and into the station where it hummed before coming to a halt beside a wide platform. Rosie slung on her pack and filed out with the other commuters.

Central East station was one of the main interchanges for the city. Identical platforms, some with shuttles waiting at them, ran neatly beside each other in a long row. Beyond them was a huge cavernous space with shops, gaming booths, electronic ticket counters and waiting areas busy with people.

The low hum of many voices echoed off the high walls, and men and women in suits rushed past Rosie as she followed the other passengers. Mothers dragged children with them and small groups of well-dressed people talked quietly. Most took a wide berth around her and anyone else that looked like they'd come from the Banks.

Rosie didn't fit here. Her clothes were too threadbare, her skin too tanned – an obvious sign of someone who couldn't afford the kind of UV protection that came with living in Central.

She walked quickly, her head up and her shoulders prickling, and pushed through the swinging doors and out into the street.

The sky was vivid blue with no clouds, and the air was so dry it sucked the moisture from her lips as soon as she licked them. Even in the shade of the station overhang the heat was like a physical presence, hot vapour going in and out of her lungs.

Central East was a residential area of low hills with

views over Newperth. The station was surrounded by a few white-barked eucalypts and large grey boulders. Beyond the sparse trees and baked earth was a grid of housing estates accessed by a narrow street that curved down to the station and ended in a cul-de-sac up against the area's huge solar energy store.

An estate hoverbus made a low humming noise as it waited for passengers, but it was mostly quiet. At this time of the day the bulk of the population was at work in the city. Smearing some balm across her lips, Rosie approached the bus. It was AI-operated and the doors swished open in a blast of cool air as she reached it.

"Destination?" an automated voice asked.

"Um, Darling Grove," Rosie said.

"Resident ident, please."

Rosie hesitated. "I'm visiting."

The AI was silent for two seconds then a short flash of blue light swept her face from an invisible detector above the door.

"Please be seated. Journey time, four minutes, thirty-six seconds."

Apparently, the machine didn't consider her a threat. Rosie sat in one of the eight seats in the oblong bubble-shaped interior. There was a soft whirring sound then the bus abruptly took off, heading up the road towards the estates. They passed a snub-nosed car at the top of the hill then turned right and sped down a long narrow lane that cut through a section of trees and rock. The high wall of Darling Grove estate was at the end and the bus let her out with the terse call of "destination" and a dim chime.

There was no one around as she typed *Shen* and the dwelling number into the keypad.

After a while a black-and-white image of Juli blipped onto the screen and grinned.

"Hi." Juli's voice sounded hollow. She waved at Rosie then disappeared again. Rosie stepped back as the huge gate buzzed and, with a click, a small portion swung open allowing her to slip through.

Ahead of her a paved road wound away through the trees and gardens that were so lush, they looked fake. Tubular solar lights were set in sunny patches on either side of the drive and every hundred metres or so was a short pole with a box on top and a number on it, marking the start of a driveway.

Rosie wiped sweat off her face with her forearm and turned down Juli's driveway. It was quiet except for the occasional sound of a bird or insect, and the heat of the road rose up through the thin soles of her shoes.

She hadn't known Juli very long. The past year had been her first at the Central school her aunt had found for her — she'd said it would be a good place to have on her resume if she wanted to get into the Orbitcorp Academy. But a girl from the Banks going to school in Central wasn't exactly popular. Hardly anyone ever spoke to her, which wasn't too bad; she'd never had, or really wanted, many friends. Her last real friend had been a boy at her old Banks school, but he'd moved away just after her fourteenth birthday. Ever since then she hadn't wanted to make friends with anyone else — especially anyone in her apartment block, where there was nothing but little kids or gang wannabes. Juli had been new also, and friendly. She seemed less stupid than the other kids, and she and Rosie were at least interested in some of the same things. She'd come with Rosie to the Old City after all.

Juli was waiting for her at the front door when she arrived. Her house, like the others, was surrounded by a wide UV barrier shade and more of the lush trees. Rosie glimpsed a private energy grid through them.

The Banks had one huge grid for the whole area and Rosie couldn't remember the last time they'd gone more than three days without some kind of power outage. She bet Juli's family never had one.

"Hi." Juli was barefoot, her hair tied up in a ponytail. "Come in. Mum's not home; we can have ice-cream."

Ice-cream? Rosie had had ice-cream about five times in her life.

She followed Juli through the entrance into the house.

Juli's home was all one level and built around a central courtyard. It had plaswood floors and big rooms with high ceilings and sliding doors made out of slats that let the breeze through.

"Did you bring the box?" Juli asked as she slid open one of the doors to the hallway and led them towards the kitchen.

"It's in my pack." Rosie closed her eyes as a blast of cool air washed over her from the kitchen ceiling fan.

"So what do you want, berries and cream or chocolate?" Juli was at the freezer dispenser.

"Chocolate."

"Excellent choice." Juli made the selection and seconds later two wrapped blocks dropped into the dispenser tray. She handed her one then jumped as three loud beeps sounded.

"Juli!" A woman's voice came out of a speaker and a face appeared on the cool unit's display screen. "I knew you'd do that as soon as I left. Hello, you must be Rosie." Juli's mum's gaze moved briefly to her.

"Hi." Rosie smiled tentatively. Juli's mum didn't look happy.

"Come on, Mum," Juli said. "It's just one ice-cream and it is the holidays."

Mrs Shen's eyes narrowed. "All right, but only one. There's vegetable mee goreng for lunch – make sure you eat that and no more junk!" She pointed a small finger at her daughter. "I will know if you do."

"Sure, Mum." Juli smiled.

"Good, I'll be home by two o'clock and don't go outside, the UV is too high."

There was a little ping and the screen went back to a picture of a tropical island.

Juli turned to Rosie and rolled her eyes. "Sorry 'bout that. She still thinks I'm five and links the unit to her com. Let's go to my room."

They headed across the kitchen and through the shaded central courtyard. Juli's room was as big as Rosie's entire apartment. She had a huge bed, a walk-in wardrobe, a virtual gaming system and a massive comnet screen set into the wall.

"Come on." Juli flopped down on the bed and activated the screen to music. A heavy repetitive beat filled the room, overlaid with lilting flute and a holo image of a black woman in a shimmering dress singing in Chinese.

"Ugh, I hate Chino-funk." Rosie sat down cross-legged beside Juli and held the ice-cream in her mouth as she pulled the box out and dumped her pack on the floor.

"Me too." Juli swished her finger back and forth over the control pad. "How about Moko?"

"He's not bad." Rosie turned the box over carefully near her ear. "Definitely something moving inside."

Juli was staring at the 3-D image of the singer gyrating in her room. "He is blasting pretty, don't you think?"

Rosie glanced up. "Too pretty."

"No such thing," Juli scoffed. "Hey, any idea what that design on the box is yet?"

"No. But I asked my aunt if I can look at her resource files. I might be able to find something when she gets back."

"Back from where?"

"Mars, or the space station. I'm not sure. She's an Orbitcorp pilot."

"Serious? You never told me. Is that why you're so good at the flight simulator?"

"Yeah, well, I guess so," Rosie said.

"Hey," Juli giggled, "remember Reub's face when you annihilated him? I swear I thought he was going to implode."

It *had* been fun beating him, thought Rosie with a smile.

"He deserved it," Juli said. "He is totally toxic." She shook her head and stared at the screen for a moment then turned back to her. "So, does your aunt live with you too?"

"Uh, no." Rosie fiddled with the buttons on the box. "She lives in Central, at the Orbitcorp complex. We don't see her that much."

"How come?"

Rosie sighed. "It's just ... um. It's complicated, you know."

"Yeah, right, families, eh?" Juli said. "Don't she and your dad get along?"

"No, well ..." Rosie hesitated. "My mum and aunt used to be close friends before she married Dad, but Mum was really against Orbitcorp and what they do — you know all the exploration of other planets. She used to say they'd destroyed Earth and were doing the same thing to the rest of the universe."

"My dad's the same. He hates them," Juli said.

Rosie nodded and said, "When Aunt Essie started working for them they had a big fight and Dad got involved and ..." She shrugged. "I don't think they've talked much since."

"Holding a grudge?" Juli said.

"Something like that. But since Mum ..." She paused, unable to say the words.

"Your aunt's been trying to help out?" Juli said.

"Yeah." Rosie gave her a small smile. "But Dad's,

well, he's kind of messed up and he doesn't like what he calls her charity. Aunt Essie basically forced him to let her pay for school."

"Parents," Juli said. "I hope I never get that stupid."

"Yeah."

For a moment there was silence between them, filled only by the music, then Juli said, "Let's open the box."

"Good idea." Rosie picked it out of her lap and tilted it.

"The buttons must open it." She pressed one of them. "A combination of some kind."

"But there could be hundreds," Juli said. "Any ideas what to try first?"

"Don't know." Rosie sucked slowly on the last chunk of her ice-cream. "We could try simple combinations, like one push on the first one, two on the second."

Juli shrugged. "Go for it."

Rosie wiped her hands on her shorts then began to press the buttons. Nothing happened.

"It wouldn't be that easy." Juli smiled.

For what seemed like hours they tried different combinations, but the box remained shut.

"We should just force it open. I think my dad has some tools somewhere," Juli said.

"No." Rosie sucked on her teeth in frustration. There had to be a way to get in. She tried another combination.

One press on the first, two on the third, then one on the fourth and one on the second button. Still nothing happened.

"Stupid thing!" Juli exclaimed and slapped her hand over the seal on the lid.

A soft whirring sound came from the box and then a click and the lid sprang up slightly from the sides.

They stared at each other and grinned. Then Rosie pushed up the lid.

CHAPTER 5

Inside the box were three objects: a small grey device, a key made of a piece of oblong metal attached to a circular disc, and a round dark green pendant.

"What the …?" Juli pulled out the device. It was the size of her palm and had a hinge on one side and a clasp on the other.

"It looks like an old digi book," Rosie said.

Juli flicked the clasp and opened it. There was a blank screen on the right and a numerical keypad on the left.

"Or a diary." Juli reached back in the box and picked up the key. It was the length of her little finger, but only half as thick, and had a series of indents and raised dots along one edge.

Juli raised her eyebrows. "Wonder what this is for?"

"Could be anything." Rosie frowned and picked up the pendant. She ran her fingers along its smooth, rounded edges. It was small – only two centimetres in diameter – with a hole near one edge, as though it were made to be hung from a chain. The shape of a triangle was carved deep into it on one side and on the other was the flaring sun with the horse and rider rearing over it.

"The same as on the front of the box," Juli said.

Rosie turned the pendant in her fingers. It was quite beautiful.

"Do you think it's from a necklace?" Juli said.

"Maybe," she said, but privately she didn't think so. It looked like it was made for a special purpose, not just for jewellery. But for what? She closed her hand around it and put it in her pocket.

"Hey, Juli." She reached for the key Juli was holding. "What does this remind you of?"

Juli frowned. "What?"

"Maybe this." Rosie pointed at the key that activated Juli's comnet.

"A comkey?"

"Yes." Rosie felt excitement building inside her. "The pattern on the side is almost the same." She pulled the comkey out of the slot, abruptly shutting off the music. "It could be someone's personal comkey."

"And if we put it in my comnet, it might link up to its home databank and tell us who all this stuff belongs to." Juli bounced up off the bed. "Let's try it."

Rosie hesitated. "It could be viral, or the Senate could link in and find out. It could belong to anyone."

"So? Who cares about the Senate? Just do it – it'll be fun."

Rosie considered it. Well, if anything went wrong, she guessed Juli's parents could afford to fix it.

"Don't worry." Juli took the key. "I'll do it." And before Rosie could stop her, she pushed it into the slot of her comnet.

For a moment nothing happened, and then the screen turned bright blue and a series of numbers and letters began appearing at the top in seemingly random order. Long lines of them filled the screen. Two lines became three, three became four, coming faster and faster, lines of them, letters and numbers, filling up the screen. Rosie watched nervously.

"This isn't right." She looked at Juli. The blue light was reflecting on her face as she tried to read the rapid sets flowing down the screen like digital water. Rosie had never seen a comkey make this happen before. Usually, a greeting came up from Microcorp, or a jingle started playing, but not this.

"I'm taking it out." She reached forward.

"No, wait." Juli grabbed her hand. "Maybe it's just searching for the right address. It could be really old."

Rosie waited, watching the screen fill with nonsense. Her stomach clenched; she had a bad feeling about this. "It's not working," she said.

"Just a minute. It's slowing down."

Now on the last line that would fit on the screen, the letters and numbers were slowing and then, when there was hardly any room left, a semicolon appeared and stayed there blinking for a few seconds. Rosie and Juli watched it, holding their breaths as words started forming.

```
Shore beacon activated. Code entered. Target acquired. Searching ...
```

"What's that mean?" Juli whispered.

The flesh on Rosie's arms prickled. "Target acquired" did not sound good.

"That's it. I'm taking it out." She shook Juli's hand off and yanked the key out of the slot. Instantly, the screen went to fuzz.

"That was weird," Juli said.

Rosie looked down at the still-warm key in her palm. The feeling that something was not right was roiling in her gut. "I wonder what 'code entered' meant. I've never seen comkeys come up with codes before, have you?"

"No." Juli pushed her own key back in the slot. "Perhaps it was just some old database that was out of commission and the comnet couldn't find it."

"But why target acquired? That sounds like ... I don't know."

"Like something out of retro-tel," Juli said. "You know like that old *Space Jump* show." She put on a deep voice and pulled a serious face. "Commander, we've found the fugitives – target is acquired. Should we shoot them with our death rays?" She got up on her knees, put her hands on her hips and pulled her chin into her neck, mimicking the commander. "Yes, Captain, shoot them, shoot them all. They are scum, they are toe jam. Squish them like bugs." She made a gun out of her hands and pretended to shoot at the screen.

Rosie smiled. Perhaps she was overreacting. They were only words and, really, what were the chances of it meaning anything? It probably was just an old database like Juli said.

"Come on." Rosie put the key back in the box. "Let's check out that diary."

"Okay." Juli giggled. They went back over to the bed and propped themselves up against the pillows.

"Do you think it's a com?" Juli said.

"Could be." Rosie opened it up and touched a small button under the screen. It flickered into static and then slowly stabilised until it was lit by a bright pink background with little stars bursting all over it.

"Pretty," Juli said. "I bet we need a code to access it."

"Yeah, but it must have been owned by a girl. There's no way a boy would have stars."

Juli leaned in and tried pressing some of the numbers on the keypad. "We'll never figure out the code."

"We got the box open." Rosie examined the side seams and corners. "My aunt might have something that could decode it."

"Yeah?" Juli picked up the box. "And when's she getting back?"

"Um, she said Tuesday at nine, but I'll check in case it's changed."

Rosie went to Juli's comnet screen and touched the icon to connect to the Grid. She searched until she found Orbitcorp and the staff listings.

"Here," she selected her aunt's name, "yeah, it says her arrival hasn't changed. It's still Tuesday morning."

"Okay, I guess we can wait until then," Juli said. "But if you find anything, you have to ping me, right away. Promise?"

"Promise." Rosie put her hand up as if she was swearing on something and Juli smiled.

"Total super." Juli rubbed her flat stomach. "Let's eat. My guts are eating themselves."

Riley pulled his hat down low over his eyes, hiding his face beneath its wide brim. He wound his way through the Banks, carrying a heavy black pack.

The sun beat down on his shoulders and the smell of salt, damp and decay filled his nostrils. The potholed streets were full of people — some going places, most not. Groups crouched together under the shade of building overhangs and porticos or sweated silently seated at tables in the cafes and noodle shops. Signs written in three languages littered the scene proclaiming everything from dumpling soup to shoe repairs. Street hawkers shouted at him as he passed, but he ignored them. He was preoccupied. Pip had pinged him early to tell him he'd found out the identity of the girl who'd found the box. Rosie Black, a Banker. Riley was hoping he'd find her and see if this box was the one he'd been looking for. He'd sent Pip out to Central East though, just in case, to check on the other girl.

He skirted a tiny park. There were a few people sitting on the square of dirt, drinking out of a communal squeezer. He was sliding past them in the shadows of a nearby building, when the com alarm in his pocket started vibrating. He cast his gaze about, then ran across the park and down an alleyway between some empty shops. Rubbish and dirt littered the ground, and a sickly sweet stench pervaded the air but he barely noticed. He pulled the com from his pocket then went completely still as the automated message blinked at him.

```
Code key activated.
```

A rush of disbelief and fear spread through him.

He dropped his bag to the ground and pulled out a slim computer, powering it up. It was risky doing it here, but he couldn't wait. How could the code key have been activated? He booted the remote antenna, his fingers racing over the keyboard, typing in codes, pinging the signal through as many exchange points as he could until he saw what he had hoped he wouldn't. There was the order.

```
Shore beacon activated. Retrieval team to
recon status.
```

Helios had got the alert as well — and acted on it. It couldn't be coincidence. That box the girls had found must be the one he was looking for. But why, why would they have used the key? They couldn't possibly have known what it was. His fingers flew over the keyboard as he searched for where the beacon signal had come from. Seconds ticked by. Then he found it. The Shen house, Central East. Rosie Black must have taken the box to her friend's house. With shaking hands, he disconnected the antenna and powered down. Time was short. Helios couldn't know about Rosie Black — yet — he had that advantage, but they would find out where the beacon signal had come from. They weren't as good as him; they didn't know its signal as well as he did, but they were far from stupid. He just hoped she still had everything.

He connected his com to Pip's number.

"Boss." Pip's face appeared on the small screen a second later.

Riley didn't bother with a greeting. "Where are you?"

"Central East. Like you wanted." There was lazy annoyance in his tone.

"Do you know where Rosie Black is now?"

"She's still in her friend's estate. I can't get in there — in case you're going to ask — security is tighter than a fish's butt."

Riley swore. Of course it was. But if he could get the box in time ...

"Listen," he said, "as soon as she comes out, you bring that girl and the box to me, and I mean right away."

"Sure, boss." He smirked. "You sound stressed — everything okay?"

"This is important, Pip. If she gives you trouble, you tell her that turning the beacon on has started some things in motion. You tell her there might be people after her."

"Beacon, boss?" Pip frowned. "What's—"

"It doesn't matter what. Just get it done," Riley said then cut the connection.

CHAPTER 6

Rosie trudged down the road back to the station. It was close to four in the afternoon and the sun was as hot as ever. There'd been no hoverbus available to take her back to the station so Juli had given her a bottle of water and a disposable UV filter for her hat. The filter emitted an invisible barrier that screened out the UV but it did nothing to stop the heat.

She grimaced as a long drip of sweat slid down the side of her face, and took a sip from the water bottle. There were no birds singing and no breeze; the leaves were drooping on the trees and the smell of dry dust and baking road invaded her nostrils. She tried to take a deep breath, feeling light-headed, and wondered if this was how Aunt Essie felt when she visited the Mars colony, Genesis. The air was still too thin up there to go outside the domes without a breather. She'd told Rosie that sometimes the breathers failed and she had to get back inside quickly or risk passing out. Rosie thought that if she walked around long enough in this heat, she'd pass out too.

The station was much quieter than when she'd arrived. There were only a few shuttles docked and hardly any passengers: just the guards, a handful of mums with young kids and a group of teenage boys who were waiting on the dock for the Central shuttle. Rosie kept as far away from the boys as possible. Rich kids from Central liked to pick on kids from the Banks, just for fun it seemed. She made her way to a seat near a closed news stream booth and shoved her hat into her bag. She checked the station display. Twenty minutes until the shuttle. She took a sip of water and watched one of the Senate guards ordering food from a noodle stall. He was wearing the regulation pale brown shirt with a black collar and had a gun and a stunner hooked to his belt, and a tiny com looped over one ear. He took a bowl of noodles from the shop owner and glanced her way as he ate.

Rosie stared down at her feet, hoping he wouldn't ask to see her ident card. Her dad hadn't had the money to renew the fee yet and hers was out of date – which meant she didn't have permission to be away from the Banks. If the guard found out, he'd take her to Central Prime for processing until her dad finished work. That was the last thing she needed. What if he searched her bag? Would he confiscate everything she'd found?

Rosie kept her eyes down and took her digi book from her bag. The textbook she'd downloaded from the library was all about terraforming and she hoped it made her look just like any other kid passing time.

She hunched down and stared at the screen, keeping a lookout from the corner of her eye. Eventually, the guard went back to his post on the other side of the station. She sighed with relief and was returning to her book when she glimpsed movement in the shadows between two of the shops.

It was hard to see beyond the garish holo advertising that projected from the gaming booth, but as she narrowed her eyes she saw a boy peer out from behind a stack of boxes. He checked left then right, keeping low. His head was covered with a bit of dark blue cloth that barely held back his shoulder-length dreadlocks.

She tensed. Was that the Feral from the Old City? What was he doing here? Ferals rarely ventured into Central. If the Senate guard saw him, he'd be toasted.

Rosie pretended to read again, but her heart had begun to beat fast with anxiety and she kept a close eye on the alleyway. The boy had disappeared back into the shadows and didn't reappear. She'd thought he might be gone but then, quite suddenly, he was there and staring straight at her.

Her insides lurched. It sure looked a lot like him. She wasn't sure what to do. What if he came over and started harassing her for money or food? Was he mad because he hadn't got enough the last time? She wished the shuttle would come.

She checked the display again — still ten minutes to go, but the Banks shuttles were often late, so it could be longer. She rubbed a hand nervously up and down her leg, feeling the round flat shape of the pendant from the box in her pocket. She'd almost forgotten it was there.

The solar lights hanging from the roof suddenly dimmed then brightened and from somewhere outside came the sound of grinding machinery; the power was fluctuating. It would be just her luck for it to go off and she'd be stuck here for hours waiting for the shuttle with that Feral boy watching her.

She couldn't stand it. Was he still watching her? She looked up but the alley was empty. No face. No movement.

She shifted on the bench. She had to pee. Great timing. The toilets were on the other side of the station past the shops and near where he'd been. The teenage boys were shouting and throwing things up at the lights now, and two of them were having some kind of wrestling match. Rosie waited, hoping the urge would go away, but after a while she could ignore it no longer. She put her book in her pack and walked briskly towards the toilets.

The ladies was at the end of a brightly lit passage, and the flat white light was flickering violently by the time she got to the end of it. The toilets were empty; the long mirror on the wall reflected only her nervous face and the row of open cubicles opposite. They smelled of antiseptic and recyc water. The floor and walls were all white and two of the toilets' sliding doors were hanging off their hinges – weird for such a wealthy area.

Rosie grimaced at her reflection in the mirror. She looked a sweaty mess. Her hair was curling up from the heat and her fringe badly needed cutting. It was almost in her eyes. She sighed and turned away and went into the second last toilet from the end and was just flushing when she heard the soft slap of bare feet on tile. She froze in the act of putting her bag on her shoulder and stood listening. She couldn't hear anything but she was sure the person was still there. The lights wavered and the faint sound of an announcement came muffled through the walls. Something about the Banks shuttle being delayed. Typical.

She cautiously turned the lock and slid the door open. Her anxious face stared back at her from the mirror.

"Idiot," she muttered. There was no one there.

Irritated, she left the cubicle and washed her hands, then tried to comb her thick hair straight with her fingers. It didn't work. She was frowning at the freckles that stood out against her tanned skin when one of the doors hanging off its hinges moved and a body came flying out. Rosie drew breath to shriek, but the boy's long dirty fingers clamped over her mouth.

CHAPTER 7

Rosie struggled but the boy was taller and stronger. His hand tightened over her mouth and he squeezed her against his chest and dragged her back into the cubicle. She tried to kick him in the shins but missed.

"Cut it out. I'm not going to hurt you," he said.

Rosie struggled harder. She jerked her arm back as hard as she could and was satisfied by a loud grunt as her elbow connected with his ribs.

"All right," he said. "I'm going let you go. Just don't scream, okay?" She nodded. He took his hand from her mouth and stepped back between her and the open door of the cubicle.

Rosie tried to wipe the feel of his dirty hand from her mouth and backed away until she felt the cold bowl of the toilet against her legs.

"What do you want? I haven't got any money." She held her bag close against her body.

He looked offended. "If I'd wanted that, I could've snatched it when you were taking a leak. You left the strap lying on the floor."

He'd been in the next cubicle when …? The boy gave her a slow smile and Rosie went pink.

He was taller than she remembered, but it was definitely the same boy. He was still wearing the same filthy jeans and stained T-shirt – surprisingly, he didn't smell bad – but it was the eyes that confirmed it. Up close they were even bluer and more disconcerting than before. And right now they were looking at her with lazy amusement.

"What do you want then?" she said.

"Maybe I just wanted to catch up, talk about old times by the river."

"By attacking me?" Rosie said. "And where is my friend's bag by the way?"

"Sold it." He leaned against the wall. "But don't worry about that. You're going to be busy. You've got a date to keep."

"I'm sorry, what?" She folded her arms.

"My boss wants to see you. He says you've got something that belongs to him."

"I haven't got anything that isn't mine," Rosie said.

But the boy shook his head. "He says you got it and he sent me to bring you."

Her insides clenched. Was he talking about the box?

"You've got the wrong girl." She tried to push past him but he put an arm up across the doorframe.

"You're a bad liar," he said, and looked at her bag. "Is it in there?"

"Nothing's in here but my own stuff." Her heart was pounding. "Let me out. I've got to catch my shuttle."

"Can't." He shook his head. "Boss wants to see you. If I don't bring you, he don't pay me."

"That's your problem. I'm not going anywhere with you."

"Yep, you are." He smiled, his teeth unexpectedly white for a Feral. He didn't seem so threatening now.

Rosie tried to duck under his arm, but he moved it down so she couldn't. She glared at him. "Get out of the way."

He smiled wider but didn't move. "It'd be better if you came with me. Boss said there's others searching for you since you turned on the beacon."

Rosie froze. *Shore beacon activated.* "What are you talking about?"

"Don't ask me. But he seemed worried when he

talked about it. And if he's worried ..." He let his words trail off, watching her.

Rosie began to feel very scared now. She knew there'd been something strange about that key.

"I have to go home ... tell my dad first," she stalled.

"No time."

"Well, why does your boss need to talk to me?" she said. "Why didn't he just have you steal the stuff?"

"So you have got it then?" He raised an eyebrow.

"I didn't say that."

"Do you think I want to be here dodging guards?" He shifted against the doorframe, looking annoyed. "You just come with me, get it sorted, and I get to go home."

"What if I don't want to?"

He straightened up. "Well, you don't have a choice." A flick-knife appeared in his right hand, the blade shining.

Rosie swallowed. She could fight fists – she'd had to before – but weapons? She wasn't sure if this boy would really use it. He didn't look that dangerous but it was better to be cautious than dead.

"I'll come if you put away the knife," she said.

A smile tugged at the corner of his mouth and he made a show of folding the blade back into the shaft and putting it in his pocket. "All right then?" He moved away from the door to let her out.

"My name's Pip, by the way." He draped his left arm

around her shoulders and pulled her tight against his side.

"Congratulations."

His smile widened. "Thanks. And don't look so worried. I won't hurt you unless you try something." He led her towards the door.

"Where are we going?" she said.

"You'll find out." Pip dragged her to the end of the corridor then made her stop. He peered around the corner.

Rosie was gripped by anxiety. It was getting late. Her dad would be home at six – he'd lose it if she wasn't there again. But how to get away?

"Move it," Pip said and held her close as they walked out, his hand clamped around her upper arm.

"You're hurting me," she said but he ignored her, guiding her to the row of shops and merging with the people lingering nearby. They wove through the meagre crowd, staying behind the bright holographic signs. The guards were nowhere in sight. Perfect, Rosie thought. They were never around when you needed them.

She wondered if she should try to run for it or scream. Pip moved his arm to hold her around the neck and his lips brushed her skin as he whispered in her ear. "Don't even think about it." He slipped his right hand across her waist, holding her even closer.

To anyone looking, they might have thought them

girlfriend and boyfriend, the hand around her waist could have been a caress.

The urge to call out was strong, but there was still that knife in his pocket. Rosie kept her mouth shut as Pip took them swiftly towards the shuttle stop.

The few people around avoided them, and Rosie thought that even if she did start screaming and Pip stabbed her, none of them would help anyway. She cast around desperately for something, some way out of this mess. They were approaching the North Coast shuttle dock. Was that where he was taking her? North Coast was on the opposite side of the river to Central. Her heart gave a leap as she saw the Banks shuttle waiting at the next dock; it must have been late as usual. For once she thanked the intermittent power supply.

Pip dragged her to the bench near the North Coast stop and made her sit beside him, keeping an arm around her.

From far beyond the gaping entrance where the lines came in, Rosie saw the gleam of silver coming towards them. She glanced around. People were starting to load into the Banks shuttle. Maybe she could just run for it.

She shifted the tiniest bit along the bench away from Pip, but instantly his arm tightened around her waist. "Where do you think you're goin'?" he said through a faint smile.

"The bench is hard."

"Is it?" There was a mocking gleam to his eye. "Do you want to sit on my lap?"

"No, thanks," Rosie said coldly.

The North Coast shuttle came to a stop at the dock. He yanked her to her feet. "Let's go see the boss."

They waited behind a couple of old ladies trying to swipe their tokens through the door slot. Only valid tokens would allow entry to the shuttle and the women seemed to be putting theirs in upside down.

She could feel Pip getting agitated. She glanced at the Banks shuttle on the next dock.

"Stop it," he muttered, and Rosie gave him a foul look just as one of the old women in front of them turned around.

"Please, will one of you help me?" She was holding out her token. "I can't get it to work."

Rosie turned to Pip. For a moment she thought he'd refuse but, with a sigh, he took the chip. "You just swipe it down."

He leaned towards the slot. "Like this," he said.

His grasp on her loosened a fraction. Seizing her chance, she twisted her arm as hard as she could and he lost his grip. Rosie jumped over the bench and sprinted towards the Banks dock. Pip was shouting after her and she heard the cries of the old ladies, but Rosie didn't look back.

The shuttle's red departure lights were flashing and she rounded the dock and sprinted to the open doors, removing her token from her pocket as she did.

"Wait, Rosie!" Pip called.

She almost faltered. How did he know her name? She swiped the token down through the slot, grazing her fingers on the metal, and leaped through the doors. They closed with a hiss and a thump and she turned to see Pip an arm's length behind, but not close enough to follow her on board. He punched the doors and said something but she couldn't hear him over the detach siren. She stood shaking, holding on to a pole and looking back at him through the wide windows as the shuttle slid smoothly away.

CHAPTER 8

By the time the shuttle got to her stop, Rosie had calmed down. She'd stopped shaking and her heart rate had returned to normal, but she couldn't get Pip's words out of her head.

Were there other people after her, like he'd said? It was hard to believe but he'd sounded so certain. She wondered briefly if she'd done the right thing by running away but he could have been taking her anywhere. There were plenty of stories in the Banks about people going missing and it wasn't always the gangs who made it happen.

She got off at her stop, feeling strange and uneasy. The Banks station had a high domed roof and doubled as an undercover market. Stalls selling everything from noodles to robots were set up in a disordered maze and the dank air held an underlying aroma of dried seaweed and fried onions.

Dim solar lights barely seemed to penetrate the unruly mass of stalls and Rosie put her hat back on and clutched her bag close as she wound her way through the crowds. Mothers dressed in long robes, heads covered, snapped at their sullen children, while rowdy Feral boys chased each other. Silent dark-eyed men crowded next to a beer stall, observing all who passed, and at a retro dealer's, children crouched on a mat, eyes glued to a huge screen, watching the bright colours of toon-tel.

Rosie felt exposed and hoped that if Pip was following her, she'd be hard to spot in the chaos. He might get on the next shuttle, or maybe he'd try it on foot, which meant she had a bit longer. Did he know where she lived?

Outside, the sun was starting to go down, and golden afternoon light softened the grubby buildings and lean-tos; the calling of the sellers from the floating markets was loud in the still, warm air.

She turned down Market Street towards her housing block. The walkways were crowded and she was constantly pushing past people and stepping over beggars. People on bio bikes crammed the street and she could smell the salty dank scent of the river. She glanced though the window of a junk shop as she passed, checking the time on the laser display clock. It was nearing six; her dad would be home soon. At least she'd make it back before him. She stopped. What about Juli? She'd not even thought about her. Would Pip try going after her?

Surely he'd never get past the security on Juli's estate. Still, she should find a comnet and warn her. She raced back the way she'd come, bumping into people and getting abused for her efforts. There was a public comnet just inside the south entrance of the station, near the stench-ridden corridor that led to the toilets, and she had a surge of hope when she saw no one using it. But as soon as she reached it, she discovered why. An out of order sign was blinking, or more like stuttering, across the cracked screen and the keypad had been ripped out. Rosie smacked the useless thing in frustration. Why the hell did people do that? It was the only one in the station and some toxic loser had to wreck it.

What to do now? Think, Rosie – where was the next closest one? She looked around the busy station. The beer stall? She took a hesitant step towards it then stopped. The stall was run by one of the gangs – there was no way they'd let her use it for free and she had nothing to bargain with. She swore. There was only one choice: she had to get home to her own com as fast as she could.

She spun around and ran back out of the station to the street. If Pip was following, she'd just given him a bit more time to catch up. Fear made her move faster and she raced along, cutting through an alleyway.

She emerged just around the corner from her block. There were few people about, just an old man poking about in a pile of rubbish and a couple of women leaning against a wall talking. It all seemed fairly normal for her neighbourhood, but something made her slow down as she approached the crumbling concrete pillars that marked the entrance to Housing Block B. Something felt wrong. There was no one in the park in the middle of the block. Normally, there were at least a couple of kids scratching around in the dirt, but it was empty. The whole place felt watchful – like it was holding its breath. There was no music playing, no voices raised, nothing. She walked slowly to the closest block of flats, the back of her neck prickling.

Housing Block B was three oblong blocks, each ten storeys high, surrounding a central area. The bottom flats were separated by low walls, but those above, rose smoothly up – small boxy dwellings with one window that looked out either on the central area or the back alley. Rosie's home was on the second floor.

Nervously, she walked past the row of ground floor flats to the central staircase. All the doors she passed were tightly closed – even the old woman who usually sat in her doorway staring and spitting wasn't to be seen. Rosie licked her lips; this kind of quiet only happened if the Senate guards or the gangs had been around.

She went up the stairs, trying not to smell the stale piss embedded in the concrete. She wanted more than anything to be in her own room with the door closed. But would that be a good enough hiding place? She pushed through the door to the second floor.

Her soft-soled sandals squeaked on the bare cement. She took off her hat and unlocked the door to her flat.

There was no power. She pressed the switch twice but nothing happened. That was strange when there was light in the hallway. She dropped her bag and hat on the floor and locked the door behind her.

The blinds were drawn but there was enough light filtering through for her to see that things were not right. Dark shadowy shapes cluttered the floor and to the right of the door the cupboard that usually sat against the wall was facedown on the floor.

Someone had been in the flat. The skin on her arms rose up in goosebumps. The door had still been locked. Gangs wouldn't do that; they would've busted the door.

She forced herself to move towards the kitchen, banging her legs against the sofa as she went. The three drawers under the bench had been pulled out and the few utensils they contained were scattered across the floor. Reaching over the sink, she snapped up the blind so she could see better.

Everything they owned was knocked over, pulled out and strewn across the living area. Rosie felt a lump rise in her throat. Whoever had been there had been thorough. The sofa was upside down, the small table near it broken, and the boxes of old clothes and precious keepsakes that had been in the cupboard removed, littering the floor with bits of their life. She could even see the digi album lying against the far wall, the spine split and the memory card half hanging out. She ran to her room.

All her belongings had been gone through. Her bed was shoved out from the wall at an odd angle, the sheets a tangled mess. They'd even pulled her precious picture of the Mars colony off the wall; it lay in a crumpled heap by her other pair of shoes.

She kneeled on the bed and checked the hiding place between her bed and the wall – the com was gone. In a panic Rosie began shoving things around, sifting through the mess, but she couldn't find it anywhere. Whoever had come in here had taken it.

She sat on the bed hugging her pillow. What was she going to tell her dad? How would she explain it? She felt like crying, but stopped the tears before they could start.

She didn't have time to sit here feeling scared; she had to contact Juli. She went back into the living area, then froze as she heard footsteps out in the corridor. It was a heavy tread, like men in boots.

Adrenaline swept through her. She launched herself across the room and grabbed her bag from where she'd left it near the door, picked up the broken digi album and ran into her dad's bedroom.

It had been trashed as well, but she didn't stop to look. Jumping over clothes and scattered articles, she dragged one of the two crates used as a side table to the corner near the bed, then stacked the other one on top. The boxes were flimsy but she was sure they would hold her weight.

She shoved the album into her bag and swung the pack on her back then climbed on top of the crates. They creaked and swayed but held. Her legs shaky, she reached up to the ceiling and dug her fingers into the groove between two of the panels.

All the ceilings in the housing block were made of interlocked panels of white plaswood, each about a metre wide. One panel in her dad's room had been loosened to allow access to the cavity between the second and third floor. It was a hiding place, their escape hole. Her dad had done it. Not long after they'd first moved in, the people next door had been broken into by the gangs. The father had been shot and the mother and two little girls raped and beaten. Rosie had seen them as the medics had taken them away; she couldn't even recognise them. After that her dad had said he wasn't going to let that happen to them and made a plan.

Rosie pushed hard upwards and the panel shifted, sliding back into the darkness above. The smell of damp and mice wafted from the hole. She grimaced but reached up inside anyway, feeling a wide beam of metal: the roof structure. She listened for the footsteps but there was no sound. The boots had stopped. But had they stopped outside her door?

She strained to hear over the sound of her own heartbeat and at first there was nothing, but then, faintly, she heard the stealthy scrape of metal on metal.

She thrust her head and shoulders up through the hole and pulled herself into the roof. Balancing on the wide beam, she reached down and pushed the top crate off the bottom one as hard as she could towards the bed. It toppled and bounced down onto the mattress then to the floor with a dull thump.

Rosie dragged the ceiling panel back, setting it into place as she heard the unmistakable squeak of the front door opening. Barely daring to breathe, she huddled in the darkness.

For a long moment it was quiet and she began to

think she must have been mistaken but then came sounds from below. There was the deep rumble of a man's voice, the scrape of something being moved across the floor in the living area and quite suddenly noise erupted. The front door banged, footsteps pounded over the floor and a man shouted in a voice she recognised – her dad.

"What the–" His cry was swiftly muffled and the sounds of a struggle broke out. Her dad shouted again and then something hit a wall hard. Rosie flinched and her hands slipped on the metal bar. Next came whimpering and she squeezed her eyes shut. She should try to help him, do something, but she was too scared to move. Thuds pounded the walls and her dad shouted out again, his cry abruptly cut off.

"Take him." Rosie clearly heard a deep voice say and then a grunt and the sound of something being dragged and heavy boots going away down the hall. Up in the dark place, Rosie stared ahead shivering, clinging to the metal beam.

CHAPTER 9

Rosie didn't know how long she'd been up there; her lower legs had gone to sleep and her knees were aching from the pressure of crouching on the metal beam. She knew she should leave, but she couldn't make herself move. Somewhere to her right something was shuffling in the dark, a mouse or more likely a rat. Rats didn't bother her, or cockroaches, but perhaps scorpions ... Rosie jerked her mind back; she was drifting – she had to focus.

She couldn't stay here. She was hungry and thirsty. But where could she go? She doubted the neighbours would take her in.

Juli's? She still had the shuttle token and she had to warn her – but what would she tell her?

With effort she moved, and stifled a cry as feeling rushed back into her legs. She massaged her calves until the tingling subsided, then pushed her fingernails under the panel and levered it up. The room was dark and quiet. A faint glow of pale blue light from the kitchen window showed in a wedge shape on the floor near the door. That meant the streetlights were on.

Rosie made out the shadow of the one crate below. She was going to have to jump down onto it. She dropped her pack through the gap, then lowered herself down as far as she could, and let go. She hit the corner of the crate. It tipped and she fell to the floor, her shins whacking against the bed frame. She bit her lip trying to stifle her cry and lay there for a second, furious at the pain, before she got to her feet. She picked up her bag and looked out into the living area. The mess was still there and the front door was open.

Who had taken her dad? Was he still alive? Don't think about it. Rosie felt as though there was a hand around her throat. She crept towards the open door. The light was on in the hall; a dirty yellow glow. She put a hand on the wall then stopped. There was a smear of something on the doorframe. Fingerprints. Blood. Something snapped inside her and, without thinking, she ran out into the hallway towards the stairs.

Panic filled her, but then her brain kicked back in

and she stopped a few steps down. What was she going to do – fight them? Her dad hadn't been able to.

What if the men were waiting for her at the bottom? She stood, indecisive, taut with fear. Then she remembered the fire-escape. She ran back. She climbed up on the sink and unlatched the window with shaking hands. There was the ladder: a thin frame of steel, leading down to the alley. Rosie swung out and began climbing down. Below, the alley was empty but for a stack of rubbish against the wall that surrounded the housing block.

Around and above her small squares of light showed most people were at home, but she knew she couldn't count on anyone helping her.

The metal felt greasy and something buzzed around her head as she reached the alley and jumped to the ground. One of the streetlights on the wall buzzed then went out, plunging her end of the alley into darkness. She clutched at the bottom of the ladder, trembling. Rosie hated the dark. It meant danger, the unknown, death. She pressed her face against her hand, willing herself to calm down. Her fear was threatening to swallow her.

High above, the thumping sound of a helijet came from the direction of Central. A bright searchlight swept across the clouded night sky. Like a white wing of light, it arced across the Banks, the helijet invisible behind it.

Rosie turned her face to it, the light steadying her somehow. Pull it together, Rosie. She forced herself forward and, keeping close to the wall, crept towards the mouth of the alley. Further along, the heap of rubbish, twice her height, half blocked the way out. As she got near, she heard a dull scraping sound come from the other side and a long shadow stretched towards her.

She stopped, frozen against the damp grime of the wall.

"Rosie?" It was Pip. He came around the stack of rubbish towards her, his hands up as if she might attack him. "It's okay. It's just me."

He'd lost his headscarf and his dreadlocks were a mass about his head. The whites of his eyes seemed bright in the darkness. "You all right? I saw 'em go into your flat – thought they might've got you but …" He stretched a hand towards her.

"What're you doing here?" She flinched back, her heart racing.

"You skipped out on me, remember? I was following you for my boss." He checked over his shoulder. "Probably a good thing too. Come on, we shouldn't hang around here."

"I'm not going anywhere with you." Rosie took a step away.

"Well, where else are you gonna go – your friend's place?" His tone was derisive. "You think they don't already know where she lives?"

"You seem to know a lot." Rosie could hardly believe he had turned up here so conveniently, ready to help her. She watched him warily and said, "How do I know you're not working with them?"

"If I was, don't you think I'd have knocked you out or something by now? I wouldn't be offering to help you, would I?"

"Oh, is that what you're doing?"

He ran a hand over his dreadlocks and said slowly, "Rosie, you've got no choice. Just come with me. The boss won't hurt you; he just wants to talk. Where else have you got to go?"

"You just want to get paid," she said.

"Sure, whatever you say." Pip sighed. "Let's just get going."

Rosie was filled with indecision. She didn't know if she could trust him, but he was right. She had no idea where to go. Aunt Essie wasn't due back until tomorrow and she didn't want to sleep on the street. And perhaps this boss guy knew something about what was happening and who had her dad.

"All right," she said quietly, "I'll come with you, but I need a comnet."

"What for? Those men who took your dad could trace it. All the public ones are linked."

"Maybe not all of them." His superior tone annoyed her and she wasn't going to give up on trying to contact Juli just because he said so.

"Fine. The boss probably has one you can use. Just come on."

"Where are we going?"

"You'll find out soon enough."

"Are we taking a shuttle?"

"Yeah, right. How easy do you think it would be to spot you on one of those?"

Why hadn't she thought of that? She bit back the smart reply that sprang to her lips. She suddenly felt very tired and despite the humid warmth of the evening, a shiver ran through her.

Pip jerked his head towards the mouth of the alley. "Coming then?"

Rosie nodded. He turned away and she followed.

The central park of the housing block was empty and they jogged silently across it and headed towards the riverfront through the maze of housing blocks and shops. They emerged in the street that ran between the markets and the jetties. It was chaotic with night-time trade. Bars were open and people wandered in noisy groups from one to another. Neon holo signs, surrounded by insects, lit up the night.

"This way." Pip stepped out into the crowds, walking fast towards the jetties.

Rosie followed, bumping into people as she tried to keep up. A man dressed in an overcoat and stinking of stale beer spat on the pavement near her, and she lost sight of Pip when a group of young men cut across her path, staring at her with leering eyes. "Slow down," she called.

Pip stopped and waited for her. "Hurry up, will you?" he said as she caught up. "We can't hang around here."

"I'm trying." She spoke through gritted teeth.

"Try harder." Pip glanced over her shoulder. "The men who took your dad could be around here somewhere and if they see you, they're not going to play nice." His blue eyes were dark and Rosie was chilled by the look in them. He knew something.

"Who are they?" she said. "Are they Senate?"

His face closed up. "Don't know." He gripped her arm and pulled her along with him through the crowd. "But they had gear – not just the laser guns the Senate have – real gear. Why do you think your whole housing block went so quiet?"

Rosie didn't reply. What was so important about what she'd found?

"Here." Pip swerved onto the road. His grip on her

slid down so he was holding her hand as they negotiated the traffic. It was oddly intimate and she would have pulled away but for the thick trail of bio bikes whizzing around them. She was clipped more than once, the bikes' drivers yelling at her or sounding impact alarms as they buzzed past. Pip didn't slow down when they reached the other side. He strode towards a dilapidated-looking set of stairs that led down to a jetty almost covered by water.

"Down here." He let go of her hand and went nimbly down the stairs. The jetty wasn't fixed to the riverbed but floated free, tied only to the stairs, and a swell made the jetty lurch as Rosie stepped down. She staggered.

"Careful." Pip caught her. He then turned and jogged down the jetty, water splashing up his legs. Rosie followed more slowly, wary of the undulating surface.

The boat they were getting on was in no better condition than the jetty. It was just a skiff. Pale green paint was peeling along its side and the mast looked like it hadn't seen a sail for years. The cabin was nothing more than a three-sided shelter and a thin man of indeterminate race was sitting in it on an upended drum, a fat candle burning on another drum next to him. His skin was sallow and wrinkled, and when he stood up he wasn't much taller than Rosie. He regarded them with a dour expression.

"Got another one?" He addressed his comment to

Pip but his eyes stayed on Rosie as he sucked on his bottom lip.

"We've just got to go over." Pip pulled a credit slip from his pocket. "The boss sends this."

The man looked at the slip, then up at Rosie again and after a moment he jerked his head at Pip. "In." He turned his back and blew out the candle then went towards the engine.

Riley paced back and forth. It was getting late; Pip should have been here by now with the girl. What was he doing? He pushed a hand through his hair. How had this girl found Cassie's stuff?

He tapped a key on the computer, reading again the message that Helios had sent out.

Shore beacon activated. Retrieval team to recon status.

It had come from Madrid, sent to Libertine City in South Bay. Someone there had sent the team out — but was that all? Was he missing something?

He paced back and forth, back and forth. The room

he was in was dark and dank, and the stink of the river mud drying on the floor smelled like sewage; he'd have to wash his boots before he went back to Central.

He stopped, his profile edged in the moonlight coming through the broken window. What if he'd been wrong?

He began to type furiously on the keyboard, spinning numbers, checking routes, hacking the net. Sweat formed on his forehead and stained the armpits of his shirt as he prayed it wasn't what he thought. But then he found it hidden in a complex sequence of numbers. They were clever. He shook his head and stared at it. There had been two messages sent. The second was buried deeper than the first, much deeper, but there it was:

```
Clean Genesis.
```

Two little words. Riley's fingers shook. This was it, they were going to destroy everything. His chance to bring them down would be gone and Cassie would never be able to come back.

Cold anger formed in his gut. He walked over to the window and stared up at the stars towards the brightest and reddest of them all: Mars, his family's downfall and their only hope of salvation. Did those girls have any idea what they'd done?

CHAPTER 10

Rosie sat under the shelter of the cabin with her pack jammed between her legs, swatting at the insects buzzing around her bare thighs. She wished she'd thought to change into a pair of longer pants, but clothes had been far from her mind when she'd jumped out of the window. Where was Dad? Was he all right? She kept hearing the sound he'd made, the way his cries had cut off, and it made her feel sick. She pushed her head briefly into her hands, pressing her palms to her eyeballs and took a long breath. Get it together, Rosie. This was no time to burn out.

She rubbed at a bite, praying it was a midgie and not a MalX-carrying mozzie, and glanced at Pip. He was leaning against the cabin entrance, his hands in his pockets, watching the dark water of the river rippling out behind them. She wondered how much this boss of his was paying him to fetch her and if it was worth the trouble.

The old man sat at the back of the boat, his eyes fixed on an unseen spot ahead of them, ignoring both his passengers.

She tapped her fingers on her knees. She didn't want to meet this boss, but he might be able to answer some of her questions. Pip had said the box belonged to him. But how? The diary was obviously a girl's and there was no name on it, nothing but initials to give a clue to the owner. Maybe his initials were CS?

She felt for the pendant in the pocket of her shorts and looked again at Pip. She hated this waiting, this not knowing. She got up and went to him.

"How far are we going?" she said.

He didn't look at her. "Not far."

"Can you be more specific?"

He shrugged and kept looking at the river. "Probably."

"Probably?" She waited, watching him, but he just scratched his arm and said nothing more. The strain of the day, all the worry and the fear came raging up in her. Furious, she pushed him – hard. He staggered back into the wall of the cabin, his eyes wide with surprise.

"Probably?" she repeated, louder this time. "My dad is missing and I'm going God-knows-where and all you can give me is *probably*."

He recovered his balance and came back at her fast. "What do you want – a map?"

"No." He looked angry now but Rosie didn't care. She was sick of his attitude. "I want you to tell me who those men were who took my dad and how they found my flat so quickly."

He leaned towards her and said quietly, "You really have no idea, do you?"

She wanted to slap him. "Why don't you explain it then?"

He shook his head, a weary, condescending look on his face.

"Did you happen to check something on the Grid while you were at your friend's fancy estate? I don't know, say look up the name of your aunt on Orbitcorp staff listings?"

"What?" Rosie felt her skin prickling hot then cold.

"Yep. It would have been easy to trace you once they figured out she had a brother and he had a daughter. I mean that's not how I found you because I checked some other sources after I saw your little face," he brushed a thumb along her cheek, "but that is definitely how they found you."

She slapped his hand away. "Who are they, the Senate?"

"Hardly." His smile became bleak.

"Then who?"

"The boss won't tell me, so how should I know?"

"Really? Are you sure about that, because you know a lot for a Feral," she said.

"Yeah?" He leaned even closer, his face level with hers. "Well, you know nothing for a Banker." He walked away to the back of the boat.

Rosie glared after him.

"Bridge ahead." The old man spoke and reduced the speed of the boat. Rosie went to the small, grimy window at the back of the cabin. Ahead of them the river narrowed and the huge curved span of Central Bridge rose up like a great black spine.

The bridge allowed traffic between the north and south sides of the river and no one crossed it unless they had gone through the Senate-controlled checkpoints on each side.

As they approached the bridge, bright lights beamed down on them from above. A blue laser roamed over the boat, examining the licence numbers painted on the side.

"Get down." Pip was suddenly beside her and pushed her to the floor behind the upturned drum.

"But it's not curfew yet," Rosie said.

"Doesn't matter. This boat's only licensed for the fishing crew. If we want to get across, we've got to hide."

"But—"

"Sh!" He crouched beside her. The boat was moving slowly under the bridge. Searchlights flooded the cabin. They huddled together, crunched up in the narrow space between the drums and the back wall. Pip's thighs pressed against hers and she felt the heat of his body through her shirt. The light surveyed the wall near his head and he ducked down so their faces were just centimetres apart. He held her gaze as the light flashed around the cabin.

"Don't move," he whispered. Uncomfortable, she looked away and stayed as still as she could.

Outside the cabin the old man was waving up at unseen people on the walkway of the bridge. He had a piece of plaspaper in his hand over which the blue laser scanned. After a moment a horn sounded and a male voice from high above intoned, "Fishing vessel D542, you are clear."

The boat passed beneath the bridge and the searchlights turned off. The old man gunned the engines higher, the boat picked up speed and they were once again moving up the swollen, dark river.

"That was close," Pip said.

He rose and put a hand down to her which she ignored.

She got up, brushing spider web off her thighs, not looking at him. Her anger at him had faded. Now she just felt nervous. He was still too close.

"We're nearly there now," he said.

"Really? So ..." Rosie glanced up but Pip was turning away.

"So be ready to jump out." He went outside the cabin to sit with the old man at the other end of the boat.

Rosie watched him a moment then followed him out but didn't join them, leaning instead against the side of the boat near the cabin. On the south bank, the Central side, the bright lights of the city's towers and hoverways lit the sky, dimming the stars. Further up, beyond Central proper, was Juli's sector – Central East – where she'd been only just this morning.

Rosie stared in its direction and hoped Juli was all right.

The boat puttered down the river, drifting closer to the north bank. Scattered clusters of lights flickered through the thick growth. Rosie had never been to the North Coast but she knew it was mostly Senate-run research stations and farms. There were a few residential areas but she'd heard they were for the workers; the people who lived there even had their own school.

Beyond the farms was the train called the Bullet that ran all the way up the coast towards the Capricorn Line and the border of Gondwana Nation – the indige lands outside Senate control. Her dad had even talked about getting out of Newperth to live up there – before the MalX. He'd said up there they could grow their own vegetables outside of a genfarm, actually in the ground. But he'd stopped talking about it when the MalX came.

She watched the bank slide past, tears stinging her eyes.

"We get off just up ahead." Pip was suddenly at her side again. She started and blinked the tears back quickly before they fell, before he saw.

"Where?" she said. "I don't see a jetty." She couldn't see much but dark scrub and there was an odd sulfurous smell in the warm air.

He leaned in closer and pointed. "Can you see it?"

She stared ahead, her eyes straining, scanning the bank, and then she saw it: a dark blob, jutting out into the water. The old man guided the boat towards it.

"Get your bag." Pip nudged her and Rosie obeyed, glad to have an excuse to put some distance between them. He picked up a long-handled gaff and jumped up onto the narrow ledge between the side of the boat and the cabin.

Rosie stood out of the way and watched the bank

come closer. The old man grunted and the engine puttered as the boat turned out of the main current and tacked across the dark water. When they were a few metres away, Pip deftly hooked the gaff onto a pylon, pulling the boat up alongside the jetty. He jumped onto it and caught the rope thrown by the old man, and the boat bumped up against the jetty with a wet thud.

"Jump out," he called to Rosie, his voice strained from the effort of holding the boat steady.

Rosie jumped. Pip threw the rope back and pushed the boat away and soon fishing vessel D542 was backing up, turning and gliding away from them. The old man didn't look back once.

"Come on," Pip said. "We can't hang around."

Beyond the jetty a steep, rough path climbed the bank and then disappeared into deep shadow.

Rosie followed Pip as he began to climb up the slope. The ground was muddy and her hands and knees were quickly covered in muck. Pip gained the higher ground, grabbed her hand and yanked her to the top without asking.

"Thanks," she said.

He barely seemed to hear as he peered into the darkness of the trees. Tall trunks surrounded them, interspersed with thick grasses and scrub, reminding Rosie of the area around the Old City. Moonlight filtered down through the canopy and, a way off, through the trees to her left, she could see lights. Somewhere an insect sang but otherwise it was still.

"This way and keep quiet." Pip started walking away from the river along a barely discernible track.

The path twisted and turned through the trees, leading them further inland away from the river and then back towards it. Finally, they emerged into a clearing. An abandoned building sat in the middle. Long, low and square, it was made of dark brick and was half buried in the earth. Grass grew raggedly around its walls, and gaping holes, where windows should have been, stared back like slitted, hostile eyes, the sills hidden underground. The roof was little more than a domed lattice of steel covered intermittently with sheets of tin, and near the building, not far from where they stood, was a burnt out hovercar.

"This way." Pip seemed nervous now and kept clenching and unclenching his fists and looking around. The boss had to be waiting for them here.

A shiver of anticipation and fear ran up Rosie's spine. What would he be like? Would he be old and fat with narrow eyes that never settled, or would he be a thug, like the gang members?

He was neither.

Pip led her to the opposite side of the building

and they dropped through a low broken window into a dark and dank-smelling room. Seated at a portable table, staring at a computer in a case, sat a man with short brown hair. Beside the computer was a lamp, half covered by a cloth, providing a small pool of yellow light.

"You're late," he said.

CHAPTER 11

The man was younger than Rosie had imagined. She guessed he was in his mid thirties and he seemed very clean. His skin was pale, his jaw clean-shaven. He had brown eyes and a straight nose and looked just like anyone from Central, except there was an intensity about him that was out of place in his blandly handsome face.

She went towards him warily, Pip beside her.

"You must be Rosie," he said. "Did anyone follow you?" His gaze went to Pip who shook his head.

"No, boss, I was careful."

"Let's hope so." Rising from his chair, the man walked towards her and held out a hand as though intending to shake hers. "Give it to me," he said.

Rosie hesitated, holding tight to the straps of her

pack. Now she was here, she was filled with misgiving.

"Please, Rosie."

Pip took hold of one of her pack's straps.

"I can get it." She twisted away from him with a glare.

"Just trying to help," Pip said, his smile smug.

Rosie slipped the pack from her back and pulled the box out. "Here." She thrust it at the man who took it as though she'd offered it willingly.

"Thank you. Where did you find it?"

"In the Old City."

"I'm aware of that. Where in the Old City?"

His face gave nothing away as he regarded the symbol on the lid.

"A tunnel, a long way in." She wanted to ask him why it was important and, mostly, what had happened to her dad, but his demeanour was unnerving.

He placed the box carefully on the table. Rosie flicked a glance at Pip but he had gone to stand by the window. He appeared tense.

"Tell me exactly where you found it," the man said quietly.

"I don't know exactly."

"And you figured out how to open it?" He hardly blinked as he watched her.

"It was just luck, really," she said. He said nothing so

she ventured a question. "Do you know how to open it?"

He pressed the silver buttons and the lid sprang open. The look on his face as he saw what was inside was impossible to read. Did he know what was supposed to be in there?

The man picked up the grey com. "Did you look at this?"

"We couldn't figure out the entry code."

He studied her closely. "We?" he said. "Your friend's name is Shen, isn't it?"

A trickle of dread shivered up Rosie's spine. "Yes. I'd like to try to contact her if you have a com I could use."

"It's too late. I'm sorry." He turned his computer towards her. "I recorded this earlier. I hoped we could have avoided this. If Pip had brought you here sooner, I could have contacted them — told them she didn't have it."

What was he saying? Her breath felt short as she gazed down at the blue screen.

Family killed in freak accident. She read the news wave in disbelief: *The entire Shen family was found dead earlier this evening at their home in Central East, apparent victims of a faulty generator switch. The explosion destroyed the main part of the home ...* Unable to read any more, she turned away feeling sick.

"You were lucky you hid when those men came," he said.

Rosie couldn't speak. This wasn't true. It wasn't happening. *If Pip had brought you here sooner ...* His words repeated in her head and a terrible feeling like bitter acid rose in her gut. If she hadn't run away from Pip, would Juli still be alive? She stared back at the screen. The news wave was paused on what had been Juli's house. The remains of the house were smouldering, the bush around it a blackened circle. She wanted to sit down. She was dimly aware of Pip standing beside her, the man frowning as he watched her.

"Why?" she said.

"It's what they do," he said.

She shook her head, folding her arms around herself. She wanted to cry. She should be crying, shouldn't she? But she only felt a dull tightness behind her eyes.

"When you turned on the beacon, Rosie, it was like starting a chain reaction. And the people who did this will start at the beginning and follow it to the end. They don't miss things."

"What about my dad?" she whispered. "Is it true they found him because I ..." She couldn't finish.

"Yes." His tone was quiet, serious, but there was no condemnation, he merely told her the facts. "I'm sorry. I saw too late you'd looked up your aunt's name. It would have been easy for them after that."

"Is he okay, do you think?"

"I don't know. But if it's any consolation, I'd say he's still alive. They probably would have just left his body in your apartment if they'd killed him."

His body. Rosie felt like throwing up. She rubbed a hand across her eyes. Juli was dead, her father gone, all because of something she'd found.

She fingered the pendant in her pocket. Perhaps she shouldn't keep it. She pulled out the small, green disc.

"This was in the box too." She held it out to him. A faint smile curved his lips, and a look of recognition lit his face as he took it from her.

"What is it?"

He shook his head. "Nothing. A keepsake." He regarded her thoughtfully. "Here." He reached into his case and pulled out a silver chain with a key hanging on it. He took the key off and threaded the chain through the pendant then held it out to her. "You have it."

Rosie didn't know what to say. It was obvious the pendant meant something to him. "I don't want it." It was part of the trouble, pretty as it was. It was one of the reasons her dad was gone and Juli was dead.

He took a step towards her and forced it into her hand. "You should wear it, Rosie. It's important sometimes to have something to remind us of the consequences of things we've done."

Was he blaming her for Juli's death and her dad's

kidnapping? "I didn't know what would happen," she said. "It's not like I wanted anyone hurt."

His calm expression didn't waver. "I know, but as you've seen, the effects are devastating and it's not going to end here."

There was more to come? Rosie swallowed and her voice sounded weak when she said, "What is the Shore beacon?"

"I can't tell you. The more you know, the more dangerous it is."

She felt like he'd slapped her. "More dangerous? My dad is gone and Juli is dead! We have to go the Senate," she said. "We have to tell them what happened."

"They can't help you, Rosie. And you cannot tell them."

"Why? We have to do something!" His calm was infuriating.

"No, I have to do something. And don't think they won't stop hunting you down. They know who you are now and they have people in the Senate. There're probably guards looking for you right now. You go to them and you might as well hand them a gun to shoot you with."

She stopped, shocked. Was that true? "But what about my dad?" she said.

"If he's still alive, they'll use him as bait. In fact they

are probably counting on you running to the Senate for help so the people they have in there can just swoop on you. Easy."

"But who are they?"

He regarded her for a moment and she thought she saw a flicker of sympathy. "They are very powerful and you are merely a small itch to be scratched out."

"But–"

"I'll send them a message and tell them you don't have what they want any more."

"But what if they don't believe you?"

"They will." He sounded so certain but Rosie couldn't understand why. If these people were so powerful, why would they believe him?

She turned to Pip but he seemed just as remote as the man. She felt like she was in a nightmare that wouldn't end. Just like when she watched her mum die. You tried to pretend it wasn't happening, but you knew, all the time you knew, it was real and you couldn't do anything about it.

"Who are you?" she said. "At least tell me that."

He hesitated a moment, glancing at Pip. "You can call me Riley," he said.

"Riley who?"

He shook his head. "Just Riley." He nodded at Pip. "He'll take you back to the city."

"What?" both Pip and Rosie exclaimed together.

"That's it?" Rosie stared at him. "But—"

"Enough." Riley's tone was sharp. "This is not a discussion. Pip, you take her back to the city by the bridge — it's the safest way. Keep her with you, out of the way of the Senate, until I contact you."

"But ..." Rosie began but the expression on his face made her shut her mouth.

"Go," he said.

She stood still, staring at him, but he ignored her.

Pip shook his head and jerked a thumb towards the window. Never had Rosie felt so powerless or so lost. She picked up her backpack and followed Pip to the window. Riley had gone back to his computer and didn't look up as they climbed out.

CHAPTER 12

Pip wound his way along an invisible path through the trees. Rosie followed, barely paying attention as she kept going over what she could have done differently that would have kept Juli alive and her dad at home. A litany of could haves and should haves. If she hadn't gone to the Old City. If she hadn't found the box. If she'd stopped Juli using the key.

"Hey," Pip said. "You got that shuttle token still?"

"In my pocket."

"Good."

They'd walked a bit further before his words actually penetrated her brain.

"Why did you ask about the token?" she said. "Shuttles don't run this late from here."

"The bridge isn't far. We can show the guards the token, tell them we missed the last shuttle back so they don't wonder why we're here. I've got some papers that show we've got visiting rights for Gentech Research Station; we can say they kept us longer."

"Shouldn't you fix your hair or something then?" she said to him. "Who's going to believe Gentech has a Feral to help them?"

Pip appeared almost offended. "They use Ferals all the time. Besides, you don't look so hot yourself." He turned his back on her.

They'd almost reached a road. The dull gleam of it was just a few metres ahead through the scrub and they stopped behind a thick clump of grass growing alongside it. The line for the shuttle hummed quietly above their heads and a solar car whirred past, its batteries glowing blue.

Pip said, "We need to get cleaned up. You've got mud on your face. Here …" He leaned towards her.

"I can get it." Rosie pushed him back.

"Hey, I'm just trying to help," Pip said, but he looked like he was trying not to smile.

"I don't need your help, thanks." She rubbed vigorously and rubbed vigorously at the smudges of dried mud on her cheek. By the time she finished she thought it probably looked worse — a big red mark instead of a muddy one. Then she turned her attention to her legs, using her bag to rub off as much mud as she could.

It had to be around midnight. She wondered how close to Earth her aunt was and how she was going to tell her about all of this. What would she say? And then there was the more obvious problem: how was she going to get to her? Riley had told Pip to take her somewhere, but where would that be? And how long would she have to stay there? She might have no way of contacting her aunt at all.

She glanced at Pip who was watching the road. There was no way she was going to just sit with him and wait for Riley. She found it hard to believe what he said about the Senate. And who was to say it hadn't been Riley who took her dad anyway? He'd seemed believable in person but now she wasn't so certain. Why should she trust a man who had sent a boy practically to kidnap her? She had to get to Aunt Essie's. If only she knew how to get to Orbitcorp from here.

"All clear, let's go." Pip nudged her. They stepped onto the road.

Moonlight cast long shadows before them. There were no lights but further ahead a sharp right turn in the road was lit by the glow of the guard station that lay just beyond it. Somewhere nearby an insect creaked noisily and from further away came the deep hum of a power source.

The air was still and humid, and Rosie could smell her own sweat as she trudged along. A heavy throbbing had started behind her eyes and she felt totally on edge. Her heart was beating too fast and thoughts were ricocheting around her mind like bugs around a light.

She could feel Pip watching her.

"What?" She didn't glance at him.

But instead of saying something, he grabbed her hand and squeezed hard.

"Ow!" She tried to pull away but he held her fast.

"You looked like you could use it," he said.

She glared at him. "What, a broken hand?"

"No, pain. Sometimes it helps you to focus."

"I am focused."

"Yeah, sure. You were spacing out."

"I wasn't. I—"

"Don't pretend you weren't trying to come up with a million ideas to get away, or go to the Senate." He smirked.

He was still holding her hand, not so tightly now though, and swinging it lightly between them as if they were on a date.

"Let go," she said, enunciating each word slowly.

"You sure?" He cocked an eyebrow and she gave him

a poisonous look. He dropped her hand and she flexed her fingers, shaking it out.

It had been a weird thing to do, grabbing her like that, and it had taken her off guard, but it had helped. She could breathe easier now and, judging by his smug expression, Pip probably knew it. She put a little more distance between them. He made her uneasy. It hadn't felt that bad, holding his hand, especially after the day she'd had. But he isn't trustworthy, she reminded herself. Forget the blue eyes and remember the knife in the station, the threats, remember what happened to Juli and Dad.

When they arrived at the security station, the guards barely paid them any heed. There were three guards but only one bothered to come out from the building where a ghostly blue glow and the sound of a tinny scream betrayed the others were watching digi-tel.

The guard skimmed Pip's papers, surveyed Rosie and motioned them forward with a bored expression. He pressed the controls to lift the laser barrier and, with a yawn, turned away and went back inside.

"Too easy," Pip muttered as they walked along the deserted bridge.

Rosie didn't reply. Her legs were starting to feel as heavy as bricks and every step was becoming an effort, while Pip still walked with the same long stride he'd kept up the entire night. Didn't he ever get tired?

Ahead, the bridge continued on a gentle incline to its apex and on the other side of the river the lights of Central obscured the stars.

She wondered how far it was to Aunt Essie's apartment at Orbitcorp and how she was going to get away from Pip. The bridge was about a kilometre long and it seemed to take forever to cross it.

She walked behind him, watching his feet, staring at the frayed cuffs of his jeans.

His feet suddenly stopped. "What're you doin'?" She blinked and looked up at him. "Keep up, will you." He grabbed her hand again briefly and pulled her forward. "The guards'll get suspicious if we don't get to the other side soon."

Rosie was too tired to resist. "Where are we going?" she said, falling into step beside him.

He let out a long breath. "Just some place Riley keeps." He was annoyed for some unfathomable reason. She glanced sideways at him. He was frowning.

If she pretended to make friends, she might be able to persuade him take her to her aunt.

"So," she said, casting her mind about for a starting

point. "Um, where are your parents?"

"Dead."

Great start. "Sorry," she said.

He shook his head and gave a bitter laugh. "No."

"What?"

"I mean, don't go thinking we've got something in common, just because your mum's dead and now your dad's missing. We're nothing alike."

"I didn't say we were."

"Yeah, but you were thinking it."

Rosie felt herself go pink. For a second, she had been. "What's your problem anyway?"

"Nothin'." He stared straight ahead, which just made her more angry. Who did he think he was? "I wasn't thinking we were the same," she said. "Why would I? You're a Feral and you know what people say about that. I'll be working on the space station while you're still running around in the Banks, stealing food like the rest of them."

His stride faltered and she saw a flash of hurt in his eyes quickly replaced by disgust. She was mortified at her own words but it was too late to take them back.

"Is that right?" he said, his eyes icy. "Well then, let's just see how you do without me." And with that he broke into a run, sprinting away from her towards the end of the bridge.

Rosie stared after him then started running herself, cursing her own stupidity. Great plan, Rosie! What was she thinking? She wanted to get away from him but not yet. Not until she had some idea where she was.

Fearful, she watched as he ran further and further from her. He reached the guard dome and passed it, his dreadlocks bouncing wildly as he streamed past. One guard chuckled and shouted out to her. "Boyfriend dump you, love?"

Rosie ignored him, her eyes fixed on Pip's rapidly disappearing form.

Beyond the lights of the dome, the road was darker and she had to slow down, her eyes not yet accustomed to the difference. There were buildings up ahead on either side, but the lamps set along the road were dimmer than the bridge – low-voltage yellow and unsteady, the power source weak. She stopped by one of them and looked around, but it was no good, Pip was gone.

CHAPTER 13

For a moment Rosie stood uncertain, then she moved out of the light towards the nearest wall, gripping the straps of her pack as though they were lifelines.

Excellent plan, Rosie Black, she berated herself, now what are you going to do?

The road ran straight ahead for several blocks between rows of dark buildings, each several storeys high. There were no lights in any of them and were most likely abandoned factories. The huge windows were partly boarded up and the fences around them were ripped, trailing rusty metal onto the footpath. The distant hum of traffic from Central was like background static but immediately around her it was quiet. Too quiet.

She thought about shouting out for Pip but it didn't seem like a good idea. Although it was quiet, she'd bet there were people about. A tinkling crash came from somewhere to her right and she spun around and scanned the dark building but could see nothing. The back of her neck prickled. There was another crash, closer this time, and she took off up the road, adrenaline chasing away her exhaustion.

She caught a flicker of fire out of the corner of her eye as she passed an alley and noticed a dark shape huddled against a wall. She didn't stop to figure out what it was. She ran as fast as she could. Ahead, the road ended at another abandoned building and she turned right, straining to hear above the sound of her own breath and pounding feet.

She didn't know how long she kept running, but eventually she had to slow to a walk. Her lungs were burning and her leg muscles shaking, and she had a stitch in her right side. Clutching it, she walked close to the walls. The buildings were apartment blocks now and across the road, protected by a metal grille, was a small shop. But there was no one around. Probably all asleep.

She came to a crossroads and stopped. She was sure the glow of lights to her left, like a white halo above the rooftops, had to be Central. She guessed she was somewhere in the Eastern Rim, the sector that formed the border between the river and Central. If she went towards the lights, she should be able to find Aunt Essie's apartment, but it could take hours.

She leaned against the wall of a building, slid down it and sat on the pavement. She was so tired. But she couldn't stay here. Just a moment's rest, that was all she needed. Time to think about what to do.

She didn't realise she'd drifted off until a door slammed somewhere above and she jerked her head up off her chest. She blinked and glanced up. Of course. Why hadn't she thought of it sooner?

High above her head, the suspension track of the shuttle line glinted silver against the night sky. It ran right to Central station. All she had to do was follow it. She groaned and got to her feet, looked once at the empty street behind, then began to follow the track towards the white glow of Central.

It was more difficult than she'd hoped. Huge apartment complexes kept blocking her way, forcing her to make detours. The streets were so empty and quiet, she began to feel like the only human left alive in the world.

Was this what it felt like on Mars when you were

out of the colony? she thought. When they strapped a breather to your face and you were away from the domes, was Mars as silent as this? Was there nothing but the hum of energy behind you and your breath loud in your ears?

The apartments gave way to corporation buildings. Small shops were replaced with glass-fronted stores, four storeys high, the interiors lit with frosty blue lights illuminating racks of goods – mostly electrical and computer supplies.

Sometimes Rosie thought she heard noises behind her and she backed up against the walls, hiding in doorways, but she never saw anyone.

After a while it was all she could do to keep walking. She didn't have the energy to worry about what was behind her; she just focused on making it to her aunt's.

The sun was starting to rise when she reached Central, the early light glinting on the massive glass dome that topped the entrance to the Orbitcorp complex. She stopped across the road and looked wearily at it. The huge glass doors were closed, the front steps empty, but there were lights on inside, illuminating the moving sculpture of the solar system that dominated the massive foyer.

Beyond the dome, behind the high walls, the rooftops of the rest of the buildings of Orbitcorp poked up into the pink-washed sky. There were apartments for the employees, offices, workshops, and beyond them four shuttle bays. Orbitcorp occupied a large chunk of Central and it was all locked tight.

Rosie backed into the deep awning of a closed robotics store. She sat slowly down, pulling her knees to her chest and positioning herself so she could see the street.

Her eyes and limbs were heavy with fatigue, her mouth was dry and she felt sick with hunger. Exhausted, she rested her head back against the cool wall; she had hours to wait. Aunt Essie was due for planetfall at nine. The public viewing gallery would open at eight and she guessed right now it was around five if she was lucky. She should stay awake in case, she thought. She shouldn't sleep here. But that was the last thought she had as her eyelids closed and her head dropped down to her chest.

Pip hid around the corner, peering out every so often to keep an eye on her.

He was surprised she'd made it. He munched on a strip of dried meat and watched Rosie hunched in the corner of the doorway. She was a mess and a twinge of guilt hit him. Her hair was all tangled and she still had mud on her shorts. She looked so small there by herself. Alone. It made him feel things he didn't want to feel. Things that could make his job harder.

Riley would be pissed he hadn't taken her to his safe house but Pip was sure he'd be able to talk him around.

He bit savagely on the dried meat. Why had that other girl got killed? It had been unnecessary. He hated it when people were killed.

He stayed watching Rosie a moment longer, then slunk away into a nearby access tunnel.

He headed to the Game Pit in the Western Rim. Built underground, it was dim, cheap and the staff would sometimes sell him beer. Plus it was off the radar – a wholly zero surveillance zone – and Senate or whoever couldn't get a look-in. It was a perfect hide-out.

He hunched down in a game pod and munched on a hot chip. It was greasy and stale and had a chemical aftertaste, but it helped him think.

It bothered him that he couldn't get the girl out of his head. Rosie hunched over in the doorway, Rosie wiping mud off her face, Rosie saying those things to him.

She had no idea about him, not really. He hated that it bothered him.

"Thought I'd find you here." A voice spoke quietly.

Pip turned to see Riley behind him. He looked angry. Pip tried to judge if he was gunning for a fight. It wasn't usually Riley's style but you never knew when you pushed someone. And he'd deliberately disobeyed him. "How'd you know about this place?"

Riley ignored the question. "Shouldn't you be somewhere else?" he said.

Pip shrugged. "She pissed me off – I had to drop her. But don't worry, I know where she is. She went to her aunt's place."

Riley put a hand on his shoulder and squeezed it hard then, leaning down close to his ear, said, "Get up."

"All right, all right." Pip got to his feet. "Why's it so important anyway? You got the stuff you wanted."

Riley put his hand tightly on the back of Pip's neck and steered him towards the door. "Where is her aunt's?"

"Orbitcorp."

"Great," Riley muttered under his breath and pushed Pip out the door. "Let's go then."

———◆———

Rosie woke to something hard prodding her side and a nasally voice saying, "Get up!"

She blinked and squinted up at a pudgy man with

a pink, sweaty face who was prodding her with the toe of his shoe.

"Get up," he grunted again.

Rosie struggled to her feet. Her eyes felt gritty and she swayed dizzily for a second.

"Move it, before I call the Senate." The man pointed to the street and she stumbled out from under the portico into the sunlight. Behind her the man mumbled something about Ferals as he unlocked the shop door.

Rosie looked down at herself. Dried mud stained her shorts, her T-shirt was grubby and creased, and the long-sleeved shirt she wore over the top was wrinkled and splattered with mud. She supposed she did resemble a Feral, sleeping in a doorway and using her bag for a pillow.

She stood on the kerb. It had to be near opening time now. Bleary-eyed, she stepped out onto the road and was almost knocked over by a hovercar. It whirred past, the driver sounding the horn and glaring at her from his climate-controlled interior.

Rosie jumped back onto the kerb. She was definitely awake now. There were more people in the street and a steady stream of hovercars were buzzing quietly up and down the road. Those she met eyes with cut their gazes away quickly as if she didn't exist. Rosie began to feel uncomfortable. She pulled her shirt over her T-shirt and watched for a break in the traffic, then she jogged across the road to Orbitcorp. There wasn't anywhere to hide so she settled for standing as inconspicuously as possible near the doors. She peered through the glass. There were people in there. Was it open?

She moved to stand directly in front of the double doors but nothing happened. She waved her arms up at the motion sensor. The doors stayed closed.

She went back down a few steps, checking left, then right. There. At the far left corner, a single door was open and a few people were entering through it.

She lined up behind three men. The last one turned and glanced down at her in surprise. "Hello. Are you an employee of Orbitcorp?" He raised an eyebrow.

"I'm here to meet my aunt." Rosie noticed a large guard armed with a gun near the entrance.

"Really?" The man looked bemused. "Then you'll need one of these." He waved a plascard at her. It was some kind of ID.

Rosie's heart sank. "But I'm just going to the shuttle bay."

"New rules. No one gets in without a pass." He gave her a rueful smile and turned away.

Since when? There seemed to be more and more rules every day. Aunt Essie couldn't have known or she'd have got Rosie a pass. She studied the man in front her.

He was about forty, with wavy black hair and caramel-brown skin, his natural colour though, not tanned.

She tugged on the back of his dark purple jacket. "Excuse me," she said quietly.

He turned to her. "You still here?"

"Could you help me? My aunt is coming in from the space station today and she told me to meet her." She hesitated. "I know I don't look very good. I had an accident – that's why I'm so dirty. But if I don't meet her, she'll be worried. She didn't know I'd need an ID card."

The man considered her for a minute. "You know you could be mistaken for a Feral, don't you?" he said.

Rosie nodded. "Yes, but—"

"But you've got much better manners than Ferals have," he interrupted. "So you might be telling the truth. What's your aunt's name?"

"Um." Rosie didn't want to tell him, but if she made up a name and he knew people, he'd know she was lying. "Essie Black," she said. "She's a pilot."

"Black?" He frowned slightly. "The name is familiar."

"Sir?" They'd reached the front of the line and the guard was holding his hand out for the pass. His eyes went to Rosie and narrowed. "She can't come in here."

"I'll decide that," said the man to the guard. His voice was sharp and Rosie felt a little scared jolt inside. But then the man smiled blandly at her.

"Come," he put an arm out, "I'll show you to the dock. Your aunt's coming in from the space station, you said?"

Rosie nodded, moving with him past the guard.

"That will be dock fourteen. This way."

He drew her across the wide foyer towards a bank of lifts.

People gave her surprised glances, quickly smothered when they saw the man she was with, and Rosie began to wonder if she should have trusted this stranger. But she was in, at least, and the time display said it was just after eight, so she didn't have long to wait. Nervously, she followed him into the shiny silver lift and turned to face the doors as they closed. Besides, what could happen to her here? She folded her arms about herself and smiled at the man in the purple suit as he selected the floor.

CHAPTER 14

It was further than she remembered to the shuttle dock. They went from the lift, down a long glass-covered walkway to another building, then down again and through another walkway, through gardens to yet another building and then another. By the time they reached the dock, Rosie was disorientated.

The man hardly spoke as they walked. He stopped once to show her to a bathroom and gave her a bottle of water, but he didn't ask her any questions other than her name.

The longer they walked, the wearier she felt. When they reached the shuttle waiting area, he led her to a seat, patted her firmly on the shoulder and left. After he'd gone Rosie realised she didn't even know his name.

The waiting area was a long glass-fronted building that looked down at the dock. Rows of blue cushioned seats, grouped in lots of four, were placed throughout the room. Behind her, near the door, was a small shop.

When she'd visited before, there had been about one hundred people to watch the landing. Now, the shop was closed and only five other people were waiting for the shuttle. They were all dressed in white jackets and conferring over coms, which meant they were probably scientists. After a single, measuring glance, they ignored her and Rosie sat by herself on one of the chairs, hugging the water bottle and staring out of the window at the empty shuttle pad.

Time passed slowly. She had a headache from hunger and closed her eyes against the glare from outside. It was very quiet and soon she felt herself nodding off again. She jerked awake and tried sitting up straighter. Her heart felt as though it was beating too fast and she put her head in hands.

Suddenly, a loud beeping filled the room. Startled, she looked up to see the scientists strolling to a door marked Disembarkation Area: Personnel Only.

She went to the window and peered up at the sky. A faint white trail of vapour was streaking down. The shuttle had made planetfall. A wave of relief struck her.

Before long she could make out the streamlined

shape of the shuttle, dropping to Earth in a controlled fall.

She watched it stow its solar sails and invert, powering up the ion thrusters to land. She could feel the rumbling vibration through the floor as it settled on the dock. A blast of enviro scrubbers burst up from the dock as it touched down to capture any hazardous particles.

She anxiously watched the exit tunnel extend from the waiting area and connect with the hatch. There were no windows on the tunnel, so she couldn't tell when the hatch opened or if anyone was coming out. She moved towards the door marked Disembarkation and waited.

After a few minutes she heard voices on the other side, the door slid back and six people came out. Among them was a woman with short, black spiky hair wearing dark green pants and a tight, black tank top.

Rosie's heart lifted. Her aunt spotted her and smiled, waving.

"Hey!" Aunt Essie dodged past the rest of the crew. "How long have you—" Her smiled faded. "You're a mess, kid. What the hell have you been doing?"

She placed her hands on Rosie's shoulders. She smelled familiar, of frangipani and spice, and her tiny diamond nose stud gleamed in the light. Rosie felt tears starting to gather behind her eyes.

"Can we go?" she said. She didn't want to start bawling in public.

Aunt Essie's hands tightened. "Sure. You okay?"

Rosie shook her head and her aunt put an arm around her.

"Okay, right." She began steering her towards the exit. "I'll make tea and you can tell me what's going on."

———•———

Aunt Essie's apartment was on the sixth floor of one of Orbitcorp's scientific complexes. It had pale green walls, one bedroom, a lounge room adjoining a white kitchen and a tiny balcony with a view over a garden. It also had a com room decked out with bio computers and shelves of gadgets and research materials.

Rosie sat in the very corner of the big cream-coloured sofa while Aunt Essie made tea. On the coffee table a miniature model of Genesis glowed softly under a dome of glass, flakes of red Martian dust flitting around the tiny representation of the colony.

"How did you get in?" Aunt Essie called from the kitchen. "I found out they'd brought in new security rules on my way back. You're supposed to have a pass and I couldn't get hold of you to tell you."

"A man helped me." Rosie took the cup of tea her aunt offered.

"What man?" asked Aunt Essie, as she sat beside her.

"I don't know."

"What did he look like?"

"Um ..." Rosie stared at her cup. "Black hair, tall."

"I wonder who that was." Her aunt frowned, sipping her tea for a moment then shrugged. "Doesn't matter, I'll find out later. First, what happened to you, kid? You look terrible. Should I call your dad?"

Rosie put her tea down. Her hand shook and the cup almost tipped as it met the tabletop.

"Rosie," her aunt grabbed the cup, "what's going on?"

"Dad's gone. Some men took him."

"What the hell are you talking about?"

She covered her face with her hands.

"Rosie?" Aunt Essie's voice was sharp.

Rosie shook her head, unable to meet her eyes. "I found this box of stuff and–" She faltered, gripped by a terrible feeling that once she told her aunt, everything would be true. Juli would really be dead, her father really gone. Just like her mum.

Aunt Essie took a long breath. "Rosie," she said. "Just tell me."

She told her. About the box, about everything that

had happened since she'd found it. The words came out stiff, washed with an overwhelming feeling of guilt, but she didn't cry and she was glad for that.

Aunt Essie didn't speak for a long moment. "It's not your fault. All right?" she said finally.

Rosie could only nod but she found it hard to believe. If she hadn't found the box, none of this would have happened.

"Okay, so Adam's been taken by these men and this guy Riley has the stuff you found?"

"Yes."

Her aunt was staring out of the window.

"Do you think he's still–" Rosie wasn't able to form the words.

"Alive?" Aunt Essie finished. "If they wanted him dead, they would have just killed him in the flat – it's not like anyone there would have stopped them. Bunch of cowards."

"Riley didn't want me to go to the Senate," Rosie said. "He thought they would have people waiting there to get me."

"He thinks the people who took your dad have infiltrated the Senate guards?" Her aunt looked thoughtful. "It's possible, I guess, but … he might be saying that to confuse you. This guy, Riley, could be behind the whole thing."

"That's what I thought, but he has the box now," Rosie said. "Why would he take Dad, and why did he want Pip to take me somewhere safe?"

"To scare you, so he knows where you are. Plus your dad was taken before you met him and then you went straight to him after, didn't you?"

Rosie nodded. But if she hadn't run away from Pip, she'd have been there before. Maybe her dad wouldn't have been taken then. Or maybe she just wouldn't have found out until later. She didn't know what think. Why were the diary and key so important?

"Riley could be wanted by the Senate," Aunt Essie was saying. "I've got a friend, I could contact him, ask him to check the database – get some help."

Rosie felt confused. Was Riley involved? He'd been so certain of who had taken her dad. But she didn't know if she should disagree with her aunt. She'd been in the Senate Elite for two years before she joined Orbitcorp. The Elite was the force the Senate sent to work for the United Earth Commission's Earth Peace Alliance and helped keep the peace both on- and off-world. She must know something.

"Rosie, tell me again what the message said when you put the key in the comnet."

"*Shore beacon activated. Code entered. Target acquired. Searching ...*" she replied. "Why?"

Her aunt was frowning. "There's something familiar about the name, Shore." She went to her com room and activated her holo drive and began searching. "Ha! Look here." She pointed to an icon hovering within the parameters of the controls square that had appeared in the air in front of the back wall. Her aunt selected the icon and the control panel disappeared and a block of green text appeared. "I knew I'd seen that name."

Rosie read the news wave sample her aunt had recorded.

Mars report: The Genesis colony has been temporarily closed due to the recent explosion of a research laboratory. Officials have still not released the cause of the explosion but are calling it an accident. Twenty-three people were killed and hundreds injured by the explosion which destroyed a main medical research laboratory on Genesis. Among the dead were renowned geneticists, Drs Margaret and Ethan Shore, who had been working on a cure for the recently discovered generation-X strain of malaria, known as the MalX, which it is feared will decimate the highly populated poorer areas of Earth.

Next to it was an image of the destroyed lab.

"They were looking for a cure?" Rosie said.

Aunt Essie hesitated then said carefully, "Yeah, kid. I know. I remember when it happened. This wave is ten years old – you would have only been six. It was huge. Everyone had to be evacuated because the domes were damaged. I was with the Elite then and we were sent up to oversee the evacuation." She shook her head, staring at the image. "It was a mess. Everything was destroyed. All their research lost – it really set them back. That was one of the reasons I went to work for Orbitcorp, to help with the rebuilding. Me and your mum fought over that. Who knew–" She stopped and Rosie felt a tight band of pain grip her. She wanted Aunt Essie to tell her more, but at the same time she didn't want to hear it.

"Why would their name be in that message?" Rosie said. "Shore beacon. What does it mean?"

"No idea." Aunt Essie swiped a hand over the information and the projection vanished. "But I bet that Riley guy does. We've got to get to my friend in the Senate."

Rosie wasn't sure if that was the best idea but what else could they do? She fingered the pendant under her shirt.

"Jesus, kid, you've been all alone," Aunt Essie said as she went towards the kitchen. "Why didn't you contact me?"

"I couldn't," Rosie said, following her aunt. "They took my com when they trashed the flat." Then Rosie had another frightening thought. "But that's not how they found me," she said. "I looked you up on the Grid when I was at Juli's."

Aunt Essie halted and turned to stare at her. "What? Why didn't you tell me? Christ, Rosie, they'll know where I live. Orbitcorp security is good, but there's no way we're safe here. They're probably watching, trying to figure a way in – or waiting for us to come out." She glanced at the timer on her wrist. "Okay, here's what we're going to do: get you cleaned up, get some food and gear, and get out of here."

"Right, yeah."

Her heart racing again, Rosie ran to the bathroom. Why hadn't she thought of that before? Of course they'd track down her aunt's address.

Stripping off her clothes, she got under the hot shower, trying not to think of how the same men who had taken her dad could be coming for her now. When was she going to stop making stupid mistakes?

When she came out wrapped in a towel, a backpack was sitting on the kitchen counter.

"Put these on." Aunt Essie handed her a pair of jeans and a red T-shirt. "The jeans might be a bit long but you can roll them up. Take the jacket on the bench as well."

"Where are we going?" Rosie took the clothes.

"Firstly, out of Orbitcorp." She handed Rosie a protein bar. "Eat this. We'll get a proper meal later. I'm going to erase my computer files – in case."

Apprehension running through her, Rosie ate as she dressed, then swung on her backpack and followed her aunt from the apartment.

CHAPTER 15

The corridor was empty, and bright sunlight bounced off the beige walls, filling the air with warmth.

They turned right, heading away from the lifts. Before they had gone more than a few steps though, one of the lift doors opened with a soft ping, and a voice called, "Miss Black?"

Rosie's insides leaped as she recognised the man in the purple suit.

"Mr Yuang." Aunt Essie's smile was forced and she put a hand on Rosie's shoulder as he strode towards them.

"I see the young lady found you," Mr Yuang said. "I assume she told you she had some trouble getting in this morning."

"So it was you who helped her. Thanks. I was just taking her out for something to eat."

"I see." He smiled and his gaze went to the bags they both carried.

"I have to run some errands," Aunt Essie said. "After being in space for so long, things pile up – washing et cetera."

"Certainly."

Rosie couldn't help staring at how white his teeth were against the caramel colour of his skin. The lift pinged again and a black-suited Senate guard stepped out. The man looked straight at them and Aunt Essie's grip on her shoulder tightened.

"I'm sorry, Mr Yuang, we really have to–"

"Yes, you must get to your errands." He walked slowly backwards towards the guard as he talked. "I won't keep you. Well done on your last mission, Miss Black." His eyes went once more to Rosie, before he turned. "You there," he called to the guard. "I have a job for you. Follow me."

"Come on," Aunt Essie whispered, pulling her away. They hurried to the end of the corridor and Rosie glanced back as they turned the corner, and saw Mr Yuang following the guard into the lift. He winked at her then disappeared behind the doors.

Aunt Essie urged her into a jog.

"You know him?" Rosie said.

"Not really. He's on contract to Orbitcorp. It's weird that he helped you this morning."

"Why?"

"I wouldn't have thought he would need to use the main entrance, that's all."

"What does he do?"

"Not sure. He deals with Genesis and the outer planet programs." Her lips tightened. "He's a big fish though. I've never seen him around the living quarters before. This way." She stopped and pushed open a door with "Stairs" stencilled on it. Their footsteps echoed in the stairwell as they ran down.

"Do you think he was really looking out for me? Checking that you found me?" Rosie said.

"Doubt it. I hardly know him. I piloted for him once – the last time I went to Genesis. He was checking on some lab stuff. It's not like we said more than two words to each other."

Rosie was worried. Something felt weird. Why would he help some kid get into Orbitcorp? And what had that wink meant?

"Keep up, Rosie." Her aunt pushed open the exit to the ground floor.

Outside, a pathway wound between gardens to a courtyard in the middle of the living complexes. They walked quickly and Rosie kept checking over her shoulder, expecting to see Mr Yuang following them. But it wasn't Mr Yuang who found them.

They'd almost crossed the courtyard when she caught movement from the corner of her eye and saw the telltale flick of dreadlocks disappearing behind a shrub. "Aunt Essie!" She grabbed her arm and tried to keep her voice low. "Pip's here."

"Where?" Her aunt was instantly alert.

"He was—" Rosie stopped. Riley had just stepped onto the path a few metres ahead and next Pip emerged from between the shrubs and caught her by the arm.

"Hey, Ro—" His words and air were cut off as Aunt Essie twisted his free arm behind his back and got him in a chokehold.

"Hands off!" she said.

Pip wheezed and let go of Rosie. Aunt Essie was shorter than Pip but it didn't seem to make much difference — he was squinting with pain and making strangled sounds.

"I think he's disabled," Riley said quietly. Aunt Essie let go and pushed Pip in his direction. He stumbled and Riley caught him, but Pip shook him off, turning to glare at them both.

"You got lucky," Pip choked out, rubbing his neck.

Aunt Essie half smiled. "If you say so."

"I think Pip forgot to take you somewhere, Rosie." Riley took a step in her direction but before Rosie could respond Aunt Essie moved between them.

"And I think you forgot your manners," she said. "How did you get into the complex?"

"You must be Aunt Essie." He held out his hand.

She ignored it. "I said, how did you get in here?"

He lowered his hand. "We need to talk."

"Is that a request or a demand?"

Riley looked weary. "I didn't take her dad, if that's what you're thinking."

"Oh, I don't think you want to know what I'm thinking."

A taut smile curved his lips. "You have no idea what she's started, have you?"

"No," her aunt said calmly, "but I intend to find out. How about we go somewhere else and talk? I'm thinking you're not too keen on being seen here anyway, right?"

Riley's eyes glittered but after a moment he gave a curt nod and stepped back, sweeping a hand out before him in a mock bow. "Ladies first."

Pip snorted.

"Come on." Aunt Essie gave Riley a cold stare and took Rosie's arm, leading the way.

The building Aunt Essie took them to was a research lab with white corridors that intersected like a rabbit warren. They passed half-a-dozen closed doors marked with numbered labels. Several men and women in Orbitcorp uniforms passed them, but no one challenged them and they moved through the building until they came to an unmarked door at the back.

Aunt Essie regarded Riley and Pip. "Now, don't touch or take anything." Her gaze settled on Pip who gave her an innocent wide-eyed look. Aunt Essie pulled a small card out of her pocket and pushed it quickly into a slot. A moment later the door slid open and they went in, the door closing behind them.

They were in a long room lined with lab tables on one side and a bank of computers and whirring test chambers on the other. The only light came from a pulsing orange orb rotating in the centre of the largest test chamber.

"This way." Aunt Essie took a step forward but Riley put a hand on her arm.

"Wait, I ..."

Her aunt threw his arm off and pushed him back against the door, her forearm against his windpipe. A knife appeared in her hand and she held it to his throat.

Rosie stepped back, shocked, and Pip grabbed her arm, for what purpose she wasn't sure. It wasn't like she had the knife.

"Don't do that again," Aunt Essie said. Riley didn't resist or make any move to fight her.

"I'm not going to hurt you or Rosie," he said calmly.

"No, you're not. You're going to tell me what's going on." She pressed the blade against his throat.

Riley looked steadily back at her and Rosie had to give him some credit, even she was a little scared of her aunt right now. "I will tell you only what you need to know," he said. "You can't persuade me to tell you anything more." Riley glanced at Rosie. "Did you tell her everything I told you?"

"Don't talk to her," Aunt Essie snapped. "What have you done with Adam?"

Pip's hand tightened around Rosie's arm but she barely felt it. Her heart was hammering as she stared at her aunt. "Aunt Essie, I don't think he has Dad."

Aunt Essie didn't look at her. "I'm not so sure."

"Listen," Riley said. "You have no idea what these people will do to her dad. You can't go to the Senate because they have connections everywhere. And even if we try to make a trade, it's too late – things have already been put into motion."

"What things?"

"That's not important for you to know, but trust me and I can help you get your brother back alive. I know where he is."

"Aunt Essie," Rosie said. "What if he's right?"

Her aunt glanced at her then looked back at Riley. Slowly, she lowered the knife. "Talk."

"The box Rosie found, the diary and the key, people died protecting them. They give access to information that can expose the people who took Rosie's dad."

"And who are they?" Aunt Essie's tone was sceptical.

"They call themselves Helios."

"Never heard of them."

"It's not a name they use openly but you might have seen their symbol around Genesis."

"The symbol Rosie described on the box? The half-sun and rider."

"Yes," Riley said. "They operate some … contracts on the colony."

"On Mars?" Rosie pulled her arm from Pip's grasp who let her go with barely a glance. All his focus was on Riley. "What do Helios do?" Rosie asked.

"Have you heard of the name Shore?"

"As in the scientists?" Aunt Essie said.

Riley nodded. "They were killed in an explosion that destroyed their lab in the Genesis colony ten years ago."

"But what do they have to do with Helios? They worked for Orbitcorp."

"Did they?" Riley said. "How do you know?"

Aunt Essie frowned. "Orbitcorp manages Genesis,

and the lab that was destroyed was owned by Orbitcorp."

"That's what it looked like," Riley said. "But Orbitcorp is a merger of many corporations. And Helios is connected to most of them. They used those connections to take over one of the labs on Genesis, to make it their own — as well as the brilliant minds who ran it."

"But what does Shore beacon mean?" Rosie said. "We checked it out but we couldn't see how it related to them."

"It's for Helios to identify them. A way to track them. It was embedded in everything they used, including that box. You see Ethan and Margaret Shore found out the work they were doing for Helios was ... not what they thought. They decided to blow the lid on them."

"So Helios shut them up first," Aunt Essie said.

Riley looked grim. "Yes. That explosion wasn't an accident. The Shores managed to get the diary and the key out before it happened. I found out about it two years ago and I've been searching for that box ever since."

"What was Helios hiding?" Pip said in a soft voice. "What did the Shores die for?"

Rosie glanced at him. He seemed angry, upset even. Obviously, this was something Riley had never shared.

"I'm not sure," Riley said. "But the diary and the

key will give me the access I need to find out. To finish what they started."

Pip's jaw tightened but Riley had turned away, not noticing the flash of bitterness in his eyes. It was clear Riley hadn't trusted him enough to tell him much of anything. That must hurt. Pip saw Rosie watching and his blue gaze narrowed. Rosie turned quickly away.

"So where is Dad then?" she asked Riley.

"They would have taken him to their original base where all their records are kept, including what the Shores were working on. They call it the Enclave. It's forty or so kilometres from Genesis."

"On Mars?" She stared at him. "Then how do we stop them? If you give them back some of the stuff in the box, will they let him go?"

"Sorry, Rosie, I can't do that. There's more than your father's life at stake." He glanced at her aunt. "Besides, I don't think it would help."

"Why not?" Rosie's anger was starting to outweigh her fear.

"Because these aren't the kind of people who keep bargains," Aunt Essie said slowly and the look she gave Rosie was bleak. "Even if we gave them what he has, it's unlikely they'd let your dad go, hon."

Rosie felt something cold touch her spine.

"I sent them a message after I met you, Rosie," Riley

said. "I told them you had given up the box to me but they refused to deal. And now they know you're being helped and will want to know who I am."

"And they will be after Rosie even more now to try to find out," her aunt said. "All because of you." Her expression darkened, like she wanted to pull out her knife again.

"I'm sorry," Riley said. "I was trying to help. It was a long shot but worth a try."

"A shot you should have—"

"It doesn't matter," Rosie interrupted. "We have to figure out how to save Dad."

They both paused.

"Rosie, these are dangerous people," Aunt Essie said.

"No, she's right," Riley said. "We should go after them."

"What?" Rosie's aunt's voice was flat and hard.

"They might not expect that. They're more likely to think we'll target the news or go to the Senate."

"You think we should go to Mars?" Rosie said, and he nodded.

"No." Aunt Essie shook her head. "No way."

"If she stays, they'll get to her," Riley said. "There's nowhere to hide."

"That's if what you're saying is true," her aunt countered.

"I have no reason to lie."

"That's debatable."

"Aunt Essie," Rosie said, "I believe him. We should go."

"She's right, you know," Pip said. "Pissing around here won't get her dad back." Rosie glanced at him in surprise but he cut his eyes quickly away.

Her aunt studied her for a long moment then turned to Riley. "If we do go, how do we stop them murdering Adam? And why do I get the feeling you're not telling us everything?"

"Because I'm not," Riley said. "I have other reasons for going – things that you don't want to be part of – but I will help you get Adam back."

"How?" Rosie said. "What do we do even if we get to Mars?"

"I'll give them something they won't refuse. Something they want badly."

Rosie wanted to ask what it was but the closed expression on his face prevented her.

He seemed to have convinced her aunt because after a short silence, she said, "Well, we can't get to the colony in a corp shuttle – too many questions."

"How about your pod?" Rosie suggested.

"It's parked in the dock at Space Islands." Aunt Essie met Riley's raised eyebrows. "I keep a room there.

I get a discount through Orbitcorp."

He didn't say anything but Rosie could see he was surprised. Space Islands was a huge hotel in stationary orbit outside Earth's atmosphere and was more like an amusement park. Her aunt didn't exactly seem the amusement park type.

"I might be able to get us on the next shuttle," Pip said. "I know a bloke who works on the luggage crew."

"We won't need him," Riley said. "I can get new ident cards and we can use them to buy tickets. It won't take long."

At Aunt Essie's appraising look, he only said, "Follow me." He pushed between them, heading for a door at the other end of the lab.

Aunt Essie's eyes met Rosie's, and Rosie could tell what she was thinking: how did he know his way around here and could they trust him?

CHAPTER 16

They left Orbitcorp through a staff exit and Riley led them down a narrow side street alongside the complex. It ended at a basement car park where the round, bubble-like roofs of white solar cars spread out before them like rows of strange lollies, clean and glowing in the dimness. Riley stopped at the first one and took a small tool from his pocket.

"It disables locking systems," he said at Aunt Essie's curious glance.

"Are we stealing this car?" She raised an eyebrow.

"Borrowing," Riley answered. The door flipped open on its top hinge. "In the back, you two," he said to Rosie and Pip.

Rosie clambered in, followed by Pip and her

aunt took the front passenger seat.

"Where are we going?" Aunt Essie asked as Riley switched on the window reflectors so no one could see in.

"To get those idents."

"Of course," Aunt Essie said. "Don't bother to actually tell me where, and by the way," she leaned over, peering at the lights on the dash, "the turbo is still on."

"I know," Riley answered tightly, and then they were moving.

It was the first time Rosie had been in a hovercar. She glanced at Pip and wondered if it was his also, but he was staring out of the window with a frown. Stewing over Riley's treatment probably, she thought. He turned to her and she was surprised to see that rather than being angry, he seemed thoughtful, even unsure. Maybe he wasn't as tough as he made out. His gaze swept over her face and she got a sudden case of butterflies.

"What?" he said.

"Nothing." She turned away, annoyed at herself.

He tapped his fingers on the seat between them and she shifted closer to the door.

Riley drove out into a busy street, thick with cyclists, cars and a few long transport vehicles. Above them a shuttle zoomed along its line and on both sides of the street crowds of people walked to and fro carrying cases or talking into their coms.

The adults in the front were quiet and the car wasn't moving fast enough for Rosie. She felt sick with anxiety and fiddled with the pendant at her neck.

Riley turned the car down a narrow street and stopped it in front of a tall building. "Right, I've got to get that stuff. You wait here—"

"Forget it," Aunt Essie cut him off. "We're coming with you. Your boy can wait." Pip made a rude exclamation at this but Aunt Essie ignored him.

"That's not a good idea," Riley said.

"Tough."

"What am I going to say if someone sees you?"

"I'm sure you'll think of something. Come on, Rosie." Aunt Essie got out and opened Rosie's door.

Riley let out a long breath. "Fine. Pip, you stay here. If we're not back in half an hour—"

"Yeah, I know," Pip said curtly. "Leave the car and go to the safe house."

"Safe house?" Aunt Essie said sharply and pushed the car door shut.

"Just a precaution," Riley said.

Rosie and Aunt Essie exchanged a look. "Okay, whatever. Let's go." Aunt Essie led the way up the stairs to the front door.

The building looked like apartments. The lobby was small and poorly lit, and the reception desk was attended by a responsive hologram of a woman of about forty. It looked at them expectantly as they entered. "Can I help you?" It spoke in a voice two octaves too low, followed by a loud spit of static. Rosie flinched and covered her ears.

"Suite 452," he said. The hologram blinked, then became a grey fuzzy shadow. Riley reached under the desk and fumbled around for a moment before coming back to them with an entry card. Behind him the hologram flickered back to normal and stared past them as though they weren't there.

"This way," he said and headed towards a lift.

They emerged on the third level into a corridor filled with people. Long windows stretched across the opposite wall and on either side of the lifts was a row of doors, all whooshing open and closed as people entered and exited. The air was cold, despite the sunlight pouring in through the windows, and Rosie rubbed her bare arms.

"Where are we?" she whispered to her aunt.

"Not sure but I saw a Microcorp insignia on some workers' shirts. Could be a research facility."

"It is." Riley had heard them. He glanced back. "It's deliberately not signed and in an apartment block to stop the competitors sniffing around."

"That's what the trick with the hologram is for," Aunt Essie said.

"A simple code deviation – I designed it."

So he's some kind of security expert, Rosie thought.

Riley swiped his card through a door lock and they went through to another hallway. They hadn't gone far when a short, balding man coming out of a door up ahead saw Riley and began to walk towards them. Rosie heard Riley swear under his breath.

"Riley," the man called, hurrying up to him. "I've been messaging you for three days. Where have you been?" He did not seem pleased, and Rosie and Aunt Essie hovered behind his shoulder, trying to be inconspicuous.

"Sorry, I had to go to over east."

"I've been waiting for you to complete that report." He looked curiously at Rosie and her aunt. "Visitors?"

"This is Dr Black from Orbitcorp and her student," Riley replied. "They wanted to see some of our new technology."

Rosie stiffened at the use of her aunt's name, but the man only gave Aunt Essie the once-over and said, "Orbitcorp snooping around new tech again, eh? You can tell your superiors it will cost them. Only the reviewed work, Riley." He gave him a warning look then left. Riley took off again, turning into another corridor.

"Why did you tell him my name?" Aunt Essie whispered as he paused at a door and swiped his card.

"I had to. There's surveillance everywhere. Why do you think I told you not to come in?" He led them into a small, musty office.

Rosie figured this had to be Riley's. A large desk sat in front of a glazed window and high shelves held myriad coms, digi books and assorted computer parts. There were no other chairs except the one behind the desk, which was clear apart from embedded computer controls.

Riley went to the desk and touched some sensor buttons. A blue image of a Microcorp logo appeared and began to rotate above the desk. He moved his fingers lightly above the controls and the logo disappeared to be replaced by lines of text and the Senate insignia of joined hands.

He turned to her aunt. "Give me your current ident."

He removed a black box from a desk drawer and put Aunt Essie's card into it.

"I don't have an ident card," Rosie said, watching as sets of numbers rotated in midair above the desk. "It's expired."

Aunt Essie looked at her in surprise. "Why didn't you tell me?"

Rosie shrugged. "Dad didn't want to, you know …"

"That's all right," Riley said absently. He pushed more buttons and a holographic picture of Aunt Essie appeared and alongside it the name Alice Branigan. "I'll just pull your details off the population web and make a new card. It will be easier than adjusting a current one. There." He hit a few more buttons and gave Aunt Essie her new ident. "Here you go, Alice."

She made a face. "Alice is the name of a woman who serves coffee at a spaceport."

"Good, then that's what you do." Riley looked at Rosie. "Do *you* have any name preference?"

"No."

"How about Cate Branigan, Essie's daughter?"

Rosie shrugged and Riley quickly tapped away. "I'll use one of my old cards, re-code it and add your name." He tapped some more and Rosie's face appeared.

"That capture was taken last year," she said.

"Doesn't matter, it'll pass." He moved the information around then placed a new card in the black box. A minute later he handed her the ident. "Right, let's go." He powered the com down. Rosie studied the image of her face on the card. Her hair was shorter, but she supposed it wasn't too different.

They made it to the lobby and out the front door without incident. But then Riley stopped dead on the top step, so both she and Aunt Essie bumped into him. The car and Pip were gone.

CHAPTER 17

Riley put his arm around Aunt Essie's shoulders as if he did it every day and grabbed Rosie by the hand. Startled, Rosie was about to speak when he said in a low voice, "Play along – there's a Senate guard across the street."

The guard was leaning against a black car, talking to someone inside.

"Do what he says, Rosie." Aunt Essie put her arm around Riley's waist and smiled. Rosie tried to smile back.

Riley led them down the steps and strolled casually towards the main street.

"Keep going," Aunt Essie whispered. "Don't look back."

Rosie walked as casually as she could. The back of her neck was prickling and she couldn't help herself — as they reached the corner, she glanced back. Her heart leaped into her throat. The man was half a block behind them.

"He's following," she whispered.

Her aunt swore and Riley increased his pace.

"Where the hell is Pip?"

Rosie was beginning to panic. "Does the guard know who we are? Could he be with Helios?"

"Maybe," Riley said. "See that group of people ahead?"

Four men were standing in a group in the middle of the pavement talking.

"Yes."

"As soon as we get around them, we run."

"No," her aunt's whisper was harsh, "we'll look suspicious."

Riley spoke through a tight smile. "He might not know who we are but if he's a Helios mole, he'll know about Rosie. He's probably recognised her. Do you want to risk it?"

"You're the one who risked her!"

Rosie's pulse was racing. They were going to be caught before they could even get off the planet.

They reached the men and as soon as they were

around them, they ran. Rosie dodged past people, trying to keep up with her aunt. She could see the top of Riley's head just ahead of them. Behind, people exclaimed as the man pursued them. Hovercars hummed past her and overhead two shuttles zipped by each other in a rush of air that made her hair lift.

"Come on!" Aunt Essie called back to her.

Rosie dodged around an old woman, then almost fell as a small robot buzzed out of a shop and under her feet. She stumbled and panic overwhelmed her as she was pushed towards the road by the crowd. She'd lost sight of her aunt and the man in pursuit was almost on her. Suddenly, a car pulled up alongside on the kerb. The side door flew upwards and she saw Pip at the controls.

"Get in!" he shouted.

She threw herself into the passenger side. Pip gunned the motor and she slammed the door shut as the car lurched forward. Her aunt and Riley weren't too far ahead and had seen the car. Pip barely slowed enough for them to jump into the back seat, one almost on top of the other.

"Go!" Riley closed the door, looking back at the guard. He was on the kerb watching them and talking into a com as Pip swerved into the line of traffic and sped away.

For a long tense moment, none of them spoke. Riley

stared out of the back window. After a while it seemed as though they had got away. No sirens sounded and the traffic moved smoothly around them.

"He might not have known who we are," he said finally.

"Let's hope so," Aunt Essie said.

Rosie didn't speak; her heart was still thudding hard, more from fear than the run. What would have happened if they'd been caught?

Pip glanced at Riley in the rear-view mirror. "He arrived not long after you went inside. I didn't want to risk him seeing me," he said.

"You should have left the car," Riley answered tightly.

"It's stolen, boss. I thought it'd be smarter to take it."

Riley didn't reply. He looked angry but Rosie thought Pip was right. The Senate guard could have checked it and then they'd really have been screwed.

"Where did you learn to drive?" Aunt Essie said.

Pip shrugged. "Around."

"Do you know the way to the spaceport?"

But before he could answer, Riley said, "Pull over in this side street. I'm driving."

Pip was about to argue but hesitated at the look on Riley's face.

Without a word he stopped the car and they swapped places. Riley drove towards a steep ramp that led to the upper freeway that circled the city. He gunned the engine, speeding up to 200 kilometres per hour. Rosie sat beside him feeling tense and wishing she'd changed places with her aunt in the back.

It took nearly an hour to get to the public spaceport. It was on the coast, to the south of the city and the freeway exit led right to the outer gates.

The spaceport covered an enormous area. It had two terminals: one for interplanet travel and another for off-world launches. Riley parked the car at the edge of the sector for the off-world terminal and they got on the hoverbus to the terminal.

The bus was full of holiday-makers: couples with matching luggage and families with noisy kids. The four of them huddled together, all of them tense, none of them speaking. The display on the bus announced there were two ships bound for Space Islands waiting to launch. Rosie hoped they'd be able to get on one of them.

The terminal was like a shuttle port without the shuttles. A line of auto check-in booths took up one corner, another line of desks sold tickets nearby and there were dozens of shops selling clothes, food and liquor. A holo sign proclaiming the latest in nausea-calming space travel drugs rotated near the entrance and ship stewards wearing Space Islands uniforms smiled brightly at people as they showed them where to submit luggage.

"We need to keep out of sight," Riley said. "Especially you, Rosie. Get between your aunt and Pip."

He shoved Pip so he was walking beside her, blocking her from view of most people in the area.

"No worries, *boss*," Pip said, his tone tinged with sarcasm. Obviously, he was still annoyed about the driving thing but Riley appeared not to care.

He took them to a retro-themed cafe and directed them to some stools along a side wall. Then he bought them each a drink and went to one of the public comnets. Rosie sucked the sweet, bubbly liquid through the straw, feeling the rush of engineered caffeine hit her empty stomach, and looked for the telltale Senate uniform. She couldn't see any, but that didn't mean they weren't there. Maybe someone from Helios had seen them already. Maybe they weren't dressed as guards.

Aunt Essie looked narrow-eyed at everyone and didn't touch her drink, while Pip downed his in a few swallows then proceeded to twist his straw into strange shapes, flicking Rosie with the remnants of liquid left in the tube.

"Stop it," she hissed. He smiled and sprayed her with

drops again. She threw her straw at him, wondering why he was suddenly so cheerful.

"Children," her aunt said quietly.

Pip raised his eyebrows at her, his eyes mischievous, and flicked her aunt, spattering liquid on her arm.

"Cut it out, Pipsqueak!" She glared at him.

"Pipsqueak?" He grinned. "Jeez, Aunty, a nickname? Does this mean you like me?"

"Sure. The way I like poison in my tea."

He chuckled and looked sideways at Rosie. "It's true, I am a dangerous addition to beverages, and highly addictive." He winked at her and put the straw in his mouth, chewing lazily on it. She stared back speechless. Was he flirting with her, now in the midst of all this?

Riley came back to them and said, "I managed to get us three berths on the second ship. It leaves in an hour."

"Three?" Pip's smile disappeared.

"You don't need to come." Riley took a sip of Aunt Essie's drink. "Besides, you've got no ident."

Pip stood up. "So I save your arse and you dump me?"

"Keep your voice down." Riley's own voice was low and controlled. "You don't need to be involved any further. I need you to stay here and keep an eye on the Senate."

"So that's how it is." Pip threw the straw onto the table.

"I'll still pay you, if that's what you're worried about."

Pip said nothing for a moment as he and Riley looked at each other. Finally, he glanced at Rosie and his lips tightened.

"Fine, no worries, boss." He gave Riley a mock salute. "See you 'round." He left the cafe, his dreadlocks bouncing as he loped off.

"Let's go wait in the lounge," Riley said.

Rosie followed them out of the cafe. She was relieved Pip wasn't coming; he was annoying and unsettling and she had enough to deal with already. Aunt Essie put an arm around her as Riley took their ident cards and swiped them through the auto check-in.

"We're a step closer, kid," she whispered. "Keep your head down."

The air in the waiting lounge smelled of vomit, fuel and air freshener, and all around them people were talking or laughing and kids were complaining. Rosie sat next to Aunt Essie and Riley sat on her other side. It felt like they were light years apart from the happy people here.

"How much longer?" she said.

Aunt Essie looked at her watch. "'Bout ten minutes. They should call it soon." She was sitting very straight, her eyes constantly roving over the crowd.

Rosie watched a boy playing with a hover-yo. Another kid, a little girl, was standing at the window with her face pressed against the glass watching the ship, which was clearly visible through the floor to ceiling windows.

A D-class sonic cruiser, the ship held 150 passengers and twenty crew and was shaped like a gigantic pill with a pointy end. It had long arms, retracted now, that would extend once they breached the atmosphere and start the rotation that would give the interior a low level of gravity. It was a classic people mover and was in her book on space travel at home. Rosie had studied it, just as she'd studied all the other ships in her hope of getting into the Academy. So much had happened, she had forgotten that this was the first time she was going off-world; she was actually going into space. Rosie got up off the chair and joined the little girl at the window to watch the ship. Soon she would be in it and far up above the Earth. For a moment a sense of wonder eclipsed her fear and she felt as small as the girl beside her — a tiny part of the universe.

"She's a big one." Aunt Essie came up behind her. "Thousands of pounds of fuel in her."

"But not enough for light speed," Rosie said. She recited what she'd learned by heart in her studies. "It's got a fusion cell core that will reach speeds of up to 10 000 kilometres per hour, zero point eight of Earth's gravity — enough to keep us from bouncing up to the ceiling."

"Top of the class," Aunt Essie said.

Rosie looked up and her aunt smiled, but it was forced and the lines of tension were deep around her eyes. Rosie's elation evaporated. She'd never dreamed her first trip to space would be to save her father's life.

A woman's voice announced their flight was ready for boarding and the three of them joined the queue that took them down the long connection tube to the ship's hatch.

CHAPTER 18

Their seats were next to a small window in the main cabin. Behind them a sealed hatch led to the sleeping chambers for trips to Genesis, or further, and in the front another hatch led into the central viewing port where a third of the ship's hull slid back to give a view of the stars and Earth far below.

Rosie gazed out the window as the seat harness automatically fit itself over her shoulders and around her middle. The ground staff looked like ants as they zoomed off the tarmac in baggage carts. The screen on the back of the seat in front of her lit up with a Space Islands ad, bright 3-D fireworks exploding silently out towards her. She used the keypad on her chair to switch it off. Beside her, her aunt was staring straight ahead and Riley was watching his screen.

Her mind was filled with worry about her dad and what they would find when they made it to Mars.

"Aunt Essie," she whispered, nudging her. "What do you think Riley's going to offer them?"

"Not here," her aunt replied.

"What did you say?" Riley turned to them.

"Nothing," Aunt Essie said quickly. "Rosie just needs to use the toilet."

Riley looked silently from her to Rosie but didn't say anything.

Rosie turned back to the window. If the diary and key weren't enough to get her dad back, what was he going to trade? There was more to everything, a lot more. What was the secret the Shores died for? If Helios had killed them for it, what else could he possibly give them?

There was a sudden roar and the lights dimmed. She lost her train of her thought as the cabin began to vibrate.

Her seat screen lit up automatically. "Ladies and gentlemen," said a pleasant female voice, "we are now preparing for take-off. For those who haven't travelled with us before, oxygen inhalers will soon be released from your seats to assist with your comfort during the preliminary breach. Please attach these like so—"

An image of a woman clipping a tubular breathing device to her nose and mouth appeared on the screen.

"Please keep these in place until we have breached atmosphere. Your restraints will remain locked for the breach. After that, you are free to move around and join us in the recreation cabin for refreshments and to view the stars. As gravity will be reduced, please take care not to move too quickly. The estimated time to our destination is three hours and seventeen minutes. Thank you and have an enjoyable flight." A chime sounded and the screen went dark.

She glanced at her aunt, nerves playing with her insides. Aunt Essie smiled. "The first time is always the best, kid," she said.

Rosie tried to smile and stared out of the window as, with a shot of steam, the ship lurched up into the sky.

It took ten minutes to exit Earth's atmosphere. Clouds slid past her window like fog. The oxygen made her head feel clear and light, and the vibrations from the force of their lifting travelled through her body, massaging the muscles in her back. Her heart was pounding with anticipation and her vision was shaky, the curved roof of the cabin oscillating, and then suddenly they were out; gravity loosened its grip and the ship burst through into the blackness of space.

For a moment there was no gravity. Rosie lifted slightly off her chair, straining against the straps of her harness, and wisps of hair drifted around her head like strange tentacles. Her aunt's spiky hair was hardly any different but Riley's dark hair was a nimbus around his head, making him look much younger. He was trying to catch a pen which had floated out of the pocket of his shirt. He smiled wryly but then a dull mechanical sound filled the cabin and Rosie looked outside and saw the edge of a long arm extending into space. Moments later a low level of gravity started forming in the cabin as the ship began to rotate. Rosie settled back on the seat and her hair dropped to float lightly around her jaw.

Rosie smiled. "We're in space."

"Uh, yeah." Aunt Essie rolled her eyes.

Riley put his pen away and pushed the slowly retracting harness off his shoulders. "Let's go to the viewing station."

"Now?" Aunt Essie said.

"I thought Rosie had to go to the toilet?" Riley said.

"Right, yes, I do," Rosie said quickly, shrugging off her harness.

They followed him up the aisle to the recreation

hatch. Around them other passengers laughed and exclaimed as they acclimatised to the lower gravity, bumping into each other and the chairs. Rosie couldn't help feeling as though she'd come to a party to which she wasn't invited. The people around her were going to Space Islands for a holiday; she was going to stop someone killing her dad.

The viewing port in the recreation chamber had been opened and the whole curved wall of one side of the ship was a window out to space. Rosie stared out at the endless black vista, sparkling with faraway points of light and the blue orb of Earth. The ring of atmosphere was dense with cloud and pollution but it was still a beautiful sight – almost unreal.

"This way." Aunt Essie shook her arm and Rosie tore her gaze away. They crossed the wide expanse of the ship, leaving Riley standing alone in the crowd.

"Careful," he whispered to her as she passed him.

His words immediately made her regard the other passengers around her with suspicion. But none of them seemed remotely like they were here for any other purpose than to have fun. A couple in a corner weren't smiling though, they were … She stopped and stared. She couldn't believe it. How had he got on? Standing with his back to her, half hidden behind a group of people, was Pip.

She pulled free of her aunt's grip and, moving awkwardly in the low gravity, went towards him. It was difficult to move quickly as, with each step, her feet seemed to arrive in a slightly different place to where she intended. So it was more of a hopping, skipping motion. Pip turned and saw her when she was still an arm's length away.

"Rosie." He didn't appear surprised and she noticed he'd managed to clean himself up. He had on a clean white T-shirt and jeans with only a few patches and even a pair of boots. The white shirt made his brown skin and blue eyes stand out even more. To her irritation, Rosie's heart beat faster. He stepped forward and yanked her towards him, causing her to slam into his chest.

"Ow!" She pulled out of his grip, crossing an arm across her chest.

"Sorry."

"What're you doing here?" She glared at him.

"Told you I got a cousin in baggage." He grinned, then lost his smile. Her aunt was right behind her.

"Hey, Aunty," he said.

"Pipsqueak. You just turn up everywhere, don't you?" Aunt Essie looked at him with narrow eyes. "How did you get on?"

Pip shrugged. "Just talented, I guess."

"Or stupid." Riley joined them. "I told you to stay."

Pip's expression became defiant. "I came to warn you, boss," he said in a low voice. "I saw some people getting on who looked suspect. A guy and a girl – I'm sure they're not right. I thought they must be some of you-know-who."

"I saw them," Riley said.

Aunt Essie turned on him. "Why didn't you say something?"

"And have you all watching over your shoulders? Besides, Pip's wrong. They're not with Helios. I haven't seen anyone on board who might be. It's odd."

Aunt Essie poked him in the chest. "This lone ranger crusade has to stop, Riley. In case you've forgotten, we're all in danger here."

"I haven't forgotten."

"Oh, really? You could have fooled me. I need to know what's going on. And I mean everything. What if something happens to you or me? What the hell are Rosie and Pip going to do?"

"I can take care of myself," Pip said.

"Well, Rosie's not a Feral, Pipsqueak," Aunt Essie said. "And you overestimate your ability."

"I'm not helpless," Rosie said, feeling irritated.

"I know you're not," said her aunt. "That's not what I meant. I think it's time we found out what all of this is about, don't you?" She turned back to Riley.

"I've told you all you need to know."

"You mean all you want to tell us." Aunt Essie leaned towards him. "Why should we keep following you if you're going to keep us in the dark?"

Riley's mouth twitched. "All right, but only you. You two go sit over there and wait." He indicated a set of empty chairs a few metres away.

Rosie was about to protest but her aunt stopped her.

"It's okay, Rosie," she said. "I'll fill you in after, hon."

"You might change your mind about that," Riley said.

"We'll see." She put a hand briefly on Rosie's shoulder then walked a few paces away with Riley.

Pip didn't appear to care. He just rolled his eyes and slouched over to the seats and sat down. Rosie joined him but kept an empty seat between them. He smirked and, annoyed, she watched her aunt and Riley standing close together. Riley had a hand on Aunt Essie's shoulder and was talking close to her ear.

Her insides were stretched taut as wire.

"Typical," Pip said. "Mr Mystery strikes again."

Rosie ignored him. She couldn't see her aunt's face, but she was standing very still as she listened. Every so often she nodded and said something back. What was it that he didn't want her to know?

She could feel Pip watching her. It made her

uncomfortable and she tried to pretend he wasn't there, but then he moved into the seat next to hers.

"What do you think he's saying?" She could feel the warmth of his breath near her ear.

"Don't know." She didn't look at him.

"Your aunt thinks he's hot," he said.

"What?" She turned to him. "She does not. She was going to stab him."

Pip shrugged. "Girls always do weird things like that when they like a guy." He smiled and put his hands behind his head. "I've had girls try to beat me up, throw things at me, even call me names," he winked at her, "but they're all just after the same thing."

Rosie stared at him in amazement. His T-shirt was riding up, exposing a line of tanned stomach and the muscles in his arms bunched as he leaned his head in his clasped hands. "You're deluded," she said and got up. "I'm going to check out the view."

She tried to move too quickly, almost stumbling as her feet failed to make proper contact with the floor.

"Careful." Pip grabbed her arm and stopped her from tumbling. "I'll come with you, leave the lovebirds alone."

"No, thanks." Rosie tried to pull away but succeeded only in pulling herself closer to him.

"Oh, come on, Rosie. Don't be like that. I was just

teasing." He tried to put an arm around her waist but she pushed him away.

"Stop it, Pip. Can't you be serious about anything?" She was suddenly angry. "What are you even doing here? You don't care about me or my family. You're just here to get more money out of Riley or something. Why don't you just piss off!"

He looked at her like she'd hit him.

"What?" she said savagely.

His smile was gone and there was emptiness in his eyes now. The brightness had gone and there was a bleak desperation in his gaze, a sadness. Rosie felt as though she'd got a glimpse of the real Pip and he looked older, worn.

"You know," he said quietly, "I wish I could. I'm really sorry about your dad, Rosie. I didn't–" He clenched his lips together as if he'd been about to say something he shouldn't.

"What?" She reached out to him, trying to take his hand, but he shook his head and walked away.

She stared after him. What had just happened? She watched his tall frame disappear from view as a chattering family swarmed towards the viewing window. He didn't seem to have any trouble moving in the lower gravity.

"Where's he going?" Aunt Essie came up beside her.

"Don't know."

"He won't go far." Riley had followed her aunt. "Come on, let's get some food."

"As long as you're buying," Aunt Essie replied.

Apprehension filled Rosie. The tone of her aunt's voice had changed: she sounded friendly towards him now. What had he told her to make her change?

Unsettled, she fingered the pendant as she followed them to the ship's restaurant. Would her aunt tell her what he'd said? She was getting a feeling she might not and it made her feel very alone.

CHAPTER 19

Pip didn't show up again for the rest of the trip and Aunt Essie didn't tell Rosie what Riley had said. They'd sat in the recreation area and watched everyone else and at no time had her aunt made any move to get her alone to speak to her.

Rosie began to wish she hadn't chased Pip off – at least if he was there, they could have been in the dark about everything together. She felt ill about what she'd said to him and couldn't get the look of hurt on his face out of her head, or what he'd said. Despite what he'd done, he'd been doing it under orders from Riley – and he'd saved their skins in the city with the car. They could have been caught if it wasn't for Pip and she'd treated him like he was nothing. Was he off somewhere now feeling as alone as she was?

She needn't have worried though. They docked at Space Islands ten minutes ahead of schedule and he was waiting for them in the disembarkation chamber, the nonchalant grin back on his face. "Here I am, boss." He winked at Aunt Essie. "Aunty, having fun?"

"Pipsqueak, what a pleasant surprise," her aunt said.

"You miss me, Aunty?"

"Like the black plague." She smiled in exasperation.

Pip's eyes went to Rosie briefly but she could have been anybody. His smile was easy, as though he had no problems in the world.

Rosie watched the hatch that was slowly opening and felt stupid. Idiot. Why had she thought she'd upset him? Clearly, he was fine.

A voice was announcing their arrival over the intercom and telling them that people would disembark in groups of ten at a time and be picked up in the hotel's transports.

Rosie had studied the Space Islands complex almost as closely as she had studied the spaceships. It was built like an enormous wheel. At its core was a long tube of docking bays – the gravity maintained at Earth levels – topped by the hub, a transparent-roofed zero-G dome where you could play sling ball, ride the catapult or even don wings and "fly". Extending out from the central core were seven spokes, each one a long tube connecting to the outer wheel of the hotel proper, where normal gravity was maintained along with the rooms, gardens, a water park and restaurants.

Their ship had docked at level eight, two floors above the spoke entries. Aunt Essie was twitching with impatience as they waited to leave of the ship. Finally, she turned to Rosie and said, "I'm not waiting for this." She nudged Riley. "If I use my own ID, we can get out of here faster. They know me here anyway."

Riley nodded.

"This way." Her aunt began pushing through to the front of the queue, ignoring the protests. Rosie kept her head down and followed, conscious of Pip right behind her. Her aunt spoke to a man in uniform at the front and handed him her original ident. He waved them through.

"Check it out," Pip said as they emerged onto a wide walkway.

The docking bay was a massive circular open space, about as large as two football fields, crisscrossed with connecting metal walkways and platforms that seemed to float in midair. Looking over the chest-high balustrade, Rosie could see all the way down to the other floors, and above them, all the way to the curved base of the zero-G dome hundreds of metres overhead. It made her dizzy. Spaced around the inner walls were more airlocks that allowed passengers to enter the hub from the ships docked outside. Next to each airlock were smaller hatches which gave maintenance crews and robotic repair systems access to the outer airlocks.

An open-sided cart sat whirring quietly on the walkway near their hatch, waiting for its passengers. The sides flashed colourful images of Space Islands' attractions and a small pod-shaped robot hovered in the air nearby, a spiel of information sounding from its microphone as the other passengers climbed into the cart.

"Follow me." Aunt Essie turned to a narrower walkway that led to the centre of the hub. People in white uniforms were moving back and forth along the various walkways, many accompanied by buzzing robotic pods. Far across the other side and a level down, a long line of passengers in carts were rolling up and waiting to enter another ship.

They reached a central platform and turned left, heading for a smaller hatch, which turned out to be a lift. They all filed in and after pressing a button, her aunt said, "We should go straight to my room. I can request my pod be cleared for launch from there and the service kiosk isn't too far away. We'll be able to stock up on oxy tubes and some food for the trip. If we do it that way, no one will know there's anyone else but me going."

"Doesn't security check on your ship before it leaves?" Riley said.

She shook her head. "I get easy clearance because of my job. I'm always coming and going, same as other staffers on Genesis and the station. They only check the cruisers and colonists now. We're all just assumed to have clearance."

"No wonder it's so easy for Helios," Riley said.

The lift chimed and the doors opened into one of the spokes. Fifty metres of walkway led to the outer wheel of the hotel. The roof was curved and set with long clear panels so you could see the stars, and there was no gravity. Rosie knew the spokes were a zero-G zone but she wasn't prepared for the reality. As soon as the lift doors opened, they all drifted up from the floor, floating out into the spoke. She couldn't suppress her gasp of surprise as the weight left her body. Wisps of hair floated around her face and her pack suddenly weighed little more than a feather.

Pip let out a loud whoop and tumbled out of the lift, knocking Rosie as he floated up towards the roof. She bounced off him with a shriek and her aunt grabbed her foot.

"Sorry," Aunt Essie said, "I forgot none of you have been here before. Riley, do you need a hand?" Riley was slowly tumbling end over end.

"No, no." He stretched himself out, putting a hand on the roof and stopping his tumbling. "I'm fine."

Aunt Essie pulled Rosie back down to the floor, trying not to laugh.

"Hey, Rosie," Pip called as he drifted down, "bet I could toss you like a ball!"

"What, no!" she protested but it was too late. Before her aunt could stop him, Pip had picked her up and pushed her away from him down the spoke.

"I'm going to kill you!" Rosie yelled as she somersaulted away. But in truth, it was fun. The stars whirled above her, then below her, then above again as she rolled around and around down the spoke, bumping harmlessly into the padded walls.

"Rosie, stretch out," Aunt Essie called after her.

She could see them floating behind but she didn't want them to catch up. It was wonderful, like swimming underwater, the weightlessness, the freedom of it, and all about her, the stars, brilliant in the black. She laughed and then gasped as hands grabbed her waist and legs wrapped around her. Pip had caught her from behind. For a brief moment he tumbled with her and she felt his body warm and bumping against her back, an arm about her waist.

"Slow down," he said softly in her ear, stretching her out, his hand on her thigh. Her stomach lurched and she thrust him away from her. Then Aunt Essie and Riley were beside them and her aunt was glaring at him.

"Enough, Pipsqueak," she said, but he only shrugged.

"What? I was just having fun."

"We're not here for fun," Riley said and grabbed the neck of his shirt. "Come on." He floated ahead towards the hotel hatch. Pip gave Rosie a smile and a wink as Riley towed him away.

Aunt Essie cast her a knowing glance. Embarrassed, Rosie trailed her aunt through the hotel hatch into an airy vestibule. The hatch sucked shut and she took a sudden short breath as full gravity hit her.

"Just give yourselves a minute to get used it," her aunt said, but Rosie barely heard her as she saw Pip leaning against the wall next to Riley waiting for them. He gave her a slow smile. She looked away, her cheeks warm.

"This way." Aunt Essie led them out of the vestibule.

Rosie kept pace with her aunt as they crossed some kind of garden or relaxation area. There were plants everywhere and people strolling around dressed in light clothing. The air was warm and moist and the sound of water falling and birds twittering blended with the hum of talk and laughter.

"How far is it to your room?" Riley said.

"Not far. There's an inner wheel shuttle up ahead."

"Good. This has all been too easy – it's making me

nervous." His voice was low and tense and Rosie followed his gaze as he checked behind them. Pip looked back at her, his expression unreadable. She quickly turned around as Aunt Essie stopped at a grey door.

"Here." She swiped her ident through a lock and the door slid into the wall to reveal a narrow car with four seats buzzing above a flat track.

Her aunt and Riley sat in the two front seats. Rosie climbed into the back, Pip close behind. The door to the corridor closed and they were moving forward, the car whooshing along through a white tube that followed the circular curve of the wheel. The seats were close together and she swayed into Pip as the car zipped around a corner. He barely seemed to notice; he was distracted, his body tense.

"Pip?" she said softly. "I'm sorry, you know, for what I said before, on the ship."

He shook his head. "Forget it." His fingers drummed on the armrest between them.

It was as though he hadn't really heard her. She put her hand on his. "I mean it – I'm really sorry."

For a second she thought he was going to give one of his smart-arse replies, but he glanced down at their hands instead, then lifted his gaze to hers. Her heart suddenly beat faster and she started to move her hand.

"Don't." He put his other hand over hers and slipped

his fingers between hers. "Rosie," he said then stopped.

She swallowed, barely noticing if they were still moving or not. "What?"

"It's just," he kept looking down at their hands, "if something happens—"

"Like what?"

He paused, took a breath and then seemed to change his mind. "Nothing." He let her hand go. "It's nothing – don't worry about it."

Rosie willed him to look back at her, but he kept staring ahead and then Aunt Essie said, "We're here." The car began to lose pace and the moment was gone.

They stopped in front of another door that opened to a corridor and a clear wall through which Earth was like a giant Christmas bauble in space. But Rosie's stomach was in too many knots for her to enjoy the view. What had Pip been about to tell her? She wanted to ask him, to touch his arm as he stood so close to her, but he had gone very quiet. He stared at the floor and waited for her aunt to open the door.

The apartment was compact and neat. In the sitting room was an oval window with a view to the stars.

Riley went straight over to the comnet patched into the wall near the bedroom door, and Pip strolled to the window. She hoped now she could get Aunt Essie to tell her what Riley had said. Rosie grabbed her arm as she was going past her to Riley.

"Aunt Essie," she whispered. "Can I talk to you?"

Her aunt paused, watching Riley who was busy linking up to the hotel's net hub.

"We don't have time right now," she said. "Can it wait?"

Rosie sighed. "Yeah, okay. Where's the bathroom?"

"Off the bedroom." Her aunt called to Pip as she went to help Riley, "Hey, Pipsqueak, make yourself useful. There's some food in the kitchen, fix us something to eat."

"What do I look like, a chef?" He turned from the window.

"Just do it."

Rosie went into the bedroom, shutting the door, then went to use the toilet. When she came out she crossed to the door and was about to open it, when the sound of her name made her pause. She could hear her aunt and Riley speaking in low, barely discernible voices. They were sitting at the comnet just outside the door. A trickle of unease ran down her spine. They were talking about her.

She pressed an ear to the door. They were arguing, Aunt Essie disagreeing with something he'd said.

"We can't tell her about the Genesis Project," she said. "It's too much for her. She already feels guilty enough."

"She deserves to know," Riley said. Then his voice became inaudible. Rosie strained to hear.

Her aunt spoke again, anger plain in her tone. "No! She's been through enough already. Her friend is dead; her dad's gone. How much more do you think she can take? I won't tell her hundreds will die because of that damn beacon."

Rosie went hot then cold. She backed away from the door and sat on the bed.

She couldn't have heard them right. She put her elbows on her knees and rested her head in her hands. The pendant swung out from under her shirt and she watched it dangling. Hundreds will die.

She wasn't sure how long she'd been sitting there when her aunt called out to her. Her heart leaped in her chest. The door opened and her aunt poked her head in.

"There you are. What're ..." she trailed off as she saw the expression on her face. "I'll just be a minute," she said over her shoulder. She came into the room and shut the door behind her. "Rosie, what is it?"

Rosie's voice shook as she said, "Why didn't you tell me?" For a moment she thought her aunt would deny it, but then a defeated expression came over her face.

"You were listening?"

Rosie nodded and Aunt Essie let out a long breath and sat on the bed beside her. "Rosie–" She got up again and began pacing back and forth before her. "I'm not good at this," she said. "How much did you hear?"

"Hundreds of people. You said hundreds of people were going to die because of what I did."

"They *might* die – might," she said. "There's a difference."

"That's not what you said to Riley. You said *will* die. Is that what Riley told you on the ship? That it's my fault, that I've—"

"No. This is why I didn't want to tell you. You're blaming yourself."

"But it is my fault. I found the box. I let Juli put the code key into the comnet."

Her aunt sat back down again, rubbing her face with her hands. "Hon, these people – Helios – they started all this, not you."

"Yeah, but it wouldn't have happened if I hadn't found the box. Now Juli's dead and Dad's gone. He could be dead too. I just …" She felt like she wanted to cry but she pushed back the tears. *There's no use crying, Rosie Black.* She felt a sudden aching hollowness inside. "I deserve to know, Aunt Essie, I'm not a little kid any more."

"No, I guess not." Her aunt sighed. "All right, do you remember Riley saying Helios had built a base on Mars called the Enclave?" Rosie nodded. "Okay, well what the Shores were working on was part of something

Helios is still doing there. They call it the Genesis Project. They've been doing experiments – tests. If the Senate found out they were doing it, they would not be happy."

"But what is the Genesis Project?" Rosie said. "What were the Shores doing?"

"I don't know, but Riley thinks it's a new generation of experiments built on what the Shores did – and since the beacon was turned on Helios has become very nervous."

"Because they think Riley will expose them with what I found in the box?"

"Yes. And because of that he says they issued an order to clean Genesis."

"What does that mean? Are they going to attack the colony?"

Aunt Essie didn't answer right away. "No, not the colony. It means they're going to destroy their labs, the Enclave – with everyone who works for them inside."

For a second Rosie felt nothing. "Hundreds of people," she whispered.

"Yes," her aunt said softly.

She stared at her hands. "What's Riley going to do?"

"Try to stop them."

"How?"

"I'm not sure. He keeps saying that what he has to

trade will save your dad and allow him access to Helios. That he'll get to them that way. He has a plan but he won't tell me what it is."

"He doesn't want us involved," Rosie said. She felt strange; along with the fear, had come a profound sense of clarity. Consequence. She remembered one of her first science classes. For every action there is an equal, or opposite, reaction. Who had said that? She couldn't remember but it didn't matter. This was the consequence of what she and Juli had done.

"We should help him," she said. "After we get Dad back, we should help him."

Her aunt didn't reply as sadness filled her face. Rosie felt a leap of fear and realisation. Something caught in her throat. "You don't think we can save Dad."

Aunt Essie looked away. "These people ..." She shook her head. "If they will kill hundreds to protect themselves ..."

Rosie knew what she left unsaid. Why wouldn't they kill one man? It made the well of pain inside swell, threatening to spill over, to immobilise her with grief as it had done when her mum died. But she refused to believe it. They had to have some hope.

She grabbed her hand. "Aunt Essie, we—" Her words were cut off by a loud crash from the other room. They stared at each other.

"That didn't sound good." Her aunt moved swiftly to open the door. Riley was holding a hand to the side of his head while behind him the outer door was sliding shut. Shards of thick glass lay scattered on the floor.

"What the hell happened?" Aunt Essie rushed to his side. "You're bleeding."

"Yeah, I guessed that," Riley said.

"Sit down." Aunt Essie pointed to the sofa. "I'll get my medikit." She went back into the bedroom.

Riley moved awkwardly to sit. Blood was trickling down the side of his face and a bruise was forming near his temple. Rosie looked around. "Where's Pip?"

"Gone to his master like all good dogs, I expect."

"What?"

Riley gave her a bitter smile. "Seems Helios had an inside man after all. We really were being followed."

Aunt Essie came back and sat beside him. "Let me see it," she demanded. He lifted his hand. A long jagged cut ran from under his hairline down one cheek. He screwed up his face as her aunt wiped it clean and mopped up the blood.

Rosie sat down on the sofa. She felt as though she'd been punched in the stomach. Pip was one of them. He'd been working for Helios all along.

"He took the code key," Riley said.

"What?" Her aunt stopped swabbing. "How the hell did he get that off you?"

"I was careless." He flinched as she spread skin repair foam over the cut.

"What about the diary?" Rosie said.

"No." He shook his head and patted a fastened pocket on his shirt. "Here."

She was relieved. "Well that's okay then, isn't it?" Rosie said.

"Without the key the information in the diary is useless. It only has the codes for the Enclave's internal labs. It will get us through the complex but we need the key to get the Shores' information from their system." He stopped. "There could be a back door in, another way to break their computer hub." But he didn't sound certain.

Aunt Essie packed up her kit and handed it to Rosie. "Put this away."

Rosie took it automatically and went to the bathroom. She couldn't believe Pip had betrayed them. She shoved the kit back into the cupboard and slammed the door. How could she have been so stupid as to think he cared about her? Idiot. She kicked the cabinet then caught a look at herself in the mirror.

She was a mess. Her face was pale and dirty, her hair tangled. She brushed it out with her aunt's comb, pulling the strands down savagely again and again, getting more furious at herself as she began to cry while she did it. When it hung unknotted about her face, she pulled it back into a single ponytail and wiped her tears away. She splashed her face with cold water.

"Rosie?" Aunt Essie appeared in the doorway. "We have to go."

She nodded and wiped her face. Her aunt watched her.

"Hurry," she said quietly, "we need to get to the pod."

Rosie went back into the lounge room. Her head was throbbing as she swung her pack onto her shoulders. Aunt Essie and Riley picked up their own gear, their faces hard and set. She kept seeing Pip smiling at her — that slow smile. It was like a spike going through her heart. At least now she knew what he'd been about to tell her. *Oh, by the way, Rosie, if I happen to betray you all, don't get mad. It's not personal*, or some crap like that. He'd probably been putting on all that hand-holding stuff.

Her aunt went to the sofa and reached underneath. She pulled out two guns. She handed one to Riley. "In case."

He put it in the waistband of his trousers.

"Come on." Her aunt led the way. Rosie followed, thinking of how she wanted to slap Pip's handsome, lying face.

CHAPTER 20

The hallway was empty but Aunt Essie was taking no chances. She pushed Rosie between her and Riley and led them at a jog towards the end of the corridor, then stopped. "Wait," she whispered. "Did you hear that?"

Rosie heard a faint thudding vibration coming from around the corner.

"Sounds like heavy boots," Riley said.

"Follow me to the corner." Her aunt's face was grim.

They crept quietly along the corridor until she put her hand up again. Rosie flattened herself against the wall next to Riley.

Aunt Essie peeped around the corner. "They're here already," she said.

"How far is it to your pod?" Riley whispered.

"Around the corner, where the corridor turns right, there's an access door that goes under the spoke to the docking bay. The pod is on level three, bay five."

"On the other side of those men," Rosie said. Her stomach was in knots at the thought.

"Yep." Aunt Essie dropped to the floor and risked another glance. She pulled back quickly. "There're three of them. We're going to need a distraction to get past. It's the only way to the pod from here." She chewed on her bottom lip. "Rosie, you remember my lessons in how to fly the pod?"

Rosie's heart contracted. "Yes." What was she planning?

"Good, just remember not to give her too much juice or she'll fly uneven, and watch the cells, they're getting old."

"Essie," Riley said, "what are you doing?"

She gave him a hard smile. "Getting you to Genesis, Riley. I'm the most expendable – if they get you, my brother doesn't have a hope."

Rosie suddenly understood what she was going to do. "No!" She gripped her arm but her aunt pulled her hand off.

"Cowards don't make the Academy, Rosie," she said sharply. "I'll be okay. Don't worry."

Dread filled Rosie as she stared at her aunt. Wasn't

Riley going to stop her? But he wasn't moving and Aunt Essie pulled the docking pass key from her pocket and pressed it into her hand. "This will open the accessway doors and the hatch. The password's 563. Now you run like hell when you hear me shout, okay?" Rosie nodded and saw a blink of fear in her aunt's eyes as she met her own. "You'll be okay, Rosie. You can do this." Then she was straightening up and looking over her head at Riley.

"You keep her safe or I'll break your neck." She pulled out her gun, drew a breath and was gone. Rosie's heart was hammering and she didn't know she'd moved until Riley pushed her back against the wall. She couldn't see what was happening but she could hear. There was a man's grunt of surprise, followed by the concussive whump of a pulse weapon.

"Go!" her aunt shouted.

Rosie and Riley ran down the corridor. Ahead of them a man lay on the floor, another was on his knees, blood dripping from a cut on his head, and Aunt Essie was grappling with a third.

"Run!" Aunt Essie roared and elbowed the man in the face. She turned to kick the kneeling man in the head, but he caught her boot and flung her against the wall.

"Aunt Essie!" Rosie slowed but Riley dragged her towards the door at the end of the corridor.

"The pass key, Rosie!" he shouted.

Her fingers shaking, she swiped the thin slice of metal through the key slot and pushed the door open. Behind them a muffled shot sounded. Rosie turned back to see her aunt lying on the floor with one of the men standing above her, his weapon drawn. Her aunt was clutching her stomach. There was blood on the wall. Time seemed to slow. She couldn't move, couldn't breathe.

Beyond her aunt, two more people were running towards them.

"Rosie, wait!" It was Mr Yuang shouting at her and Pip was behind him. His face was pale as he stared at her. Fury filled Rosie and she tried to go back, but Riley grabbed her, pushed her through and slammed the door. He shot the lock with her aunt's pulse gun.

"Move!" he shouted, and dragged her with him.

The accessway was narrow. It sloped down until it turned a corner then levelled out. It led straight to another door with a number three on it. They were under the spoke. *Aunt Essie.* Rosie's hand shook as she slid the pass key through the lock and pushed through to the docking bay. Walkways made of metal grille stretched away on either side and in front. She paused. Which way was bay five? There, a sign above pointed left.

She turned, running to the outer hull. The metal quivered under their feet and people turned to stare at them as they raced across the bridge. Behind them shouts echoed across the cavernous space.

"They're on the other side," Riley said.

She didn't look back. She felt numb, her terror all but driven away by her focus on one thing: escape. She led Riley to the outer walkway that ran alongside the hatches. Through the slit in the hull she could see three ships docked; the last one was her aunt's pod.

"The hatch," she said as she raced towards it. She could hear pounding feet now but didn't turn around.

"They're coming," Riley said.

The crash of boots on the walkways was like an orchestra of chains. Riley aimed the gun and pulled the trigger. Concussive snaps of sound sang.

"Rosie!" His voice held a warning.

She punched in the code and the hatch hissed open.

They jumped over the outer hull into the pod and Riley locked the hatch behind them as a pulse slug slammed against the metal.

Rosie sealed the pod's doors and ran through the small cargo bay and up the stairs to the bridge. She knew her aunt's ship well. Every time Aunt Essie had brought it home she'd let Rosie sit in the pilot's chair and drilled her through a hundred different flight plans. "If you want to be a pilot with Orbitcorp, you've got to be ready for anything," she'd said.

But Rosie had never actually flown it. Her heart was pounding as her whole focus narrowed to the pilot's seat, the nav console and the controls.

"Sit there." She directed Riley to the copilot's chair. She strapped herself in, then began the checking sequence. Aunt Essie ran a tight ship; all the controls were green, good to go.

"Jesus Christ," Riley was muttering as he strapped himself in. "That was Yuang."

But Rosie barely heard him as she concentrated.

"Okay," she whispered. "Nav com green. Ignition." With a shaking finger, she pressed the button and the engines rumbled into life. "Disconnect dock." She glanced at Riley, then realised he didn't know how. "Pull the blue handle towards you." She pointed and he wrenched the docking grip back. She took hold of the steering arms as the pod floated free and the docking arms retracted back into the hotel.

The com suddenly buzzed into life and a voice began hailing them. "This is Space Islands command, pod class thirty-three, you do not have permission to launch," it crackled. "Kill your engines immediately. You are endangering docking craft. I repeat, kill your engines! This is Sp–"

Rosie switched off the com and slowly pulled back on the steering, damping the starboard engine to perform a textbook reverse turn. The black was before her, dusted with stars.

Coming in ahead was a massive cruiser and on their left a recreation shuttle approached the dock above.

"Hold on." She pushed the steering forward, firing up the core at the same time. The pod sprang ahead, forcing them back in their seats.

"Watch the cruiser!" Riley shouted as they sped towards its left flank.

Adrenaline ran like cold fire through her veins and Rosie banked hard. The pod swerved on a thirty-five degree angle, almost sideswiping the shuttle. It was so close she could see the shocked face of the pilot as the pod blasted past them and shot out into open space.

Her hands were clenched hard on the steering arms.

"Do you have the coordinates for Mars?" Riley said.

"Yes." She nodded. Her head felt stiff and strange. "They should be programmed in." She turned to the nav com and called up her aunt's log. "Here." She transferred the information to the flight plan.

"You can let go now," Riley said quietly. Slowly, she uncurled her hands and called up the rear-view port on the computer screen, staring as Earth became smaller. And it was only then, as she watched it receding, that she remembered they hadn't had time to refuel.

With a bad feeling in her gut, she checked the tanks.

The trip to Mars would take forty-eight hours — there wasn't enough fuel.

Pip kneeled by Rosie's aunt. Blood was seeping from where the grunts had shot her and she was shuddering as he pressed down hard over the wound.

She glared up at him through narrowed eyes. "Trying to finish the job, Pipsqueak?" she hissed.

He ignored her. "Any of you got a nanoplast?" He said to the grunts.

"What are you doing?" Yuang watched him.

"I need to stop the bleeding."

"I realise that, but why?" Yuang crouched down, peering at Essie as though she was a peculiar exhibit in a museum.

Pip thought hard. He had to be careful here. If he said the wrong thing, Yuang would let her die. He could still see Rosie staring at him. "Because she's a better bargaining chip than Rosie's dad," he said. "Rosie and Riley won't want to let her die. They'll give up their plan for her."

Yuang touched a finger to Essie's cheek and she rolled furious eyes towards him. "The child — well, yes, this woman is the only relative she has left, *relatively* speaking, but Riley," he smiled coldly as if he'd made a private joke, "he's been waiting for this for half his life. It's his chance."

"I saw the way Riley looked at her," Pip said desperately. "He cares about her."

Yuang stood up. Pip kept his hand pressed against the wound. He wasn't sure if Yuang believed him. He wasn't even sure if he was right but he knew Rosie would never forgive him if her aunt died. And he couldn't stand the thought of that. Essie's eyes were closed now, her breathing faint.

"All right, I'll humour you for now." Yuang motioned to one of his men who pulled a small medikit from a pocket in his pants. "Patch her up and if she lives, we'll see if you're right."

Pip took the patch from the grunt and placed it carefully over the wound, making sure the nanoplast sealed and stopped the blood. He stood back and watched as one of the men picked her up.

"Come," Yuang put a hand on his shoulder, "we have a ship to catch."

CHAPTER 21

Rosie slammed the lid down on the store, kicking it shut, then crawled back out of the access tunnel.

"There's not enough fuel. It'll get us close but not all the way. About fourteen hours out from Mars if we're lucky. Damn it!"

She sat next to Riley on the steps leading up to the bridge and rested her head in her hands. She had a headache and was sweating from crawling around inside the narrow space.

"I checked the food supplies," Riley said. "There's a stack of protein bars, some vitamin shake powder and a few packs of soup. Not great but enough to last us. The robotics team must have filled the water tanks, 'cos they're okay."

"Yeah, that's protocol whenever a ship docks," Rosie said, "but it won't do us any good if we run out of fuel. Without fuel there's no power and without power there's no life support."

Riley was silent for a long time. Rosie stared at her shoes.

After a while he said, "That man, Yuang, if I'd known he was involved–" He shook his head. "This changes things."

For the first time he looked less than confident and it worried Rosie. "Does he know you?" she said.

"You could say that." Riley was staring ahead with a bleak expression on his face. "And he recognised me. I thought maybe he wouldn't but … he was always a smart bastard. He probably didn't know it was me though until just now or he would never have let us get this far already."

"Who is he?" Rosie said.

"A true believer."

"A believer of what?"

"In what Helios is doing."

"You mean the Genesis Project? I overheard you and Aunt Essie," she said. "She told me what you said."

Riley said nothing for a moment, then spoke quietly. "I wish to hell you hadn't been the one to find the box, Rosie. It should have been me."

After what he'd said to her back on Earth, about wearing the pendant to remember what she'd done, she thought he blamed her for everything. "It's not your fault," she said awkwardly.

"But it is, Rosie. I should have tried harder. Searched harder."

"But how could you even know?"

"Because it belongs to my family. My name isn't Riley. It's Simon, Simon Shore. Margaret and Ethan were my parents."

Rosie stared at him. Things began falling into place: his secret hide-outs, watching the Senate, what he knew about Helios.

"You should have told us," she said.

"It was safer for you not to know. In case."

In case she'd been caught, he meant. Rosie felt anger surfacing again. It hadn't helped her aunt. "So they're after you then?" she said.

"Yes."

"How come they haven't found you?"

"They did. Once. But I didn't know about the box then – my sister had it. I hadn't spoken to my parents for some time when they were killed. We were what you call, estranged." He shot her a bitter smile. "I was in the Asiatic States. Yuang found me there. They thought I'd have what they wanted because I was the older one.

By the time they'd finished with me, my sister had disappeared, the box along with her. She was only nine years old. I didn't even know she'd had the stuff until she managed to get a message to me two years ago." Angry disappointment filled his eyes. "She wanted to know why I hadn't done anything. She thought I had the box. Whoever she sent to get it to me must have got caught or something, so they hid it." He shook his head, staring away from her. "God knows what she thinks of me. I couldn't get a message back."

"Where is she now?" she said.

"Safe, but it's too risky to contact her. I've been searching for the box and hiding from Helios ever since." He shook his head. "I thought Yuang was dead."

"What's the Genesis Project?" Rosie asked.

"Helios's big secret." His gaze was weary. "The Genesis Project is their way of finding a cure for the MalX. But the way they do it – they experiment on humans, extract DNA, have test subjects, for as long as they live anyway."

Rosie felt ill. "Aunt Essie said they are going to clean Genesis."

"Yes." Riley looked at her, his face expressionless. "Kill their test subjects and their remains. Wipe clean the evidence, just in case we succeed and get proof to the Senate and the UEC about what they've been doing.

They think that nothing to see, means nothing to tell. But that's not their biggest secret."

"It's not?" How could there be something worse than what they were doing to hundreds of people?

"No," Riley said softly. "Their darkest secret is the one only a few in Helios actually know about. They created the MalX, Rosie. That's the secret my parents died for – the secret they were going to expose."

She stared at him. "How?"

"An experiment. They were playing with DNA, with a virus, trying to harness a chemical that mosquitoes produce which they thought could cure any number of Earth's diseases. But there was an accident, a mistake. A shipment sent back to Earth had the wrong cargo. Infected insects escaped into the atmosphere, but instead of trying to fix the accident, they covered it up."

"The mozzies bred," Rosie said faintly.

"My parents found out." He shrugged.

And they were killed, Rosie thought. "Without the code key there's no way to get the information they died for," she said.

"Yes. They'll destroy it all. There'll be no proof."

"Unless we can stop them," Rosie said. "But we don't have enough fuel to get to Mars."

"No."

They both fell into silence. Rosie tried to digest

everything he'd said. What did it all mean for her family now?

"What are you hoping to trade for my dad?" she said.

He didn't answer but when she looked at him he didn't need to. Of course, the diary wouldn't be nearly as valuable as him. Rosie knew the right thing to do was to argue, to try to stop him sacrificing himself, but she couldn't voice the words. "How?" she said.

"I was going to do it with your aunt's help. I was going to exchange myself for your dad. There're things I know about them and they want very badly to ensure my silence. While they were distracted with me, she was to break in with the code key and get my parents' files, but now I don't know, it's–" He exhaled sharply then stood up, pacing in frustration. "This was my best chance of bringing them down, of getting the information that will prove what they did to my parents, of giving my sister a chance for a normal life. I can't–" He faced away from her, visibly struggling for control. "I don't know how to get into their system without the code key. And now he has your aunt – I should have stopped her. I should have known Pip wasn't right."

"He tricked all of us," she said.

He turned back to her, a hard bitter determination in his eyes. "I don't like being conned."

"So what are we going to do?"

He shook his head and sat next to her again on the step. "I don't know."

They sat in silence a moment, the only sound the whirring of the ship's engines.

"Do you think Aunt Essie's okay?" Rosie whispered. "Will they help her? They won't let her die, will they?"

Riley didn't look at her. "I don't know."

Rosie squeezed her eyes shut tight for a moment, trying to stop herself from crying.

"They're going to Mars, aren't they?"

"Yes. I'd say so."

"We have to get to Mars," she said. "We can't go back to the hotel."

"No, we can't. But I don't—" He stopped and frowned. "Wait, the pod has an ion core drive, doesn't it?"

"Yes."

"And if we ran it at full capacity, would it get us to Mars?"

"Maybe, but we'd have to divert all the power to do it. Including what we need to run life support."

Riley tapped his fingers on his knee. "With the ion core drive at capacity our travel time to Mars would drop to, what, thirty-two hours?"

Rosie did the calculations in her head. "About that, but we might not make it to planetfall. We might only make it to the outer atmosphere. We'd crash."

"But Mars's atmosphere is thinner than Earth's and there's less gravity. There's a good chance we could survive."

Rosie didn't know what to say. Was he right? She kept seeing Aunt Essie lying on the floor, her blood leaking out. She hugged herself, staring ahead at the wall of the pod. One of her aunt's spacesuits was hanging on a hook, the legs trailing on the floor.

"Rosie," Riley said. "We have to keep going. You know that, don't you?"

"I know." Fear was like a lump in her guts but she didn't want it to win, she didn't want *them* to win. She took a long breath. "We could use the suits," she said.

"What?"

She pointed at the spacesuit. "There's more of them. Aunt Essie always keeps the breathers fully loaded too." Her mouth twisted in the semblance of a smile. "Be prepared, she always says. But each one only carries twenty-two hours of oxygen. We'd be ten hours short."

"How many suits are there?"

"Three."

"We could share the air from the third."

It was possible. It was also possible they could use up all the air and still not make it. They could just die here, in space. One way or another, the fuel would run out.

He was watching her closely. "I think we should try

it. I'll modify the suits so we can share the air."

"All right." She got up and headed back up the stairs to the bridge.

"I'm sorry your family got caught up in this, Rosie," he called after her.

She paused and knew she should say something, but she couldn't. She was sorry too. Sorry she'd ever seen the box. She trudged up the stairs to the bridge and sat in the pilot's chair and began checking through the ion drive settings.

Her head ached behind her eyes — sharp stabbing pains like she'd been sitting up for days playing AI games. She drank some water and began setting up the diversion of all power to the ion core drive.

As she worked, her mind kept going over and over what Helios had done. They were murdering her family, one by one. Her hands shook as she reconfigured the drives, diverting power. Well, they weren't going to kill her.

She was so caught up in her thoughts she almost didn't see the amber light blinking on the console. Only when she reached for her water did she spy it. She froze. It was the long-range beacon.

She slid over to the view port and flipped on the screen. There was a ship behind them. Ten thousand kilometres behind and moving much faster than they were.

"Riley!" she shouted through the ship's com. "There's a ship behind us."

"How big?"

"Bigger than us. I think it's an F-class."

He ran up the stairs, carrying the suits. "It'll be a Helios vessel for sure." He handed her a suit. "How far behind are they?"

"Maybe five minutes. Do Helios ships have core drives?"

"Some of them," Riley said tightly, watching the screen closely. "How long till the power can be diverted?"

"I have to manually override the life support."

"Go do it. We might be able to outrun them."

Rosie thrust her legs into the suit and ran down the stairs, shoving her arms into it while she ran and zipping it up. The life support system was behind her aunt's sleeping quarters in the belly of the ship. It was dim down there and smelled of engine and sulphur, but she squeezed through the small space and crawled to it. She was hyper aware of the minutes ticking away as she pulled out the controls and switched the system to manual override. *Please let me do it right*, she prayed, then pulled the plug. The constant whirring suddenly stopped. She had about ten minutes of air left before she needed a breather. She crawled out and jogged back to the bridge.

Riley was strapping himself into the copilot's chair. Rosie hesitated. She'd never tried to pilot on full core drive before. Not even in a simulator.

Riley handed her a helmet. "Rosie, here."

She jumped. She'd been staring at the console.

Rosie took the helmet and snapped it on over her head. She fitted gloves over her hands and clipped them to her sleeves. Then she sat down and strapped herself in. Once gravity failed, the straps would be the only thing holding her to the chair.

"Switch the power over," said Riley. "They're coming!"

The Helios ship was closing fast. She turned on her breather and grabbed the controls and began the sequence, flipping everything to the ion core drive. The pod began to oscillate and rumbled beneath her as all the power was sucked into the vast energy vortex. Gravity disappeared and she punched the core drive to full capacity.

CHAPTER 22

Pip sat on the table next to Rosie's aunt, his knees pulled up to his chest, watching her. She was very pale and still. The only indication she was alive came from the slight rise and fall of her chest.

The nanoplast had stopped the bleeding and Yuang had allowed her to be injected with some blood and tissue replicators, but that was all. He'd strapped her to the med bed and left Pip to watch her. If she died, Rosie would never forgive him.

He picked up the small medigun and shot her with another dose of nano-repair cells and watched the slow beep of her heart on the monitor.

When Yuang had given him his orders, he hadn't expected any of this to happen.

He had only asked him to watch Riley and to report on him. But Yuang hadn't known then who Riley was. He'd thought he was just some guy poking around in things that may or may not be important. Now everything was messed up.

He leaned his head back against the cold hull of the ship and closed his eyes. He hadn't slept for two days and things were starting to get – clouded. Rosie was clouding him up. Messing with his reasoning. It had been harder than he'd thought to betray them. Only the thought of why he was doing it had kept him on track. Do the job and he could go home.

That was still how he thought of the Enclave: home. The place he'd grown up, safe, or so he'd thought. He hadn't been back since he was ten. Eight years he'd been on Earth. He missed Mars: the smell of the sulfurous air, the red dust and the clean, warm corridors of the Enclave. He should be happy to be going back – relieved to get away from Earth's stink and the threat of the MalX. But part of him was uneasy.

Before his parents died, the Enclave had been all he'd known. Now it was different. He'd seen things on Earth that didn't add up to what he'd been taught. Ferals that Helios took and didn't bring back. Riley saying there were things about Helios that even he didn't know. And now what was happening to Rosie's family.

He rubbed his eyes. He had a headache and was nauseous from hunger. He should look for something to eat – there would probably be some protein bars in the galley. And he should ask Yuang for a shot of the antiviral, just to be certain. It wasn't a real cure, but Yuang had said it would stop him getting the MalX while he was on Earth. Now he was going home, surely Yuang should give him one more, just in case.

Essie made a soft noise and her hand twitched under the straps. He gave her another shot of the nano cells, and was discarding the empty pill case when one of Helios's soldier drones, a grunt as he called them, appeared suddenly in the doorway.

"Oi." The stocky red-haired man filled the exit. "Yuang wants you up top." Like all the other grunts this one was wearing all black with a gold Helios insignia stitched on the collar of his shirt. And, just like all the other grunts, he'd been pumped so full of muscle enhancers he looked like a no-neck walking bag of rocks. Dangerous and just short of stupid, the grunts followed orders like rabid dogs and had implants that downloaded straight into their cerebral cortices so they could use any weapon they came across. They could run for days and also liked to hit things: animals, walls, him.

Pip slipped the medigun under Essie's mattress. "Coming," he said and he followed him out.

"She still alive?" The grunt jerked his head towards the medical bay.

"Yep."

"Pity, she kicked me in the balls."

"What balls?" Pip retorted and received a slap to the side of his head, which sent him slamming into the wall.

"Don't be stupid." The grunt grabbed him roughly by the arm. Pip's head was swimming and he felt bile rise momentarily in his throat. The grunt ignored his staggering and shoved him into the ship's lift.

Pip's head was still ringing from the blow as they got to the bridge. His insides were loose with nerves. What did Yuang want from him now?

"Get a move on." The grunt prodded him in the back.

"Piss off!" Pip tried to shrug his hand off but the grunt only laughed and pushed him again. Anger boiled in Pip's gut but he knew better than to fight back. He still had the scar on his thigh from the last time. He settled for quiet abuse. "Small-balled freak," he whispered under his breath.

Yuang was standing with his back to him in front of the wide view port, staring out at the streaming stars.

The *Cosmic Mariner* had the best tech money could buy. There were no buttons or switches on Yuang's bridge, all the controls were 3-D and AI-integrated. Yuang's pilot,

Nerita, rested, half reclined, within a curved transparent dome. An elegant helmet of fine wires sat on her dark shaved head and a single glinting eye cover connected her to the ship's operating computer. Her hands moved in the air in front of her, manipulating constantly changing images of amber light that projected up from the floor.

Next to her the copilot sat in front of a slim podium and next to him another man was surrounded by a semicircular console that controlled the ship's weapons. Nerita glanced at Pip as the grunt shoved him into the room, but didn't smile. She was less nasty to him than the rest but was still to be treated with caution.

"Come stand by me." Yuang called to him without turning. "Leave us, Reave, and shut the hatch." The grunt grunted and gave Pip a final push forward then left.

"We've caught up with your friend," Yuang said, turning to him at last.

"She's not my friend."

Yuang smiled. "Of course she is. You're just not a very good friend to her. How is our patient?"

Pip shrugged. "How should I know? I'm not a doctor."

"Is she still breathing?"

"Yes." Pip was uncomfortable talking about Rosie's

aunt. What if Yuang guessed he'd given her the extra stuff? "What are you going to do about Rosie and Riley?" he asked, trying to change the subject.

"Well, they still have an item I want, since you didn't manage to get hold of everything." Yuang let the comment hang, just long enough to make Pip nervous. "But I don't want to scare them," he continued. "Shore will know what this ship can do. We are going to follow them, at a distance, until we reach Mars, then I'll offer them a choice."

"What choice?" Pip didn't like Yuang's tone.

Yuang looked at him. "Sometimes people need to be given a reason to do something. I will offer them two alternatives. One of those alternatives is handing over the diary that you were supposed to retrieve."

Pip swallowed. He knew what the other alternative would be. He'd seen what the weapons on this ship could do. A bunch of Ferals had stolen a shuttle once to escape the Enclave. They hadn't made it more than a thousand kilometres out of the atmosphere. Their deaths had been soundless, a burst of light and heat.

Yuang had said all of them had been infected with the MalX. That they had been planning to infect as many people on Earth with it as they could because they believed it was a plague sent by God to cleanse the Earth. Yuang said the MalX had driven them insane.

Pip didn't want to end up like that. Unlike some of the other Ferals they tested, he had no immunity. Yuang had tested him himself. He'd seen the results. He could die as easily as anyone else.

Pip looked at the streaming stars, wondering how far ahead Rosie and Riley were. If they would only listen to Yuang. Pip had known him since he was a kid. Yuang had been like an uncle or an older brother to him since his parents had died. He'd made sure he had everything he needed. A room in the dorms, food. He was the one who visited him when he had no one. When he'd been sent to Earth it was Yuang who'd cushioned the blow, said everyone had to be tested and this was his test. Surely he wouldn't actually kill Rosie and Riley? As soon as Yuang had what he wanted, he'd let them go. And Pip could stay in the Enclave and everything would be like before.

Yuang watched him. "They cannot be allowed to stop what we are doing, Pip," he said. "You know that. We are trying to save them as well as the rest of Earth. If they cannot understand that ..." He shrugged and put a hand on his shoulder. "I am trying to save many lives, not just a few. Remember your parents? I wish I could have saved them."

"I know." Pip tensed. "Let me talk to her," he ventured. "She might listen to me. Let them land on

Mars and I'll go back to them. I'll get the diary."

"You would get nothing. You betrayed them, Pip. You overestimate your charm. Besides, I don't want to risk losing you." He squeezed Pip's shoulder, almost affectionately, then clasped his hands lightly behind his back. "If they don't hand over what I want, I will be left with no choice."

"But what about the diary?" Pip said.

"Perhaps it is safer disposed of. Anyway, enough talk." Yuang turned away from the view port, guiding Pip with a light hand back towards the door. "Go back to the mediroom and check on the woman. We may need her to encourage them yet. I don't want to resort to violence unless I have to. Remember why we are doing this, Pip. Remember your parents." He pushed him towards the exit. "I'll send Reave for you when we reach Mars."

CHAPTER 23

Rosie closed her eyes against the stars, seeking some respite from the constant light. The suit felt bulky and she was battling claustrophobia. The helmet was lightweight, but it wasn't that comfortable and smelled of stale rubber. She tried to control her desire to rip the thing off her head. There was no air left in the ship and only the basic systems were operating to stop it from becoming a vacuum. It was also freezing. Without the stabilising effect of life support, the temperature in the ship had dropped to minus thirty and she could feel the cold through her suit. The pylonic fibres stopped her freezing to death but they weren't made to be worn for thirty-two hours. She wondered how much colder she'd be by the time they made it to Mars.

If they did.

Images came to her of the ship veering off course, straight into the burning atmosphere; the ship exploding as they hit the Martian soil. Her aunt wounded, clutching her stomach. Her dad somewhere else, waiting for rescue that never came, or worse, already cold.

"Rosie," Riley's voice crackled in her ear. "It's time to rotate the fuel cells."

She didn't respond. She didn't want to move right now.

"Rosie!"

"Okay, okay, I'm going." Without all the ship's computer systems on, they had to rotate the fuel cells by hand or they would overload and implode. She unclasped the straps and floated out of the bridge and towards the access tunnels, pulling herself along using whatever handholds she could find. She kept seeing Pip, looking at her with that pathetic expression on his face after he'd seen her aunt lying in a pool of blood. As if he was surprised. As if he didn't think he was responsible. Shame and humiliation filled her again as she realised just how stupid she'd been – holding his hand, going all girly over his blue eyes, thinking he felt the same. Idiot.

She climbed down the short ladder and into the tunnel. She had almost finished rotating the cells when Riley's voice came through her com. "Rosie, there's something going on up here on the console. Some lights flashing. Have you finished yet?"

"Nearly." She pushed the last cell into place. "What do you mean, lights flashing?"

"If I knew, I wouldn't be asking you. Just get up here."

She exhaled in exasperation but bit back her smart retort. "I'm coming now." She flicked the cell operations back on and drifted back to the bridge.

"You took a long time." Riley looked worried as she floated to her chair. "These lights have been blinking on and off for the last few minutes."

"I had to change four cells," she said defensively. "It takes a while."

"Not that long. What are these lights?"

She checked the console then said with alarm, "It's the low-frequency sensor. It's picked up a moving body behind us."

"A ship," said Riley and swore.

Rosie's heart sank and she said desperately, "Are you sure? Could it be an asteroid or space junk?"

She switched the view port to the sensor sweep.

Riley peered at the grid and the small dot the sensor had picked up. "It's moving in a predictable trajectory. It's got to be Yuang. He's caught up, must have a core drive, or something comparable. He'll be right on our tail when we reach Mars." The stars reflected in the glass panel of his helmet as he looked at her. "How good a pilot do you think you are, Rosie?"

"Are you kidding? This is the first time I've done it for real."

"Well, you're going to have to try as hard as you can because we have to come up with a plan that's going to get us to Mars, and on the ground, before Yuang catches up with us."

"But don't you want to talk to him?"

"Yes, but on my terms, not his," Riley said. "Yuang's ship will have weapons, you can guarantee it."

"So what do we do?"

"He's waiting for us to get closer to Mars."

"Why?"

"Besides the fact he can't fire in hyperspace, if I know Yuang he'll want us to be an example to others. He wants us to be in range of the Enclave's monitoring systems so the Ferals there can see what happens to those who defy Helios."

Rosie felt a chill. "What do you think he'll do?"

"Most likely he'll shoot out our engines, disable us so we are forced to allow him to take over the pod or risk the ship imploding."

"Are you sure?" Rosie said.

"Not one hundred per cent, no, but I got to know him — far better than I'd like — when I was captured."

There was something in his voice that made Rosie ask, "That's not all, is it?"

Riley hesitated. "No. If Essie's still alive, it's likely he'll use her as leverage."

Something felt like it was slowly constricting her chest. "But if we give up, then he'll have all of us," she said.

Riley slowly nodded and suddenly, it all began to sink in. If they gave up, they lost any hope of helping the people in the labs, any hope of exposing Helios. Her aunt's sacrifice would be for nothing.

"Aunt Essie wouldn't want that," she said, her voice unsteady.

"No. She wouldn't."

She stared at the console, panic starting to rise in her chest.

"Rosie." His voice was calm, steady. "Slow down. We don't have much air left."

She realised she was starting to hyperventilate and tried to slow her breathing. "Have you got any ideas?"

"Not yet."

She thought hard but she couldn't seem to get past the part about giving up on her aunt.

They both sat in silence for a while, until Riley pulled her around to face him. "Okay. First option: does the pod have any emergency escape craft?"

"One," she answered. "But I diverted all its energy to the drive. There's no power left in it. We can't use it. We wouldn't survive. Planetfall would kill us."

"Pity." Riley was studying the controls of the flight deck.

He turned to her. "Okay, so how do you think you'd go controlling the pod in a freefall?"

"What!"

"Our original plan was to make maximum speed to Mars then squeeze the power off, using what little we had left to cruise in and land, but what would happen if we started conserving some power now?"

"We'd slow down and they'd catch us."

Riley shook his head. "Yuang could have caught us already. He's waiting until we get there. If we slow the drive a little, we'll have a slug of energy left when we get there."

"To do what?"

"We'll use it to burn our thrusters out and create a heat shield to confuse the missiles. Yuang won't be able to lock on to us. And if we do it at the right time, just as we hit the atmosphere, the burn of our re-entry will cover us enough to get to the ground."

Rosie was afraid he'd been going to say that. "But we might not have enough power left to control the landing at all."

Riley said nothing. He didn't have to; they both knew that if the heat shield didn't work, they'd be dead anyway.

"But what about my dad and aunt? If we don't make it ..."

"If we're gone and the diary is destroyed, he might let them go." But he didn't look at her as he said it.

"Yeah, right," Rosie said softly.

"I'm sorry, Rosie, that's all we've got."

"Yeah." She felt strange, detached.

"There's always the chance that he won't be able to resist talking to me," Riley said. "We have a lot of ... history. He probably won't fire unless he has to. It might buy us time to make it. And we could make it. Then, once we land, we'll get you to Genesis. I have some friends in the colony who can help. You can hide and I'll go see Yuang at the Enclave. I'll make him let your aunt and dad go."

Sure, whatever. She stared out at the stars. He made it sound so easy. She wanted it to be easy. She wanted her aunt to be okay, her dad to be here with her, and her mum back. But that was a fairytale; this was reality. Reality was Helios and the MalX, Pip betraying her and Yuang waiting to kill them. And she'd be damned if it was all going to be for nothing.

"If we do this and we survive," she said, "I'm coming with you. I want to help you stop Helios."

He gave her a long, level look. "Rosie ..."

"No." She glared at him. "My mum died from the MalX, my friend is dead, probably my aunt as well and for all I know, so is my dad. Helios has killed everyone I love. I am not going to hide in the colony while you go off and get yourself killed. Besides, how are you going to do it alone?"

"I'll find a way."

"How? Once you offer yourself up, they'll probably kill you. If we can figure out a way for me to get in, while Yuang's busy with you, I could try to get some of the information we need or at least stop the selfdestruct. We have the codes." She knew she was right. A strange recklessness had come over her. She knew she could die but it didn't seem real, any of it. She just had to act.

"Rosie, it's too—"

"Dangerous? Riley, we can't just let all those people die. I'm good at computers; I've been top of my class for the last two years. I can get in. I can stop the selfdestruct and maybe I can even figure out a way to get the lab files without the code key."

"And what happens if you get caught?"

"Then I guess I join the rest of my family," she said bluntly. "But if you tell me the codes and give me some idea of the layout of the Enclave, perhaps I won't." She met his stubborn stare. "Who else have you got, Riley?"

His jaw tightened. No one was the answer and she could see that he knew it.

With slow movements he pulled his sister's diary from his pocket.

"I don't know how to activate it," she said.

He punched in the password. "I don't have the Enclave layout but we can come up with a rough idea. I know a bit about it." He watched her as she took the diary and began scrolling through the codes. There were eight including the selfdestruct deactivation sequence. She thought she should be able to memorise them.

"If I find someone else at the colony, the deal is off," he said. "I do have some friends there."

"Fine," she said, but really, who was he trying to kid? It was just her and him. She paused, not sure what she'd committed herself to, then began readying the ship and reciting the code sequences in her head.

CHAPTER 24

Pip sat staring at Essie and tapped his fingers on his knee. For the first time he wished he was back on Earth. He couldn't think straight up here.

Yuang confused him. Sometimes he thought he was pleased with him but then he was sure he despised him. He couldn't seem to get a handle on him any more.

When he was a boy, and Yuang had only been an assistant, he had been kind to him. He would often visit and tell stories about the time before the MalX, before the Melt and the flooding of the world. Sometimes he'd bring chocolate. But one day he'd stopped coming and he hadn't seen him again for two years. Then he was different.

And then Helios had started sending Pip to Earth to

live with the Ferals. It had been a shock, going from the clean, dry Enclave to the stinking shanties by the river. Pip didn't like to think of it, that first trip. He'd been a skinny pale brown boy, left alone with a group of people he didn't know who smelled worse than the dank, bug-infested river. He'd been terrified they were going to leave him down there to catch the MalX and die. Yuang had kept telling him he was trying to convince them to let him go back but now he was starting to wonder if he had really tried at all.

Essie twitched on the bed and muttered something.

He checked the door for grunts, then leaned over and stared down at her closed eyelids. Suddenly, they opened.

She squinted up at him. "Pipsqueak?" Her voice was hoarse and barely above a whisper.

Pip didn't know what to do. He just looked at her.

"What are you staring at?" She grimaced and tried to move. "Hey, what's going on?" Her voice got louder and she struggled weakly under the straps.

"Sh!" He checked the passageway then locked the door. He stood by her bedside, not quite sure what to do next. He should call Yuang.

"Let me loose."

"Can't."

Essie sighed. "Where's Rosie?"

"She and Riley got away."

She seemed to relax a little after he said that. "So where am I?"

Pip knew he should tell her that Rosie and Riley hadn't really got away, that Yuang had plans for them, but he didn't.

"The *Cosmic Mariner*, Yuang's ship." He looked at the wound in her side, covered in thin white meditape. "Does it hurt?"

"Give me a gun and I'll show you. Where are we going? Mars?"

"Yep."

She closed her eyes and was silent for so long, he thought she'd gone back to sleep. She hadn't.

"Pipsqueak." Her eyes opened again. The whites were dull, even after the shots he'd given her.

"Don't call me that."

"Well, you are one. You're a little shit who stabbed us in the back. How long have you been working for Yuang?"

"I don't work for him."

"Yeah, sure." She coughed lightly. "Keep telling yourself that, whatever makes it easier."

"It's never easy," Pip mumbled.

"What?" She tried to turn, but the straps across her chest prevented her.

"Nothing."

"Listen, Pipsqueak, you may be a stinky little Feral but I don't think you planned for things to get this bad, did you?"

Pip didn't answer her. He knew what she was doing. They'd had lessons in the Enclave. They were taught what to do if they were ever caught. Make friends with the enemy, and that was just what Rosie's aunt was doing. She must have learned that in the Elite. But he couldn't think of her as the enemy – she was Rosie's aunt. Rosie who might die. Would Yuang really do it?

"How far ahead of us are they?"

"What?" He frowned, trying to keep his mind on the job. He was supposed to be watching her.

"Rosie and Riley, how far ahead of us are they?"

"Don't know," he lied.

"Pipsqueak, come here where I can see you." He didn't move and she let out a frustrated sigh. "What am I going to do, talk you to death?"

Reluctantly, he moved so he was standing where she could see him. She did look like crap. But she was talking, so he supposed what he'd done must have helped.

"You know, Rosie liked you, Pip. She thought you were her friend."

"Her mistake," he said.

"You just want to believe that because you feel guilty. I saw the way you looked at her." Essie flinched and closed her eyes again briefly, as though something was hurting her. Pip wondered if he should give her another shot, but she opened her eyes again before he could move. "What do you think is going to happen here? Do you honestly think they're just going to let me go? They can't hand me to the Senate, can they? And they can't keep me tied up here."

Pip shrugged. He wasn't sure what Yuang planned to do. But even if he did know, what could he do about it?

"You know something, don't you, Pipsqueak?"

"No."

"Liar, I can see it all over your face. What is it? Is it to do with Rosie?"

Pip stayed silent, and a look of weary disgust came over her. "So, you're not going to do anything, are you? You're just going to hang us all out to get shot, or worse. Bloody Ferals." She turned away.

"Well, what am I supposed to do?" Pip said.

"I don't know, Pipsqueak," Essie said resignedly. "Just do whatever you like. Save your own skin — it's what you're best at."

Pip turned away from her, angry. He paced back and forth. What did she know about what he'd had to do to survive? If he didn't save his own skin, he'd have been dead years ago.

"That's right," she taunted him. "Just worry about yourself. Don't worry about all those people in the Enclave who are going to die. Don't worry about them."

He went back to her bedside. "What do you mean?"

She looked at him with narrow eyes then a glint of amusement crossed her face. "You don't know, do you?"

"Know what?"

She let out a harsh, low laugh. "About what he's planning. Yuang. Even if he gets the diary from Riley and stops him, he's still going to detonate the place."

"What?" He was starting to get a bad feeling.

"Poor little Pipsqueak. Do you really think Helios would risk anything getting out about what goes on there? He's planning to take what he needs then make it go away – with all witnesses."

Pip felt hot and cold at the same time. Yuang was going to destroy the Enclave? "You're lying," he said.

"Yeah, sure I am." Her tone was caustic. "'Cos good old Yuang would never lie to you, would he?"

He grabbed the edge of her bed, his knuckles going white from the pressure. He knew what she was saying was probably true. He felt it in his gut, a glaring truth he'd been trying not to see.

"Even if I did unstrap you, you can't stop him," he

said. "There are a hundred grunts on this ship, plus the crew. They'll find you before you get anywhere near the bridge and then you've got to get to the weapons and …" Pip stopped. He realised he'd said too much. She'd made him angry on purpose.

"Weapons?" she said, and her gaze measured him. "Why would they need to fire weapons? He's got them in his sights, hasn't he?"

Pip turned away from her, running a hand over his dreadlocks. Why had he let her make him mad?

"Pipsqueak! You look at me. Yuang's caught up with them. He's going to fire on them, isn't he?"

Pip exhaled. "Only if they don't stop."

"And he was planning on using me to force Rosie to stop?"

Pip couldn't answer her. But he didn't need to.

"So," she said, "he threatens to slice and dice me to get Rosie and Riley to give up. And what about Adam, her dad? Do you know about him?"

"No."

Essie was silent for a minute and Pip wondered if the wound was hurting her again, and why he should care so much. But before he could ask she said very quietly, "Have you ever killed anyone, Pip?"

He half turned back to her, his arms crossed over his chest. One time he'd come close but he didn't want to think about it. He'd been hungry and the kid had taunted him over and over.

"I don't think you have," Essie went on when he didn't answer. "And even if you think it's not going to be you pulling the trigger, or pushing the button, if you let it happen, it's the same thing. It changes you, Pip. Do you want to be that person?"

He could feel her eyes on him as he stared at the floor. It was very quiet in the mediroom. The only sound was the ever-present hum of the ship, vibrating steadily as it cruised through the stars. He remembered the whites of the kid's eyes staring at him in the dark. The glint of the knife in the moonlight and the rotten stink of the river. He thought of Rosie's angry, accusing gaze.

He took a long breath but didn't move. If he let Rosie's aunt go, what would Yuang do to him?

CHAPTER 25

The air in Rosie's suit was getting thin. They'd swapped to the last breather from the third suit now, and she was trying not to inhale too deeply. If everything went according to plan, their chances of surviving the atmosphere breach and freefall were good, at least forty per cent. If things went badly, the chances of survival were up there with ploughing into the sun at full tilt in a tin can.

She tried to stay focused on keeping the pod steady — and trying to miss the really big rocks when they made it to Mars.

"Rosie, I'm going to need you to go back into the fuel cell chamber when we get close," Riley's voice sounded flat through her com and she could hear the hiss of the breather releasing air into his helmet.

"How close?"

"Close enough to see the atmosphere."

That close? She'd barely have time to make it back to the bridge.

She reset the nav controls. "You want me to change the cells around to make them uneven?"

He nodded. "We need to increase the pressure enough to burn out the thrusters."

Without blowing ourselves up, she thought, or getting hit by Yuang's missiles.

She didn't understand how Pip could work with someone like Yuang. How could he do it, knowing what was going on? Or did he actually think Helios was doing the right thing?

Riley suddenly made a low noise. He was staring intently at the view screen in front of him.

"What?"

"Yuang's hailing us."

Rosie's insides jumped.

"Can you put it on the holo projector?" he asked her.

"Yes."

"Do it."

She depressed the touch pads and a transparent image of Mr Yuang appeared, with a greenish cast, on the console between them. He smiled when he saw her.

Rosie tried to slow her racing pulse. Behind was a super high-tech-looking bridge with a black woman at the controls. Rosie had stupidly hoped to see Aunt Essie, or Pip, just to prove to him she was still alive.

"Yuang," Riley said.

"Simon Shore," Yuang replied. "So nice to see you again. You always did have a talent for survival."

"No thanks to your predecessor."

Yuang frowned. "Believe me, Simon, I would not have allowed them to torture you as they did if I had been in charge."

Riley's breathing was sharp in her com and Rosie looked at him in alarm.

"Easy to say now," he said. "What do you want, Yuang?"

"What does everyone want? A place of comfort, an end to fear, but that is irrelevant. The question is, Simon," he emphasised Riley's real name, "are you willing to kill this young woman to achieve your end?"

Riley paused and glanced at Rosie. "That's your plan, is it? Shoot us down, make us choose between surrender or death?"

"It's up to you, Simon," Yuang said. "It's out of my control."

"Shifting the blame?" Riley looked back at Yuang. "You used to be a better man."

"Things change, times change. There is too much at stake here now, Simon."

"But it's your hand on the gun, not mine. Besides, nothing is certain. I believe a famous man once said that."

"Famous and deceased," Yuang replied.

"Where is Essie?"

"Alive for now, but as you said, nothing is certain. You could ensure her safety."

"But what of the others – the lives in the Enclave? Who will ensure theirs?"

"You can, if you want to." Yuang paused. "What do you think, Miss Black? Do you trust him?"

"More than I trust you," she said.

He smiled. "And yet you know so little about him. About the many he has sacrificed in the name of his cause."

"You mean the people you've trampled to get to me," Riley said.

"You could have saved them by giving yourself up."

"Like now?" Riley's tone was filled with scepticism.

"You've already let Rosie and her aunt lead me right to you," he said. "Why not cut your losses now, before more people are hurt?"

So that was why he'd let her go when she'd seen him at Orbitcorp. Rosie met his cold smile with a frustrated glare as she remembered his wink. Riley continued talking to Yuang: going on about something to do with the past, debating about the greater good. Then, without turning to her, he tapped one finger lightly on the console.

Her heart almost stopped as she saw the indicator flashing – Mars was close. She could see it now, the spherical shape patchy with its man-made atmosphere clinging like a semidetached shroud. Rosie drifted backwards until she was at the door of the bridge, then she turned and pushed herself away from the doorframe, arrowing down towards the hatch. She had three minutes max to change the cells and it felt like it took twenty. The cells floated so slowly from their chambers and she had almost ground her teeth flat with anxiety by the time she sneaked back into the bridge.

Riley and Yuang were still talking but their voices were harder now, and as she settled back in the pilot's chair, Rosie got a shock. Pip was standing at Yuang's side. She could see just one side of his face. He looked nervous, scared almost. She didn't think he could see her, or at least he was acting like he couldn't. Yuang was speaking and she tuned in, trying to work out what she'd missed.

"You can help her, Riley. Surrender and we can talk. Don't make me fire on you." Riley gave a bitter laugh.

"I don't think Essie will be as easy to outwit as you think. You look nervous, Yuang."

"And you're playing for time." He smiled. "I'm a step ahead of you though, Simon. She has nowhere to go and you know what I'll do when I catch her. This ship isn't endless. Hasn't Essie been through enough for you?"

Rosie's heart leaped. Had Aunt Essie got free?

Riley kept talking, keeping Yuang's attention. "You're enjoying this game, aren't you?" he said.

"Life is a game, brother," Yuang replied.

"And the pieces fall according to fate, do they? How do you know I don't have some of those lab results ready to go to a source in the Senate, or the news? You don't know what else was in the box, do you? If something happens to me, perhaps I have left instructions for the information to flow."

Yuang smiled, but Rosie saw the tension around his eyes. "A good bluff, Shore, but there's still your sister. I can find her."

"No, you can't. She's beyond even Helios's reach."

"Nothing is beyond our reach."

Riley seemed disappointed but not surprised. "I see you've become the perfect Helios clone. Well, I guess there's nothing more to say but, see you in the next life." He flicked a switch and the hologram blinked out.

He turned to Rosie. "Ready?"

"No." She put shaking hands on the pod's controls and made sure her harness was secure, then dialled up the thrusters.

A dull whine started to fill the cabin and the ship leaped forward. Mars was suddenly hurtling towards them at terrifying speed. It was freezing but sweat was gathering in the headband of her helmet. Then lights began blinking on the dash and she saw the flashing of a weapons lock warning. An alarm rang through the cabin. Yuang was going to fire. She gripped hard to the pod's steering and looked at Riley. His face was set and hard, his eyes bright.

"Now, Rosie!" He had to shout over the siren.

She let go of the right steering arm and punched it to back-burn. The force threw her back in her seat and she uttered a short shocked scream.

A massive roaring sounded and the pod shuddered so much, she could barely control the steering. Suddenly, the pod veered hard left. It was all noise and chaos and then a streak of bright light flared the cabin to white and Rosie stared as a missile shot past them. It had missed. Yuang had missed. The heat shield must have worked. Triumph filled her and she turned to Riley, grinning – then they hit Mars's atmosphere. The pod shook and screeched as the force of the planet's gravity took hold.

"Hang on to it!" Riley's voice was a scratched shout. She grasped the steering arms, the vibration working through her body as though she was having a fit. The air in her helmet was thin and she began to feel light-headed. A strange whining, grinding noise was coming from somewhere. Lights were blinking all over the console and the force of entry was pressing her back hard into her seat. All she could see through the view port was a streak of grey as they plummeted towards the planet's crust.

Their angle of entry was all wrong – they were breaking up!

Riley's voice came through her helmet com, shaky and full of static. "The trajectory! Rosie, change angle."

"I know!" she yelled. Did he think she was an idiot? She pulled hard on the sticks. It was like trying to shift an elephant stuck in mud. "Help me!"

Riley smacked his hand down on the button on his chair that activated the copilot controls. Nothing happened. He swore and punched the control again and again, but the sticks remained stowed. "Damn it."

Rosie tried to quell her spiralling panic. The ship shuddered violently, and the vibrations from the steering felt like they were shaking the bones in her arms loose. She needed Riley's help. "Use manual!" she screamed at him. "Pull them out!" She tried to point her elbow at the lever in the middle of the console. He understood and stretched towards them. But his seat harness had locked him in tight. He couldn't reach it. The sensors must have decided that as the copilot, he was safer strapped tight against the seat. Riley didn't hesitate. With a loud grunt, he unbuckled his harness and, hanging on to his chair with one hand, reached for the control release with the other. The intense shuddering of the pod threatened to throw him against the wall, but he held on, his face grim, and pulled on the release. A set of extra steering sticks ejected smoothly up on either side of his seat. He gripped them and pulled back hard.

He was almost too late.

Rosie heard the outer hull start to buckle and then, slowly, the pod's nose rotated and straightened out, the shuddering eased. They'd done it. Riley turned to her with a triumphant grimace as he held on tight, helping her keep the ship in line. She grinned back, a feeling of elation flowing through her. But then she saw the view screen as they plunged out of the atmosphere.

Everything seemed to happen at once.

A loud alarm went off in the cabin, collision lights blinked rapidly and terror ran through her as she registered the sheer face of red rock in front of them.

She didn't even have time to scream. Instinctively,

she pulled the pod right, with all her might, but it was too late.

The ship slammed into the rock at a forty-five degree angle. From the corner of her eye, she saw Riley being flung from his chair. He slammed into the console and was then thrown behind her. Her seat harness held, but the force of the crash snapped her neck forward and she could barely breathe as the reinforced straps squeezed her rib cage.

The cabin filled with the sound of tearing metal. The outer hull ripped open and a massive fracture cracked the view screen.

Desperately, Rosie fought for control as they skidded through scree, rocks thumping off the sides of the ship. Then suddenly the rock ended and there was nothing but air.

For a split second the pod soared free of gravity. Then it dipped and dived straight down into a deep canyon.

Rosie saw a silver gleam of water at the bottom and smudges of green rushing up towards her. Glide in! her brain screamed at her. She punched down on the controls to deploy the emergency crash glide wings, but nothing happened. They must have been sheared off with the outer hull. Then the engines cut. For a moment there was no sound but her ragged breath and the air whistling past. She stared, frozen in fear and disbelief, as they plunged towards the river. The last thing she saw was the console as she smashed into it.

CHAPTER 26

Rosie woke to the sight of exposed wires and dangling ceiling panels. She was still strapped into her chair but it had been ripped from its footing and she was now on the floor of the bridge.

Her helmet was on her head, but the faceplate was gone and she was inhaling thin, cold Martian air. Miraculously, her helmet was still active and she saw a small blinking red light indicating her breather was empty. Moving slowly, she pulled off her gloves and unclasped her helmet. Everything ached. Her head throbbed and she tasted blood as she let the helmet thud onto the floor. It felt as though she'd been hugged by arms made of steel. The skin on her face was tight. Tiny cuts stung where the faceplate had shattered, but nothing felt broken. The chair harness had saved her life.

She lay there for a second, just breathing, until she remembered Martian air was not as oxygen-rich as Earth's. A human could survive for forty-five minutes at most before dizziness set in and then slow death. She struggled to undo the seat straps, flung them off and staggered to her feet. Immediately, a wave of dizziness made her drop to her hands and knees, retching. She hung her head down, closing her eyes until the spots of light went away along with the urge to vomit. When she could stand it, she lifted her head.

The bridge was a mess of piping and shattered equipment and all systems were dead. There were no lights, cold air was brushing against the back of her neck and the sound of running water came from outside. The view port was gone and through the gaping hole she could see a rock face, tangled creepers and a glimpse of cloud-covered sky far, far above. The faint light coming through the gap was the only illumination.

She crawled down to the locker at the bottom of the bulkhead near the door. Already she was feeling the effects of the lower oxygen. It was like she'd been running a race and was trying to fill her lungs with air, but no matter how hard she tried, she couldn't quite get enough. She wondered how long she'd been unconscious. Wrenching open the door, she scrabbled around, throwing out packets of wires and repair patches until her hand closed on what she needed. Rosie ripped open the cover and pulled out the breather. She fitted the nostril cap over her nose then clipped the thin tube and recalibrating device over her ear. She took a long breath and the breather switched on, using the electrical energy of her breath and body to alter the air composition. A rush of oxygen flooded into her nasal tubes and down to her lungs. Her head cleared and she began to feel better.

She took another breather out and put it in her pocket. Then she looked around for Riley. She remembered him being flung through the air as they crashed.

"Riley?" she called. There was no reply. Dreading what she might find, she headed through the hatch into the interior of the ship.

Her path was strewn with wreckage and the ship was lying partly on its side, the floor slanting away beneath her feet towards the river. She tried not to think about how deep the water might be.

It was hard to see in the gloom of the ship's belly but she found him at the bottom of the stairs leading to the cargo hold. He was lying facedown, one leg hooked up on the balustrade, his right arm twisted at an impossible angle. He wasn't moving. She crashed down the stairs, her legs unsteady. Was he even alive? She stripped off her gloves and fumbled with the catch on his helmet, but it wouldn't budge. Beginning to panic, she pulled off his gloves as well and checked for a pulse on his wrist. She felt a tiny pump against her finger – weak but there.

She searched the dark deck, looking for something to lever the helmet off. She found a jagged wedge of something metallic and jammed it as hard as she could under the catch. The sharp edges cut her fingers, but the catch opened and she carefully wiggled the helmet off his head.

He was very pale and his eyes were closed, but he was breathing. She fitted the breather then examined him to see if she could spot any blood in the dim light. His leg had been cut and had bled through onto his suit, but looked dry now. Perhaps he'd just grazed it. The arm, however, had to be broken.

She wasn't sure what to do. Should she try and move him? What if he was bleeding inside? She bent down next to his ear. "Riley?" she spoke hesitantly. "Can you hear me?"

But he was totally out of it. She went around to his right side and, avoiding his twisted arm, tried to turn him onto his back, but he far was too heavy. She gave up and settled for shoving some foam that had come loose from his chair, under his head so at least he was off the floor. Then she sat back against a buckled cargo container and put her head in her hands.

The nausea had returned. It was getting colder and it would be dark soon. She knew she should get up and find some water and check outside, but her body felt like it was made of lead. She needed to close her eyes – just for a minute – until the nausea passed.

When she woke, it was utterly dark and she was lying on the floor. She opened her eyes wider, trying to see something, anything, but the blackness pressed against her. She got to her feet, hyperventilating and disorientated. Where was she? She registered the breather on her face and almost pulled it off, but in another blink, it all came back to her: the crash, the river, Mars.

She took a step and fell on top of Riley. He moaned and she sprang up, terrified she'd hurt him more. She couldn't see a thing. It was too dark. She needed light – light and air. Shaking, she scrambled up the stairs towards the bridge. A faint wash of moonlight was coming through the hole where the view port used to be. She lunged forward, tripping over the debris of the crash like a drunk.

She leaned against the ruined console and looked up

at the sliver of night sky. The two moons of Mars, Phobos and Deimos, spread a dim glow across the black. Seeing them helped. She stood for a minute taking long, relieved breaths. The panic faded and she felt slightly foolish. She hadn't freaked like that since she was a child. She had to pull herself together. She sat on the floor and tried to focus on her situation.

It was very quiet. Unlike Earth there were no mosquitoes buzzing, no voices, nothing but the sound of water running past the pod somewhere outside. She closed her eyes for a moment. Her head was throbbing dully and she was thirsty; she should find some drinking water.

The pod creaked: a long, croaking groan of metal moving. Her eyes snapped open and she sat very still, listening, straining to understand what it was. After a moment it came again and, slightly, ever so slightly, the ship shifted and she heard a rock fall away outside and plop into water.

She got to her feet. This was bad. The pod was cooling down, the metal contracting. They were slipping.

Fear gave her purpose. Rosie dived under the pilot's console and rummaged around the debris. She pulled a light rod out from under a tangle of wires and twisted the ends so the chemicals merged. The rod shone with a flat white light. Holding it in one hand, she climbed awkwardly onto the console and shuffled up the sloping screens then hooked her arm around the gap in the view port and peered out.

The pod was wedged, nose first, in a crack in the canyon wall. The ship tilted slightly up towards the rock but the bulk of it appeared to be in the water.

There was no bank that she could see that they could get out onto – only striated rock and shadowy overhangs. The rock walls were channelled with long cracks, with spiky tufts of some kind of grass growing out of them.

She twisted to the left and held the rod high, trying to see the water, to judge its depth. The light illuminated black water, swirling swiftly past the ship. The canyon was about fifty metres wide. She could just make out the far side in the grey moonlight and she saw it continued in a relatively straight line before turning away to the right out of her sight.

As far as she could see, almost half of the pod was submerged. If it slipped down much more, the current would catch it, pull it right out of the crack and it would undoubtedly sink. They had to get out.

She slid back inside and rummaged in a locker behind where the pilot's chair used to be. She found a handheld geocompass and a broken com. She tried the compass. It gave a low ping and the screen lit up. It was still working. Relieved, she began to scroll through its databank to find the settings that would allow it to operate on Mars.

As far as she could tell, it looked like they'd landed in a tributary that ran into the Marineris River, Mars's longest and deepest waterway. The Marineris wound through a massive canyon system that was 4000 kilometres long and seven kilometres deep in some places. The Genesis colony had been built off one of its tributaries at the foot of the Tharsis Mountains. But how far were they from the mountains? The bad angle of their entry had knocked them off course; they could be anywhere from a few to hundreds of kilometres away.

She waited for the compass to fix their position. Genesis was the only habitat on Mars that had a working community. The United Earth Commission had started to build another city near the Crystal Lakes, but the last news stream she'd seen had shown it still had no water or food production. The only other human sites were the mines, but they were far to the south near the pole and she was sure they were a lot closer to Genesis than that. At least she hoped so.

The geocompass hummed quietly in her hand and she concentrated on its wavering image. A map appeared followed by coordinates and she let her breath out in a small sigh. Genesis was twenty-eight kilometres south-west. That was a long way to walk – *if* they could get out of this canyon, and *if* Riley could walk.

She put the compass in one of the pockets of her suit and went back into the belly of the ship.

CHAPTER 27

Pip followed Yuang through the vacuum-sealed doors into the Enclave's vestibule.

Since they'd lost the pod, Yuang had been in a foul mood. He was shouting orders to the grunts to track where the pod had crashed, yelling for someone to get him in contact with the colony, and generally causing everyone to scurry about like rats running from pest control.

Gingerly, Pip stretched his neck. His head and jaw were aching and he felt ill. Yuang had figured he'd helped Rosie's aunt get loose and as soon as he got to the bridge, he'd blindsided him. Pip hadn't seen the fist coming before it connected with his head. He'd gone down but got up quickly. He had been mad enough to think about retaliating – Yuang and he were the same height and he was fitter, stronger – but the look in the man's eye had stopped him. He hadn't even looked angry. That was the most unnerving thing. He gaze was just cold – cold and deadly – and Pip had got the message. Loud and clear. Yuang could do anything to him and no one would stop him; no one would question it.

"Never betray me again, Pip," was all he'd said, and Pip had backed off.

When Yuang had discovered that Essie had messed with the weapon guidance system, he'd really tried to become part of the furniture, although that hadn't stopped one of the grunts from pounding on him just a little, for the heck of it.

He wondered briefly if he had concussion. He'd had it before and remembered it had made him throw up. He really didn't want to throw up. He'd rather that the first place he saw on his first visit home wasn't the mediroom. Because that was where he was, he had to keep telling himself: home.

But it didn't feel the same.

The gardens surrounding the Enclave were thicker, the trees taller, and there were new buildings. The original Enclave, where he'd grown up, was a low hexagon of domes connected by half-submerged corridors, hunkering down in the soil and covered with a radiating substance, which hid them from prying eyes. Now, four smaller clusters of buildings had been added, built behind the original against the high ridges at the foot of the mountains.

It smelled the same – the corridors scented with antiseptic lemon – but it was almost too clean after the murky richness of Earth. He'd forgotten what it was like not to wake up to the odour of decay and sweat, the scent of frying onions embedded in his skin and clothes.

He felt displaced and hated it. He'd wanted to be relieved to be home, to feel cloaked in the comfort he remembered from childhood, but there was no one left here to welcome him. All the children he'd grown up with were either dead or sent somewhere else. Most were dead.

Yuang told him many of them had contracted the MalX.

He felt cheated. Why hadn't Yuang told him before? Some of them must have been dead for years now. He could have told him.

Yuang stopped at the door into the Enclave proper and turned to the grunts dragging Essie, half conscious, between them.

"Take her to room nine." His gaze went to Pip. "You go with them then meet me in the refectory. We have much to talk about."

He pressed his thumb to the lock, the door slid open, and he walked away down the long white hallway. Pip hesitated then followed the grunts. The rooms and corners were familiar to him, yet strangely altered. Everything looked smaller. When they walked by the corridor that led to the dormitories he felt the need to see his old bunk, his room. But he was being watched. Hidden surveillance laced the Enclave like a spider web, every nook and cranny subject to some kind of watchful eye. Yuang would know if he deviated. So he followed the grunts down the silent corridor through more doors and into another hexagon of rooms and halls, but this one was unfamiliar and he figured they must be in the new section.

It wasn't white. The walls were a dull, pale orange and there were no windows. It wasn't as clean either. There was something metallic in the scent. They stopped at a door marked with a number nine and dragged Essie inside.

As soon as Pip entered, he wanted to run out again. The room was large. Around the walls were lines of desks and holo coms and all manner of scientific equipment. Machines whirred in a low undercurrent, and at odd moments holo coms would come on, translucent green shapes and graphs hanging in the air. There was no one else in the room apart from them and one other:

Rosie's dad. Clad only in a pair of briefs, he reclined, half upright on a long red chair, eyes closed, in the middle of a totally enclosed transparent tent. Tubes ran from his arms and torso to medibots that hovered near him, monitoring his life signs. His head had been shaved and a series of small pods attached to his skull.

Essie saw him and struggled weakly in the grip of the grunts, swearing at them. Pip moved forward barely hearing her. Rosie's dad had the MalX; he would recognise it anywhere. His skin was covered in curls of pink rash that formed over his chest and legs like waves, and already his limbs were starting to waste. Pip was horrified. It took weeks to get to this stage. He'd seen him on Earth when the grunts came for him; he'd been fine then. There was only one way he could have become so sick, so fast, and the thought of it turned his stomach. Someone had deliberately infected him with a massive dose and Pip knew exactly who would have done it.

CHAPTER 28

"Riley." Rosie kneeled on the floor by his head. "Wake up."

She touched his left shoulder.

"I'm awake," he said, but didn't open his eyes.

"Can you move?" She tried to keep the urgency out of her voice. "We have to get out. The ship is going to slip into the river."

He made a deep grunting sound and frowned. "I think my arm is broken."

"Yeah, but—"

He tried to get up and roared in pain.

Rosie reached out to help him.

"No! Don't!" He hung onto the balustrade, white-faced and panting, and spoke from between clenched teeth. "I'm going to need a … sling or something."

"Wait there." She ran down to Aunt Essie's quarters. Her aunt's gear was everywhere, thrown into chaos by the crash. Rosie sifted through the mess. "Found it!" she shouted and raced back with a medikit. Inside were antivirals, syringes, vitamin surge pods, a kind of mask, and other vials, but no sling.

"Any material," Riley panted.

She flew down the stairs and pulled the sheet off the bunk. Using the same bit of metal she'd pried his helmet off with, she ripped a piece off it into a rough square.

"You'll have to … help me. Pain …" Riley nodded towards the medikit.

"Pain relievers?" She found a small medigun. She went to put it to his left arm, but he stopped her.

"No. There." He pointed to the broken one. Rosie hesitated. "Works faster, straight in the nerves." His face was distorted with pain. "Rosie, come on!"

Rosie jabbed the needle into his shoulder. He yelled and closed his eyes, his breath coming in gasps.

"Now the sling," he said after a minute.

They got it right after three tries and by then Riley was sweating. But with his arm tied against his body, he was breathing easier and seemed to be in less pain.

"So, do we know where we are?" he said.

Rosie showed him their location on the geocompass.

"There's no way we can get up those canyon walls with your arm like that," she said. "We're going to have to make some kind of raft and use the river. If we can get to where this tributary meets the Marineris, we might be able to get out of the canyon at this point. I think the walls might be lower there."

Riley nodded, weakly. "Sounds good. Do we have any water?"

Rosie was taken aback that he had agreed so readily to her plan. "I'll find some." She went to the narrow galley just off the cargo bay. The food lockers were buckled and the supplies strewn across the floor. Many of the packets had burst open. Rosie crunched across a carpet of dried food and searched for as many intact bottles of water and packs of food as she could. She was worried about Riley. He hadn't even looked at the geocompass to double-check her bearings. It wasn't like him. She located a backpack and filled it with the water and food and took it back to him.

He sipped his water slowly and didn't complain when she unwrapped a protein bar and put it in his hand. That worried her even more.

"What are we going to use for a raft?" he said.

"I don't know." Rosie surveyed the cargo bay. Why didn't Aunt Essie carry an inflatable? Then she was struck with an idea. The bay was full of plastic cargo carriers that had come loose from their webbing. "The carriers." She flicked the light around so it played across the bright red containers. "We could tie them together." They would need an oar as well, but the current was going the way they wanted to go, so it shouldn't be too difficult.

"Good idea," he said, although he didn't sound enthusiastic. "We don't have any coms, do we?"

"No. All busted."

"You sure? Maybe I can fix one."

Rosie sighed. "I'll get one." She went to the bridge, coming back with the broken one she'd found earlier. "Here." She handed it to him. Weariness washed over her again and her head ached.

He flipped off the back of the com. "Got any tools?"

Rosie retrieved her aunt's toolbox. She ate some food and watched Riley fiddle with the com for a while, then she got up and began to drag cargo carriers together.

For a time they didn't speak. Rosie kept dragging containers, listening for any suspicious metallic scraping noises and worrying how long it would be until Helios found them. Her muscles ached and she was still hungry despite the three protein bars she'd consumed. All she wanted to do was sit down and go to sleep. But they had to get out of the pod.

The hull creaked and she dropped a container on her foot. "Ow!" she yelled and kicked it, suddenly furious with it and herself.

"You okay?" Riley said.

She pulled the container to her pile, shoving it savagely against the others. "You mean apart from my whole family possibly being dead and being stuck at the bottom of a canyon?" she said. "Yeah, I'm just fantabulous. A-1, thanks."

"Considering that, you are doing pretty well," he said. His calm response sucked the anger out of her.

She swayed on her feet then slumped down on one of the containers. "Do you think they're still alive?"

He stopped, a tiny screwdriver paused above the com, and met her gaze. "The chances are slim."

Rosie's chest tightened. She was glad he hadn't lied. Tears made her sight blurry and she closed her eyes for a minute, trying to deny them, but they spilled out anyway. She wiped them away with the back of her hand, not looking at him.

He went back to fiddling with the com and said quietly, "You could use the harnesses from the seats and the cargo restraints to tie the containers together."

It was a good idea. She took a deep breath then went to look for the straps.

It took nearly an hour to fasten the straps around

the eight containers. It made a reasonable-sized raft, big enough for the two of them. Riley did what he could to help her, instructing in a good knot to use so they held, but he had trouble staying on his feet and had to sit down. He'd got the com working though and Rosie couldn't help being impressed. He knew a lot about the mechanics of coms and devices; maybe he could teach her one day — if they survived.

It was starting to get light by the time they'd finished. Their plan was to slide the raft out of the side cargo doors and paddle downriver towards the colony until the com was in range.

Riley said he had some friends on Genesis who could help. If he could contact them, they might be able to get a rover to come get them when they got to the junction of the Marineris. If they could find a place to land. If they could get up the canyon wall. It was a lot of "ifs" but they couldn't just sit here.

Rosie slung the pack with the food and water onto her back, then found a waterproof bag Riley could seal the diary in. He wrapped it carefully and zipped it into the front pocket of his spacesuit. They had both kept the suits on to help stay warm.

"Ready?" he said.

She nodded.

The pod was on more of a tilt now, the back section

sitting lower than before. The cargo bay doors were at the back end of the ship, ten metres away from the bottom of the steps where Riley was sitting. Rosie pushed the raft down towards them easily enough, the slanted floor helping her progress, but she was worried about the water outside. How deep were they?

"I think we're still just above the waterline," Riley said.

"What if we're not?"

"We are," he said firmly.

She'd cobbled together a paddle from a length of pipe and a broken slice of a container. She picked it up from the floor and shoved it under the straps that held the raft together.

"Where's the com? If it gets wet ..."

"In here with the diary." Riley patted the zipped pocket. "The suit should keep them dry."

Rosie hoped the suits would keep the cold out as well. It was autumn on Mars and even though they were near the equator, it was still only about seven degrees outside. "Come on, let's get the door open."

He walked slowly down to the higher end of the doors. They'd decided earlier that Rosie would have to be at the end where the water would rush in. Risky though it was, if she slipped, Riley stood a better chance of holding the raft.

Riley said, "If you feel it start to go, you jump on, and I mean fast. I'll get us out somehow."

She gripped the manual door release. "I'm ready."

"You packed the medikit, didn't you?" he asked.

"It's in the pack."

"Good." He unlocked the door. "I'm going to need those painkillers. Okay. Pull!"

Rosie heaved. The door began to slide open, her side slower than his. He had hold of it with his left hand and his face was screwed up in pain as his injured right arm brushed against the wall.

Water began to flow in around Rosie's feet. It was freezing, the cold seeping into her boots. Riley's side was still dry, but the wider Rosie opened her door, the more water came in, until it was halfway up her calves and rising. The raft began to lift, banging against the floor of the ship and the roar of the water through the canyon was massively loud.

Rosie let go of her door. She grabbed the raft and pushed hard, swinging her end towards the gap while Riley pulled.

"Rosie, get on!" he shouted.

But before she could, there was a sudden terrifying shriek of metal against rock and the pod slipped. A great rush of water flowed in and knocked Rosie off her feet. She lost her grip on the raft and went under. Her chest seized. The water was so cold, it was like being pinpricked by thousands of icicles. She flung her hands out in panic scrabbling for a handhold. The bag on her back caught on something and the stairwell rail almost hit her in the face. She clung to it and dragged herself up to surface, coughing and spitting.

"Rosie!" Riley's face was contorted with pain as he hung on to the raft that was on the verge of being swept out of the doors. Metal shrieked around them. The ship was breaking loose.

"I'm losing it!" Riley shouted.

She leaped towards it, managing to grab one of the straps.

"Get on!" He yelled. Rosie threw herself across it and he gave the raft a mighty heave then followed, landing on top as it was swept out onto the river.

Rosie clung to the raft's straps, shivering. The current whisked them away downstream faster than she'd anticipated. She looked behind and a moment later saw the pod sink in a glut of bubbles and a last scrape of metal. A mix of fear and exhilaration flooded her.

She was wet and freezing, but they were alive. She turned to Riley but the words died on her lips. He lay on the raft, his eyes closed, and he wasn't moving.

CHAPTER 29

"Riley?" Rosie crawled towards him then realised the raft was heading straight for the canyon wall. She pulled the paddle out from under the straps then shoved it into the water like a rudder. The raft tossed and bobbed in the current and it took all her concentration to control it. She balanced on her knees and dipped the paddle in left, then right, shuffling from one side to the other as she tried to steer them on a straight course. The water dragged hard at the paddle and she was terrified they'd tip over.

"Riley!" She shouted at him several times, and finally he moved his hand the tiniest bit.

"Okay," he said weakly, but didn't open his eyes. It was better than nothing.

After a frantic dance of shuffling and dipping, Rosie managed to steer the raft towards the centre of the river, where the water ran swift but smooth. They settled into the strong central current, floating in a relatively straight course.

Her knees sore, she sat back on her heels to catch her breath, inhaling deeply through the breather. Her arms and back were aching, her fingers so numb from the cold she could barely feel the paddle any more. With slow movements she shrugged the backpack off her shoulders and looked up at the sky that was cloud streaked and getting brighter by the minute.

It was just past dawn and a pale red glow was suffusing the rim of the canyon, highlighting the redness of the rock. The canyon walls rose almost half a kilometre above her head and down where they were, the light was still soft.

A thin mist was coming off the water and the air was cold, her breath frosting in front of her. Water had penetrated part of the way into her suit when she'd been pushed under. Her forearms, lower legs and neck were all damp and water had got into her boots; her socks were soaked. A chill was settling in her bones. But when she looked around, her discomfort faded as it suddenly struck her that she was actually on Mars – she was here, she was actually here.

Even after all her study, she'd not been able to comprehend Mars's actual existence until now, or its staggering beauty. The planet was still wild, and here in this relatively small canyon, humans had barely touched its natural beauty. Perhaps no one had actually ridden this river, no one had seen that particular slab of rock, that tuft of shrub. She could be the first.

Riley's groaning brought her back to reality. She turned around. He did not look good.

"Painkillers," he rasped.

She carefully wedged the oar in a crack between the containers and reached into her pack for the medikit. Her fingers met soggy protein bars. Yuck. But wet food was the least of her worries. Riley was very pale and lay half curled, his breathing laboured. Did people die of broken arms? She didn't think so – something else had to be wrong. He might be bleeding inside.

She stuck the needle in his arm, pumping it quickly. He didn't make a sound. Worried, she put the medigun away and pulled the geocompass out of her pocket. It was dead. The water had got in. Damn it! But at least she had an idea of how far they were from Genesis and what direction it was. Riley's eyes were closed. He shouldn't go to sleep.

"Riley," she said. His lids opened. "The com, is it working?"

Slowly, he unzipped his pocket and pulled out the com. He inspected it, pressing some buttons and squinting. "Okay," he said.

"How long till we can try to contact your friends?"

"'Bout an hour."

"Right, um ..." She tried to think of other things to say. She'd read it was best to keep people awake and talking when they were injured. Or was that just for certain kinds of injuries?

"Who are these people in the colony who might help us?" She picked up the oar again.

"Friends," Riley said faintly. He scrunched his face as though in significant pain.

Rosie's insides lurched. "What are their names?" she said loudly, steering them wide of a partly submerged rock.

"Jo and ..." He opened his eyes, squinting at her. "Chris, her partner. They work in the colony."

"Right, and what do they do there?"

"They're scientists. Rosie, it's okay. I'm not going to pass out. You don't have to keep talking to me."

"Maybe I'm just bored." She glanced at him.

He gave a small cough that was almost a laugh. "Okay." He exhaled slowly. "I'm going to sit up."

"Are you sure?"

"Don't be so worried. I'm not going to die."

"Not yet," she muttered, but he heard her.

"Yeah? Well …" He paused as he pushed up to a sitting position. "I'm not dying today."

Rosie pulled hard on the oar. "Let's hope no one is."

Riley didn't reply.

They rode the raft in silence for a long time. The sun rose higher and light finally penetrated into the bottom of the canyon, bringing some welcome warmth.

Rosie turned her face up to it, still shivering. Putting down the oar, she spread her damp hair as best she could with her fingers. It hung past her shoulders in a tangled mess but at least it might dry.

Even when the sun hit midday she doubted it would be much more than twelve degrees. Mars was still a cold planet by Earth's standards.

She picked up the oar again. The current was pulling to the left so she could sit almost comfortably in one spot now.

They drifted on and she ignored the hunger pains chewing at her stomach, wondering idly instead if the river water was safe to drink. She was just bending down to cup her hand when a burst of static came from behind her. Startled, she turned and saw Riley had the com out and was manipulating the controls. His face was tight with concentration. "Keep the raft steady, Rosie."

"Sorry." She turned back to working the oar. "Got anything?"

He was adjusting the frequency, the static growing louder, then softer until it faded altogether.

"What the ..." He tapped the com on the edge of his hand. "Come on!"

Glancing back, Rosie saw a faint green glow reflecting on his chin from the tiny view screen. A sharp crackle sounded then a voice came from the speaker.

"Hello? Hello, who's this?" It was a male voice, youthful and slightly high-pitched. "Riley?" He had a lilting accent. "I can barely see you. Is that you?"

"Chris," Riley said, "yes, it's me. I need you to—"

"Are you on Mars?"

"Yes," Riley said impatiently. "I need you to pick us up."

"How did you get here? When—"

"I don't have time to explain." Riley cut him off. "Just keep track of this signal and get some transport out to us."

"Us?" Chris's voice went up again but then he must have noticed the expression on Riley's face. "Okay." He became all business. "I'll get Jo. I reckon you're about half an hour away. We'll find you."

"Thanks." Riley turned off the screen, switching the com to low power. His face was pinched and grey. Rosie thought the drugs must be wearing off. "We'll need to get close to the wall when they find us," he said.

She looked up at the high canyon walls.

"Closer? And how the hell are we going to get up those cliffs?" she said.

Riley closed his eyes briefly. "Don't worry. Chris will think of something." And with that he crumpled over onto the raft.

Rosie stared at him for a moment in surprise then saw the com slipping out of his grip. She lunged towards it, catching it before it bounced into the water. She clutched it to her chest. That was close. Heart hammering, she lay with the oar in one hand, the com in the other. She had to check Riley. She sat up and leaned over him. He was still breathing, if unsteadily. She zipped the com into the top pocket of her suit and began directing the raft towards the wall of the canyon.

The canyon become wider and the current swifter, as they travelled closer to the junction with the Marineris River. Riley was still unconscious and she watched him closely while she waited for his friends. After a while the com started beeping at her.

She clamped the oar between her knees and answered it, activating the screen. "Hello, Chris?" she said.

The screen wavered and a fuzzy image of a man with black hair appeared. "Who's that?"

"Rosie. I'm with Riley – he's passed out."

Chris turned and she caught snippets of conversation with someone else. "Riley ... some kid ..."

"Hello?" Rosie raised her voice, annoyed. What the hell were they doing? "Hey," she shouted into the com, "where are you?"

He turned back to her. "Sorry, what happened to Riley?"

"I think he's got a broken arm. Where are you?"

"Not far. Look up."

About twenty metres ahead she saw a figure on the lip of the canyon high above her head.

"Can you get the raft to the wall?" Chris said.

"I'll try." She shoved the com back in her pocket and began to direct the raft. The water was moving fast and her muscles ached with the effort of trying to make the raft swing over. How she was going to keep them against the wall when she got there was another question. She couldn't see any rocks that would provide an anchor point. The wall was just one long angled slope. There were some narrow cracks higher up but at the waterline it was mostly smooth with no bank to speak of.

She got as close as she dared, the wall rushing past her, water foaming against the sides of the raft as the current pulled them along.

"Rosie," the com crackled, "look for the cable."

Struggling to keep the raft from crashing into the rock, she glanced up and saw a steel cable dangling down with what appeared to be a hook at the end. Did he want her to try and hold onto the cable? She'd never be strong enough.

"Hook it onto the ropes." Chris's voice was muffled over the sound of the water.

More than a little scared, Rosie kneeled on the raft, dragging the oar to keep the raft going towards the cable. If she missed, they'd shoot straight past. And what if Riley rolled off? She dropped the oar onto the raft. Riley stirred, groaning.

"Riley, hold on!" she shouted and reached for the cable. She pulled it down and slipped the hook under the strap across the top of the raft. The hook locked itself and as the current pulled them further along, the cable snapped taut. The raft spun around and jolted, bucking in the swift current, and Rosie lost her balance. She tumbled backwards, bumping into Riley, who had heard her shout and was hanging on to another of the straps. He stuck a leg out, stopping her from falling into the water. The com crackled. "You okay?"

Panting, Rosie shuffled back to the cable. The raft was tilting as the cable held it partly up out of the water at one end. She pulled the com from her pocket. "Okay." She squinted up to the lip of the canyon.

"Right, we're coming down to you."

A harness, equipped with anti-grav thrusters, dropped slowly down on another cable. Riley insisted she go up first and Rosie didn't argue. The ride up was quick. The light became brighter at the top where a tall thin man and a startlingly beautiful woman were waiting for her. They detached her from the harness and the woman took her to a rover parked facing the canyon.

"Are you all right?" she said, as she opened the back door. "You're soaking."

Too exhausted to talk, Rosie mumbled something positive and pulled herself into the vehicle. The woman, who had to be Jo, shut the door and went back to helping Chris get Riley.

Rosie slumped against the padded seat. Every muscle in her body ached and it was such a relief to sit down in a warm, quiet spot. The rover had its own air supply so she could take off her breather. She stared out the window, watching as Chris unhitched Riley from the harness. He looked terrible: pale and grey-faced, and she wondered how he'd managed to hang on to the raft for so long.

She pulled the one remaining glo-tube out of her pocket, then unzipped her suit and peeled it off, kicking the wet material away. Her jeans were spotted with dirt and the red T-shirt was musty with the smell of her own sweat, but it was a relief to have the suit off. She was sorry she'd left the jacket Aunt Essie had given her on the pod, which would be well underwater now. Her aunt would kill her. If she was still alive. She rested her head back on the seat. She was alive. Riley was alive. Exhaustion washed over her. All they had to do now was break into Helios and rescue everybody. Easy. With a soft groan she closed her eyes.

CHAPTER 30

Pip sat at the table in the refectory and stared out of the windows, watching the red dust swirl in the garden.

The refectory was still very much the same. It was a long room with a high ceiling, a servery at the back and a collection of white tables and chairs. The only change he could see was a terrarium in the centre of the room filled with a scene of Mars in miniature, complete with the Genesis colony and the Enclave. He remembered that Tuesdays had always been spinach pie for lunch. Pip hated spinach.

Yuang sat opposite him stirring his tea and staring out at the garden. Finally, he took a sip and said, "You've been native too long, Pip; you look shocked. Surely you've seen those with the MalX before?"

Pip didn't answer and a thin smile curved Yuang's lips. "What we do here is important. You used to believe that."

"I used to believe a lot of things," Pip said. Anger was burning his insides and his voice came out choked, growl-like.

"Careful," Yuang replied, "I might start to think you don't appreciate everything I've done for you."

Everything he'd done! Pip clenched his hands into fists under the table. "Did you infect Rosie's dad?" he said.

Yuang put his cup down on its saucer and looked at him with eyes full of weary condescension.

"It is called the Genesis Project, Pip. How else do you think we can find the cure?"

"You told me that was done in the labs. You never said anything about infecting people." Pip couldn't reconcile this cold stranger to the man he'd known as a child.

"It is done in labs but perhaps differently to what you assume. The DNA and that special protein that defends against the MalX cannot be grown in a dish. We tried." He shrugged. "This is the only way. Sacrifices are necessary. You seem to have forgotten the stakes of the game."

It's not a game, Pip wanted to shout. He was shaken

by Yuang's calm. How long had this been going on? Was Rosie's dad only one of many? The other kids he'd known before, the ones who were dead now – had the same happened to them?

"I'm saving lives, Pip." Yuang leaned forward, watching, almost earnestly. "Sometimes to save lives, you have to take lives."

"Rosie's dad wasn't immune to the MalX," he said.

"You know that for a fact?" Yuang raised an eyebrow. "Have you tested him yourself? Is that what you've been doing on Earth when I couldn't contact you? Turned into a scientist, have you?"

Pip imagined ploughing his knuckles into Yuang's face. "If he was immune, he wouldn't be sick now. You're only doing it to torture her."

"That's true. He isn't immune," said Yuang. "Neither, I suspect, is Miss Black. And you're right, I didn't infect him for purely scientific reasons. It's called leverage."

"You didn't need to do it." Pip glared at him.

Yuang smiled. "I'm not a monster – I won't let him die. I can cure him." His smile became indulgent and dangerous. "*You* can cure him."

"What?" Was this a test?

Yuang sat back in his chair, a smug look on his face. "I mean *you* can cure him, Pip. You, it's in you. You have the ability to stop him dying."

"What the hell do you mean?"

Yuang's eyes had a gleam to them now. "You're special, Pip. I couldn't believe it when I saw you developing such a strong immunity. And at your age."

"What?" Pip felt a terrible gnawing at his insides.

"How else do you think you survived all those years on Earth, living in those MalX-infested areas?"

"You gave me antivirals."

"All we gave you were vitamins and yet you survived. You are immune to the MalX, Pip. The last test we did on you a few months ago showed an astonishing development of your system. We can't explain it."

Pip was finding it difficult to breathe. "But you showed me tests, that I wasn't—"

"They weren't real." Yuang surveyed him as if he was a special pet. "I needed you to be cooperative, willing to do anything to get back here where you'd be safe. And I needed to be sure you were as special as you are."

Pip couldn't speak. What he was saying was impossible.

"I see you're shocked," Yuang said. "But it's true. You're not just immune; you're very special. We knew your parents didn't have immunity, that's why it was such a surprise to find out that you do. Your blood stops the virus literally in its tracks and unlike others with immunity, you can pass yours on. You should be pleased.

It means no more Earth trips for you. You're too precious now. We have so many tests we need to do."

"Tests?"

"Yes, tests," Yuang said. "But what you need to understand right now is that your immunity means you can stop Rosie's aunt dying when I infect her, and Rosie herself when she is captured. Because she will be – you know that, don't you?" He stirred his tea again. "There is no way she or Riley will be able to get in here and do whatever it is they think they can do."

Pip stared at him, horror growing like a tumour in his chest. Yuang was going to infect Essie and then Rosie. He was going to …

His thoughts froze as one of the things Yuang had said really sank in: *We knew your parents didn't have immunity.* Yuang had always told him he'd never been sure whether his parents were immune to the MalX or not – that he'd only found out when they caught it on a visit to Earth. Realisation struck and his stomach turned. Yuang had done the same to his parents as he was doing to Rosie's dad. He had killed his parents as part of some kind of test.

Yuang was still sitting there, smiling.

"You bastard," he said.

Yuang's smile dropped. "Yes, you would think that, after the years I put in to mentoring you."

Pip wanted to strike out, to put his hands around Yuang's neck and squeeze.

"You are the cure, Pip," Yuang said. "You are what we've been looking for."

Everything was a lie. All that fear he'd had and he couldn't even catch the disease. "And my parents?" he said.

"Unfortunate."

Pip was shaking with fury.

"And what if you don't get what you want?" he said. "What about the Enclave, the people here? Rosie's aunt said you were going to destroy it."

Yuang's eyes narrowed. "We've put too much into this to risk losing it all now, Pip. But don't worry, you'll be safely away – and I think you will cooperate with me and not try any more of your tricks. If Rosie and her family die, it will be because of your stupidity."

CHAPTER 31

Rosie was woken by the sound of whispered arguing. They were still in the rover, bumping along the uneven Martian ground. Next to her, Riley was asleep, and in front, the two who'd rescued them, Chris and Jo, were arguing in low voices.

"We can't," Jo was saying. "You know what they're like, it's too dangerous."

"But we can't just leave them," Chris hissed. "I've known him since–"

"I know," Jo interrupted. "Don't you think I know? I care about him too, but we have a child. If the Enclave–" She stopped, suddenly aware Rosie was awake.

"I heard everything, in case you were wondering," Rosie said.

Jo's mouth compressed. "It's complicated, Rosie, we were surprised to get Riley's call. We haven't seen him for three years. Things have changed. There's not much we can do." She gave Chris a sidelong glance. "We have a child. If Helios found out—"

"I get it." Rosie stopped her. They were on their own. She couldn't blame Jo – not after what she'd seen Helios do to her own family.

"What's his plan anyway?" Jo said. "He's going to the Enclave, isn't he?"

"We both are."

Jo stared at her. "He's taking you with him?"

"He can't do it alone."

Jo exchanged a glance with Chris. Rosie sighed. She was too tired to convince her. Jo saw her as a teenager who had to be protected.

"How far is it to the Enclave?" she asked Chris.

He cast a nervous glance to Jo. "It's forty kilometres from the colony."

Jo's tone was reluctant as she said, "We'll get you into Genesis – not in the rover, but somehow – and we'll get you some clothes and food, but—"

"It's okay," Rosie interrupted her. "We'll find a way."

Jo was looking at her as if Rosie didn't really understand what she was doing. "Wake Riley up," she said.

Rosie shook his shoulder and he blinked awake, bleary-eyed.

"Hey," Jo said, "we're almost there. You all right?"

"Yeah." But his voice was raspy and he moved awkwardly as he sat upright. "How are you, Jo?"

"Better than you. We're going to drop you at the south entrance. We can't take you inside with us. Helios must have someone in the Senate, because there're bulletins about you all over the comwaves. They're linking you to the death of a family on Earth, Shen or something."

Juli's family. Rosie felt the pain of losing her friend clutch at her again.

"That didn't take them long." He sounded resigned. "Do you have a gun?" he asked Jo. "I lost the one I had in the crash."

"A gun?" Jo's expression was tense with worry. "Riley, what are you planning?"

"There's information in the Enclave I need, Jo. I have to get in before Helios blows up all evidence the Enclave existed."

"Blows it up?" Jo looked alarmed.

Riley sighed and said softly, "Where have you been? You used to know how they operate."

"That was years ago. I have a family now."

"I know and I'm not asking you to get involved," Riley said. "But I'm hoping I can stop them, or at least warn them and get some people out."

"Are you sure you should be involving the kid?" Chris said.

Riley looked at Rosie. "No, but she's older than my sister was when she went on the run. And I made a promise."

"She's a child, Riley," Jo said. "She doesn't know how—"

"How dangerous Helios is?" Rosie interrupted. "Yeah, I do actually."

"You *think* you do." Jo sounded annoyed.

"Jo." Riley put a hand on her arm but she moved it away.

"Sacrificing children now, Riley?"

"I can't do it alone. Are you willing to take her place?"

A red flush appeared on Jo's cheeks. "Riley, you—"

"Jo," Chris said. "Leave it. You won't change his mind."

"We'll be out of your way as soon as possible," Riley said, his gaze troubled, and Rosie had a sudden suspicion that he might be revising his promise. He had another thing coming if he thought he was going to leave her behind. She'd come too far now to go back, and there was no way she was leaving her aunt and dad at the mercy of Helios – no matter how much it scared her.

The Genesis colony was constructed as a collection of interconnected domes and covered ten square kilometres of Martian soil between the edge of the Marineris River and the soaring, craggy peaks of the Tharsis Mountains. As they approached it, Rosie glimpsed the tops of the four enormous transparent domes that edged the river, housing the public buildings and administration centres of the colony. She'd studied all the interactive pamphlets and maps Aunt Essie had on the place and felt like she knew it almost as well as anyone living there. She knew the domes were linked by a series of wide arched thoroughfares planted with trees and shrubs imported from Earth. The scientists and top administrators had their own palatial domes east and west of the public area, all facing the river, while everyone else was housed in ordinary domes that faced out to the Tharsis Mountains and were connected to the colony by long covered walkways and cycleways.

There were four airlocked entries into Genesis: one provided access to an openair platform that overlooked the river; two others, east and west, were in large hangar-sized domes that stored rover and maintenance vehicles;

and the last was at the southern end allowing access to the gardens in the valley.

It was there, behind a band of eucalypts, that Jo and Chris dropped them.

Rosie watched them drive away with some apprehension. Since Riley was wanted by the Senate, Jo had reluctantly given Rosie directions on how to get to their home in the colony. Rosie would meet her in a few hours and Jo would give her some food and painkillers, while Riley borrowed a rover and drove it around the perimeter. Rosie would then meet him in one of the farm hangars and they'd take the rover to the Enclave. Jo had used a sling from the medikit in the rover to stablilise his arm and given him some pain relief shots, but that was all, and Rosie worried about leaving him alone. What if he collapsed again?

She adjusted her breather and rubbed her hands up and down her arms and tried to convince herself she wasn't freezing. Jo had given her a sweater and Riley one of Chris's jackets. The sweater was dark green and slightly too long for her, and the jacket a bit tight for Riley, but they were better than nothing. By night the temperature would probably drop to zero.

They crouched behind a line of trees and scrub at the side of a dirt road and surveyed the airlock fifty metres away. The area around the entrance was clear, but between them and the airlock were patches of thigh-high greyish-green shrubs and uneven rocky ground. A dozen or so people were heading along a road that curved up from the valley farms. The road fell away sharply and it appeared as if the people were coming up out of the earth as they climbed up the steep incline.

"We still don't have a plan," Rosie said.

Riley was silent and she turned to him and saw something in his eyes she didn't like. The look of a decision already made.

"What?" She spoke with caution.

"Rosie, I don't think you should come with me."

"Riley, you–"

"I've been thinking about it," he interrupted her. "Jo's right, I am sacrificing you."

"She's not right," Rosie insisted, but he only shook his head.

"She is. I shouldn't have got you mixed up in this. This is my fight, not yours."

"It's not just your fight," she said. "And you haven't lost. We've still got the codes in the diary."

"But they're not much use without the code key. Without that I can't get any of the proof about what Helios has done."

"But you can stop Yuang from blowing up the Enclave," Rosie said.

"Not if I'm locked up, and I won't let you try to do it for me. It's too dangerous."

"So you're just going to give up? What about my dad and Aunt Essie and all the other people in there?"

"I will go to Yuang and exchange myself for them. I'll tell him he has no need to destroy anything, that I have nothing. I can convince him of that, I know I can. He'll release your family, then you will leave Mars and forget about Helios."

"Just like that?" She glared at him. "Dad and Aunt Essie might not even be alive any more."

"Yuang won't have killed them yet – he needs to make sure I don't have anything. Besides, he has to follow some rules as well; he has bosses to answer to."

"But I memorised the codes," Rosie said desperately. "I can do what Aunt Essie was going to do – I can get in and stop the selfdestruct, turn on the evacuation alarm, help people get out."

"No." His lips thinned to nothing more than a line. "If they catch you – and Rosie, they will–"

"They'll kill me?" She was too angry to be scared.

His voice was firm but quiet. "They'll torture you to punish me."

"Right, like what happened to you?" she said bitterly. "Do you want to tell me about that?"

He paused, saying nothing.

"That's what I thought."

"Rosie, I've changed my mind."

"Changed your mind! Riley, you're hurt. How are you going to do this alone? You promised. I–"

"Rosie, stop." His expression was fierce, pained. "When Helios caught me three years ago they shut me in a cage. They broke my ankles, stripped skin from my body and injected me with surgical nanoblasts programmed to target my vital organs ..." He paused. "By the time friends managed to get me out, I was sure I was going to die. I wanted to die. It took nine months and five surgeries for me to recover. I don't have my own liver any more – I have one that was grown in a lab – and I still have to take injections to kill any nanoblasts that may have replicated themselves and be hiding in my system. So, no, I can't – I won't – expose you to that. I should never have let you come this far."

Rosie's heart thudded against her ribs. She could barely imagine what it had been like for him but she couldn't just give up. "What if Yuang's already done that to my dad, or Aunt Essie?" she said.

His expression softened. "What if that happens to you? Rosie, I think your family would rather you lived."

She looked away. He was probably right but that didn't stop the way she felt.

"You can do one thing," he said. "This will go better

if I tell Yuang I'm coming. When you go into the colony I want you to find a public comnet and contact him. I'll tell you what I want you to say – and you need to stick to that and say nothing else. Don't get drawn into conversation with him."

"That's it," she said, "that's all I'm allowed to do? Then I just wait?" She couldn't keep the resentment out of her voice.

"It's the safest way. You stay with Jo and Chris. I'll take a rover from the farms in the valley out to the Enclave and your aunt can bring your dad and herself back in it."

"If Yuang agrees."

"He will."

Rosie wasn't sure of that but it was pointless to say that to Riley. He'd made up his mind but that didn't mean she had to do what he said. She couldn't believe he was going to give up so easily and let Helios get away with it. There had to be another way – she just had to think of it.

"So how do I contact Yuang – in the directory, is he?"

Riley ignored her sarcasm and handed her a scrap of paper. Scribbled on it was a series of numbers. "Enter these into the comnet, and it'll connect you."

"Where'd you get this?"

"Rosie–"

"All right." She sighed with irritation. "I'm ready."

He watched her closely. "You sure?"

"Are you?" she retorted.

"Keep your head down and when you get to the airlock make sure you follow someone in. Don't look around. There'll be surveillance."

"I'm not stupid."

Riley's calm didn't waver. "I'll meet you in the hangar."

"What if you pass out again?"

"I won't."

"Sure, you're in great health – nothing wrong with you."

Riley's jaw twitched but he didn't reply.

"Is the com still working?" she asked.

He pulled it out of his pocket. "Yes, do you want it?"

"No, just make sure it's on in case you pass out and I have to come find you."

"That won't happen. I told you–"

"You feel fine," Rosie finished for him. "But you don't look fine." There was a film of sweat on his brow and she had seen him wincing when they squatted down.

"Rosie," his tone was even but with an undercurrent of annoyance, "just listen and I'll tell you what to say to Yuang."

CHAPTER 32

It was ridiculously easy to get into the colony. No one questioned her, no one did more than glance at her; she just followed some people in. Perhaps it wasn't unusual for a young woman to be seen coming in from the farms.

Inside the hangar was a huge space topped by the high curved roof of the dome. It was filled with rovers, machinery and people going about their business. At the far end a set of automatic doors led to the rest of the colony.

Rosie took off her breather and hurried towards them, wending her way around slow-moving vehicles and groups of people. On her right were several storehouses and on her left enormous coolrooms, their metallic doors gleaming in the soft light that came from the crystal globes installed in the roof. Everyone appeared too busy with their own work to bother with her and she made it through the doors without any trouble.

On the other side was a walkway. Like in the public domes, the walkway was a double layer of curved pyloglass, sunk deep into the Martian soil. It was lined on either side with small shrubs and led towards a connecting dome and more walkways.

There weren't many people about here, and as she walked, she kept trying to think of what she could have said to change Riley's mind. Why couldn't he see that she could help him? She knew the codes; they could still get in. It was such a gamble for him to think that Yuang would let her family go and stop the destruction of the Enclave because he gave himself up.

She emerged from the walkway into one of the large connecting domes and paused inside the entrance. The dome was essentially a hub connecting eight walkways that led to other parts of the colony. Four comnet booths rose from the floor in the central area arrayed around a two-metre-high, 3-D AI directory pillar. Two young boys were messing around with the AI, laughing and waving their hands through the semitransparent figure of the woman, and there was a man seated on a bench hooked into a virtual workstation. Around the central perimeter, streams of people moved purposefully in and out of the walkways. Rosie couldn't see any sign of a Senate uniform among them. A screen embedded high in the wall of the dome was showing images of the clear Martian day outside, complete with oxygen levels and predictions for windstorms. It was eight degrees outside, but it was warm in the dome and the air smelled faintly of pollen and iron.

"Move along there." Someone spoke behind her and she jumped and turned around. A middle-aged man with a greying beard looked down at her with a smile.

"Sorry." She stepped to the side but he was already moving away. Her heart was racing. She had to get this done and get out.

On the far side was a shuttle station that provided transport within the colony. Four carriages were lined up next to the low platform. They looked like elongated eggs with the tops sliced off. After using the comnet, Rosie was to take the blue line to Arcadia where Jo would be waiting for her; then they would take another to the western hangar.

Rosie walked as calmly as she could to the comnet booths, choosing one partly concealed by a potted plant. The com had a wide flat screen and a sound'n'speak device slid out of the booth as she put her palm on the screen. She slipped the fine curl of wires over her ear and waited impatiently as the five-second intro advertisement played.

The screen faded to pale red with an array of options. She ignored them all and called up a virtual keyboard then typed in the contact override Riley had provided that would divert to Yuang's com. She started sweating as she watched the screen suddenly flick off then come on again. There was a soft crackling sound in her ear then a blue tinted image of Yuang filled the screen. His expression was aloof and suspicious.

"How did you ..." he said then stopped as he saw her. "Miss Black." He smiled in a way that made her scalp tighten. "What an unexpected development. I was worried about you – both of you. Where's Shore? Is he in one piece?"

"He's fine," she said quietly.

"He always had a knack for survival." He was behaving as if they were old friends. "So what can I do for you?"

"I want to see my aunt and my dad," she said, repeating what Riley had told her to say. "Show me they're alive."

Yuang raised his eyebrows. "Manners, please."

"Show me!" she hissed through her teeth.

"No." His tone was flat, his smile gone. "But you may have my word they are alive – for the moment. Do you have something for me?"

Riley had assumed he would say that. She was

supposed to tell Yuang that Riley would come to him, and that if he released her dad and Aunt Essie in exchange, Helios would be in the clear. She was supposed to just set up the meeting and switch off the com – but she hesitated. What if that wasn't enough leverage for Yuang? What if, when he got Riley, he still detonated the labs?

"Miss Black?" Yuang eyed her with some amusement. "I don't have all day."

Rosie took a breath. He didn't know what had been in the box. He couldn't be sure if she was lying or not. "Release my dad and aunt at the north gate of the Enclave. Riley will meet you there."

"Will he?" Yuang watched her. "Giving himself up for them, is he?"

"Yes."

"How noble." His tone was condescending but the look in his eyes was not.

"Him in exchange for my family and an end to plans to destroy the Enclave," she said.

"Interesting," Yuang replied. "And the other contents of his parents' box?"

"He will bring them," she said, then added, "all that he has."

Yuang frowned. "All that he has? Are you implying something, Miss Black?"

Rosie swallowed hard. "I took something out, before, on Earth. He doesn't know about it but I think it's important."

"What?" His tone was cold now.

"A piece of plaspaper," she said. "It was some kind of shipment order for stuff going from Mars to Earth around ten years ago. Something about malaria vaccines and new test doses. I hid it before I met Pip."

"Where?" Yuang's expression was frightening, even through the screen, but Rosie kept talking. She had to make him think she had something, even though she had no idea if a record of the shipment that had brought the MalX to Earth even existed.

"It's safe," she said. "But if someone found it ..." She let him think what he might.

He watched her closely, his gaze narrowing. "And why should I believe you?"

"Because you can't afford to have any information leaking out, can you? And if someone saw that document, they might wonder about how the MalX really got to Earth."

He smiled, a slow scary smile. "That's brave, Miss Black. If you're telling the truth. Brave but stupid. Does Shore know what you're up to?"

"Let my dad and aunt go and stop your plans to destroy the Enclave or someone might see it," she said.

"Oh, I was planning to let them go," he said. "They are of little use to me now since they've brought me what I need anyway. Shore is a big fish, Miss Black, and we will talk when he comes to me. But as for you," he smiled again, "there was a reason he told you to deliver your message to me fast and then shut the com off. A reason a smart girl like you should already know."

Rosie felt a leap of fear as she realised he was right. She had taken too long.

"Miss Black," Yuang said, "meet Gerry."

The hairs on the back of Rosie's neck lifted. Someone was standing behind her. She heard nasally breathing. "Need a ride?" a man said.

Her heart boosted like a rocket ship. She ripped the earpiece off and sprang forward, pushing past a couple using the next com, but he had hold of her arm before she went more than a step.

"I don't think so." He pulled her so hard, her head snapped back and she bit her tongue. He was big with clammy hands and white-blond hair, cut short against his skull.

"Let me go!" Rosie shouted. "Help!" She looked at the couple, but they were moving out of the way.

"Now, come on," Gerry said, "I told your mum I'd catch you next time you ran off."

"My mum's dead!" Rosie squirmed and twisted in

his grip. "Help me," she pleaded to the couple.

But their eyes were set on the golden insignia of Helios on his breast and they backed off fast.

"She always gets like this," Gerry was saying to them, a smile on his face as he dragged her away. "Hates astrophysics." He chuckled.

"I do not!" Rosie shouted furiously. "Probably know more about it than you. He's kidnapping me!" she screamed, but no one wanted to interfere.

He pulled her close, leaning down to whisper in her ear, the smile still on his face. "Don't be bad or you don't get to see Daddy."

"Your breath stinks," Rosie replied.

He looked sidelong down at her and grunted. "Tough, eh? Won't last long."

Rosie just glared at him. Her heart was beating so fast, she couldn't breathe properly.

Gerry dragged her at a fast pace down a walkway and into a living dome. What looked like an ordinary home for someone flashed past as he dragged her through to an outside airlock.

He thrust a breather at her. "Put this on and don't do anything to make me hurt you."

It was frigid outside, the sun was dropping and a red light dressed the bare earth. A few metres away a three-wheeled vehicle was waiting, another man at the controls.

"Get in." Gerry prodded her and she climbed into the back. He sat beside her, squashing her against the side.

"Go." He tapped the shoulder of the driver.

The vehicle trundled up a narrow track towards the Tharsis Mountains and away from the colony. Wedged into the back, Rosie watched the massive bulk of the ranges filling the sky before them and felt a moment of panic and despair. Would Riley guess what had happened? Would he still turn up? She had no idea and could only hope Yuang believed her about the plaspaper. If anything, it might buy them a bit more time.

CHAPTER 33

Pip watched. Keeping still and silent, he moved in the background, staying in the shadows of the walls, listening in doorways and using all the tricks he'd taught himself to survive on Earth.

Being a Feral made you a target and he'd become very good at being invisible. It was amazing what people could miss. As big and muscled as Yuang's grunts were, they were far from bright and most of them were spinning on enhancers.

Pip gritted his teeth, feeling the hatred oozing like river mud. Even Yuang was a bit stupid. He'd thought that telling him he was immune to the MalX would keep him docile, on the leash. If it was even true. He wasn't sure what to believe now but somehow the idea that he might be immune made some sense. He'd helped Essie screw up Yuang's plans and normally that might be enough to get him a one-way ticket through the airlock. Maybe he *was* special. And Yuang thought the threat of not letting him cure Rosie and her family would make him do whatever he said.

Yuang was deluded if he thought that. As far as he could tell, he didn't think he could do much for Rosie's dad anyway, and her aunt wasn't looking too good either, which was a pity, because he'd liked her. But Rosie … Fury surfed cold through his veins as he watched Essie through the gap in the vent. That was not going to happen to her.

He smiled grimly as Essie spat at the grunt attaching her drip. The spit landed short but it was satisfying nonetheless. She shuddered for a while as the sedation took hold and Pip watched until she subsided then he crept away.

He'd heard they'd picked Rosie up at the colony and he wanted to see for himself when they brought her in.

Silent as snowfall, he melted into the corridors of the Enclave and into an unused room. It looked directly out onto the back area where the rovers came in. He crouched low and crooked a finger under the blind and waited for Rosie to arrive.

They threw her in a tiny room and slammed the door.

It was pitch black. For a moment Rosie panicked. She couldn't draw a proper breath. She crawled forward until she felt the wall, then sat back against it.

The wall was hard against her back but surprisingly warm. She pressed her cheek and the palms of her hands against it and told herself not to think about what Riley said Yuang had done to him. She told herself he'd only made it up to scare her into staying behind. She concentrated on wondering where Riley was, if he'd noticed she was gone. Was it sunset yet? Was her family still alive? She thought hard about them, pictured her aunt and her dad, and after a while she could breathe again. She curled up and waited.

After what seemed like forever she heard the sound of voices. She sat up and listened carefully, but could barely hear more than a murmur.

The door opened, the light intense after the blackness and she put up a hand to block it, squinting in the glare.

"Who is it?" she said.

No one answered, but a dark shape came towards

her and large hands reached out. It was Gerry again. She struggled but it was pointless. He dragged her out of the room.

Blinking, she stared around her. They were in a corridor, painted stark white, and the glare of it hurt her eyes. How long had she been in the dark? Her mouth was dry with thirst, her stomach empty.

"Come on." Gerry wrenched her arm hard and she cried out in anger and pain.

They passed doorways: most closed, a few open, some with lights on, some in darkness. She caught glimpses of tables like a schoolroom, darkness, cupboards, darkness, blue eyes watching, darkness.

Her breath caught. Pip? She tried to turn around but Gerry swung her a casual slap to the side of her head, rocking her skull. She cried out and on instinct punched him back. It was like hitting rock and he laughed at her.

They stopped at a door. He swiped a key through the lock and pushed her through so hard, she sprawled onto the stone floor.

"Ah, Miss Black."

Rosie looked up at Yuang standing in front of a blackened window that ran the entire length of the wall. "A pleasure to see you."

She'd bitten her lip and could taste blood. With

shaking fingers she wiped at her mouth and got slowly to her feet.

He came towards her, his arms folded casually across his chest.

"Please, you look tired, sit." He indicated a white chair between them. It was the only furniture in the room, apart from a tall cupboard in the corner near the door.

She backed a step away and remained standing.

Yuang seemed amused. "Please yourself."

"What do you want?" She sounded weak and scared.

He tilted his head to one side. "I think you know. Where is Shore?"

She didn't answer and Yuang sighed. "I'm disappointed, Rosie. I know you're smarter than that. Top of your class in astrophysics in fact. You scored ninety-seven per cent on your last semester test."

"So what?"

"So, a corporation like Helios is always on the lookout for bright new minds."

"Why, have they run out of people to kill?"

"I'm sorry you think that, Rosie. We are scientists, not monsters." He came closer. "Did you doubt me when I told you your family is alive?"

Rosie's heart jolted. "Where are they?" She was annoyed to hear the fear and desperation in her voice.

"Would you like to see them?"

"Yes." She could feel tears forming and angrily tried to stem them. She was finding it hard to stay on her feet now and swayed slightly.

"Come." He put a hand out to her but she flinched away. "Look at this window, it's a view port."

She noticed then he had a small device in his left hand. He pressed it and the black window became transparent. She could see through it into a lab, full of complicated equipment and screens. In the middle of the room was a sealed bubble and inside that two beds, one with her aunt and another with her dad. They lay still and were hooked up to monitors.

She went to the window and put her hands on the glass. They were barely dressed and there was a red rash on their legs and arms. It was worse on her dad. Something dropped inside her and she felt cold and sick. She'd seen that before. The MalX.

"As you can see, they are alive – for now," Yuang said behind her.

"You did this!" She turned on him.

"Why are you surprised? I assume Riley told you what we do here, or what he thinks we do. Normally, I would not have bothered using either of your relatives as a test subject. They are, after all, not within the gene pool of those whom Earth society so quaintly calls, the

Ferals." He smiled as though it was a good joke. "But I thought it necessary this time, as insurance."

"But they'll die!"

"That depends on you. Where is this plaspaper you say you have?"

"Why would I tell you?' she said. "There's no cure!" She could not fathom how he could be so cruel, so uncaring. Her idea to try to manipulate him with the imaginary plaspaper seemed foolish now. She was going to lose her whole family and there was nothing anyone could do. She began to cry and he watched her unmoved.

"You are right, of course," he said. "We don't have a cure — well, not one that can be administered like a vaccine. But I can cure them."

"What?"

"We have been testing subjects for some time now, looking for that special combination of genes and DNA. We were successful; we have a subject who is immune, a subject who, with a simple blood injection, could save lives." He came up to her then and whispered in her ear. "It's Pip."

Her heart felt as though it missed a beat. "I don't believe you."

He shrugged. "But are you willing to risk the lives of your father and aunt on it?"

Pip? She stared at her dad. She wanted to smash the

window and run to him. How could Pip be the cure? Why hadn't he told her?

"I know, it's hard to accept," Yuang said. "But it is true. Pip has developed a remarkable immunity – one he can pass on to others. To your father and aunt."

Rosie wasn't sure she could believe him. It seemed so unreal. But Pip had lied to her. He had betrayed all of them. Why wouldn't he lie about this as well?

She wiped the tears from her cheeks and said, "What do you want?"

"Just tell me where this plaspaper is and what Riley is planning. I can't believe he would just give himself up. Tell me everything and it will all be over. You can go home – with your family."

Rosie didn't know what to do. She felt overwhelmed, in way over her head. "Is it such a hard decision?" Yuang said, leaning close.

She flinched away from him. "You're a murderer," she whispered.

"Perhaps to you, but consider this: if you don't tell me, your family will die. And what guarantee do you have that Riley will succeed in his paltry attempt to stop me carrying out my orders? He will most likely die trying and then what will you have achieved? Not to mention that what we are doing is trying to save people. We are trying to find a cure for the MalX,

Rosie. Surely you of all people can appreciate that?"

She couldn't answer him. She put her forehead against the glass; she was so tired.

"Wanting your family to live doesn't make you a bad person," Yuang said. "And what we are doing, we're doing for humanity. The people we test are martyrs, giving their lives to ensure the survival of the human race. They are heroes. Who are you to take that away from them?"

He was insane. How could he call the people he was murdering heroes? Why had she thought she could reason with him?

"There's no plaspaper," she said quietly. "I made it up."

"Really?" His tone was dry.

"Yes, and Riley really is coming to give himself up to you – as long as you let my dad and Aunt Essie go first. He'll be waiting for you near the north gate like I said."

"So no plans to use them as decoys, perhaps with something from his sister's diary in the box? No plans to get in while my back's turned and ruin everything?"

"I told you, he wants to save lives, not end them."

Yuang appeared disappointed. He shook his head. "I'm sorry, Rosie. I just find this all hard to believe. I'm not sure about your plaspaper claim, but Shore has been trying to find a way to bring down Helios for ten years and, believe me, people working with him have died before in the process. And now, he's just going to give it up for two people he barely knows?" He turned to Gerry. "Take her to the cells."

Horror filled her. "But I told you the truth!"

"You told me what you thought you could get away with," he said. "I know Shore, far better than you think."

"No! I told you everything." Rosie tried to avoid the guard's hands. "Please." But he ignored her and Gerry's fist smashed down on her temple, turning the world to black.

CHAPTER 34

She woke in a different room. This time she was lying on a thin mattress and it wasn't dark, but the light was dull. Her head throbbed and she pushed herself up slowly, wincing with the effort. She was in a cell. Three grey walls surrounded her, fronted by floor to ceiling bars. There was a toilet, a sink and a bottle of water near the bed. Beyond the bars the room continued into shadow. But someone was there, watching her.

She stiffened. "Who is it?"

"Only me." Pip stepped into the light. "I saw them bring you in."

She stared. His dreadlocks were gone, his head shaved to leave only a dark fuzz. Without his hair the bright blue of his eyes seemed to blaze in his face. He looked beautiful, and her heart faltered. "Go away," she said weakly.

He didn't move. "They're coming for you soon."

"So why are you here, to make sure I don't get away?"

A barren smile tugged at the corner of his mouth. "I wanted to make sure you were all right."

"Do I look all right?"

"No. They've hit you." He came closer and curled his hands around the bars and a pained expression crossed his face as he gazed at the bruise on her temple, the cuts on her cheek. Such a great actor.

"Don't pretend you care, Pip," she said. "Shouldn't you be with Yuang? He says you're the cure for the MalX. His golden boy."

"Yeah, weird, isn't it? He just told me too."

"Don't pretend you didn't know."

"I didn't."

"Sure, like you don't know what Helios is doing here, like you didn't know what would happen when you stole the code key. Do you feel guilty for what you did, is that why you're here?"

"I'm sorry, Rosie. I really didn't know."

She shook her head. He just couldn't stop lying. "Go away, Pip."

But he stayed there, watching her closely. It unnerved her. "It doesn't matter what you told him, Rosie. They're not planning to cure your dad or aunt." He paused. "And he'll inject you too."

Rosie kept her face turned away so he couldn't see her fear, and willed him to leave.

"Rosie—"

"Go away!" She raised her voice. "Just leave me alone."

"Okay. Get some sleep. I'll be back later." He reached a hand through the bars. "I'm not lying, Rosie. I'm going to help you. I promise."

She couldn't look at him.

"I'll see you soon," he said, and then he was gone.

Rosie lay down, curling in on herself. She didn't want to think about Pip or his promises. She didn't want to think of anything at all.

———◆———

They came for her a few hours later. Three guards for one small girl.

Rosie couldn't stop shaking when Gerry dragged her out of the cell. His fingers wrapped around her upper arm and she felt light-headed and nauseous.

Adrenaline raced through her, trebling her heart rate so she was almost dizzy with the need to run. But there was no escape.

They took her to the lab she'd seen before. Yuang was waiting for her and her dad and aunt still lay unconscious within the plastic bubble. Rosie felt herself slipping into a kind of numbness. She couldn't feel her feet moving but she knew she was getting closer to a narrow bed set up outside the bubble.

"Strap her in," Yuang said.

Gerry picked her up and dumped her on the bed. The mattress was hard and Rosie watched as though from outside herself as Yuang approached. He began fiddling with a machine on wheels.

Gerry pushed her down and she didn't fight him. Her limbs felt heavy and detached from her body and all around was the steady beeping of the machines.

She knew she should be resisting. A small part of her brain was shouting at her, screaming that this wasn't good, that she should do something, but the message wasn't getting through to her body. The two other guards snapped straps over her ankles and wrists.

"All right." Yuang's expression was bland. "Now this won't hurt – not at first, but it is necessary. Riley will be here soon and when he arrives you will explain to him what has happened." Yuang smiled. "I'm sure he won't let you die."

Rosie couldn't speak. This wasn't happening. It couldn't be happening. It was all a mistake and soon she would wake up again in the cell, or at home, or somewhere else where there wasn't a madman and machines and the terribly loud sound of her thudding heart.

"Go get him." Yuang glanced at one of the guards.

The man grunted and turned to go, but a voice called out, "I'm here."

Rosie strained to see past the bulk of the guard. Pip was in the doorway, his hands in the pockets of a pair of dark green pants. His eyes seemed to reach across the room to her like a flare in the dark. Something contracted in her chest and for a millisecond she thought maybe he'd come to save her like he'd said he would. But he only stared at her for a moment then looked at Yuang. "Let's get this over with."

Yuang frowned. "Keen, aren't you?"

Pip shrugged and came towards them. "It's not like I have a choice."

They watched each other for a moment in silence then Yuang said, "It's on the desk."

Pip went to one of the desks against the wall. When he came back he had a pump syringe filled with clear liquid. He stood calmly, a metre from her, waiting for Yuang.

"Get her ready." Yuang nodded at Gerry.

Something snapped and a great wall of fear swept

over Rosie's body like a wave, washing away the inertia. She began to struggle. "No!" she cried out. "Don't touch me."

But everyone ignored her.

Gerry swabbed her arm then wrapped a soft tube around her bicep and slapped her skin, searching for a vein.

Pip stepped up beside her, the needle in his hand.

"You bastard," Rosie screamed up at him. "You backstabbing bastard!"

He gazed down at her but he wasn't looking at her eyes, only her arm. His lips were tight as he pushed the needle slightly and a drop of liquid came out of the tip.

Gerry was holding her shoulders down, his breath hot and smelling like onions. She struggled but the straps only cut into her wrists.

"Pip!" she pleaded with him but he moved the needle to her vein as though he couldn't hear her. "Pip!" she screamed as he punctured her skin and pushed.

She felt scarcely any pain, just a pinprick, but he'd killed her! She started to cry. How could he do this? A part of her had thought that maybe, just maybe, he wouldn't be able to because he liked her. Just a little bit? The syringe emptied into her arm. Pip took it out and threw the needle into a disposal unit nearby.

"Now," Yuang was talking to her but Rosie could

barely understand him. "There's a sedative in that shot, Rosie. Not a great deal but enough to make you drowsy for an hour or two just in case you panic and hurt yourself against those straps."

He was worried about her hurting herself?

"It will take four hours or so before you feel any effects of the disease. It shouldn't be too painful at first, but I'm sure you have some idea of what is to come."

He was starting to look blurry around the edges and she could hear herself mumbling as though from far away. *Mum, I'm scared.*

"Come on." Yuang's voice sounded like an echo as he turned away, the guard and Pip following.

No, don't leave me. She stared after them. She didn't want to be alone with the beeping machines and the roaring in her own head. Pip was the last to go and as he turned to activate the door, he mouthed something silently to her that the other men didn't see. Through her tears and the roaring, Rosie couldn't tell what it was. Hurry, or sorry, or something. She didn't care; she hated him. She tried to scream but everything slid away like the tide sucking her back into roaring waves.

Riley was having trouble breathing. His ribs were cracked and, judging by the rising and receding pain in his abdomen, he suspected Rosie had been right: there was something wrong inside. He felt weak and clammy.

For the hundredth time he cursed his own stupidity. He should have gone into the colony with the kid. He should have listened to her.

He had blacked out not long after getting in the rover, and by the time he'd come to and managed to get hold of Chris on the com, it had been way too late. Chris said she'd never showed up at their dome.

Yuang would have her. He knew he wouldn't kill Rosie himself – even Yuang had limits – but he'd leave her there with the rest when he "cleaned" the place out.

The indicators on the nav panel flickered as the com buzzed with static, the relay interfering with the old rover's engine.

"Riley, where are you?"

It was Jo. Wincing, he reached for the set and depressed the link button. "About ten minutes out," he said, trying to breathe evenly.

"Okay, hangar's quiet. We'll be waiting."

The com went dead and he dropped it on the seat. Pain stabbed his side, and every time the rover went over another rock or dip, it jarred through his body. He wiped the sweat off his forehead and tried to brace himself against the door of the vehicle.

The small beam of the headlights was almost swallowed by the dark Martian night. The moons were dim, and when he looked up through the semitransparent canopy, he could see a million stars dotted across the black. He was in a narrow valley that ran behind the colony, a lone rover trundling across the regolith in the middle of the night. He'd be easy to spot.

Riley had no idea how he was going to finish what his parents had started. If truth be told, he only had a slim chance at the beginning, but now ... He gripped the steering hard, squinting against the throbbing pain in his gut. Now everything looked hopeless.

He needed a new plan.

CHAPTER 35

The world was grey, as though she was outside in the moonlight. Everything was made of shadow. Rosie blinked. *Where am I?* She couldn't move properly; something was holding her wrists and ankles down. She felt too hot, but cold as well and she ached – all over. She squeezed her eyes open and shut, trying to clear her vision.

There was a sound, like a thumping bass, a dull monotony repeating, repeating. The sound became clearer, the pitch rising – a tenor, a soprano, a machine beeping. Something touched her arm. She rolled her head and saw Pip beside her.

It all came rushing back. She was in the Enclave and she had the MalX. She could feel it now. It was why she was so hot, so cold. It was why she ached. And Pip had given it to her. She sucked in a breath to scream and he covered her mouth with his hand.

"Don't," he whispered. "They'll hear."

He was trying to kill her faster. She struggled to get his hand off, clarity returning. He wasn't applying much force so she twisted her head and bit his finger.

"Ow!" He yanked his hand away.

"Get away from me!" she shouted. Except it wasn't a shout; it was more like a squawk, her throat was so dry.

"Sh!" He jumped on the cot on top of her and pinned her shoulders back against the bed with one arm. "I'm curing you, Rosie, so if you want to live, stop moving."

He had a needle in his other hand attached to a bag of red liquid. Furious, she flinched as the needle went in. "What are you putting into me?"

"My blood."

"What?" She stopped struggling.

"I am the cure, Rosie." He glanced at her, then back at her arm. "It's one thing Yuang didn't lie about – I double-checked myself. Now hold still. This is a special regulator needle that's going to pump some blood into you from this." He showed her the small bag full of red liquid next to his knee. "It shouldn't take too long and if you keep quiet, no one should hear. I've deactivated the surveillance."

She looked from him to the bag and back again. "Why are you doing this?"

"I wasn't going to let you die." His arm was still firmly across her shoulders and she was acutely aware his face was only centimetres from her own. He frowned and brushed a thumb lightly across her cheekbone near the bruise on her temple. "Grunts know how to hit, don't they?"

The heat in her skin seemed to spread suddenly all over and her heart rate spiked making the machine beep faster. "Get off."

"You sure?" He glanced at the machine.

"Get. Off." She spoke through gritted teeth.

Pip smiled slightly and got off. He began undoing the straps holding her down.

She sat up as soon as he untied her and immediately fell back as a bout of dizziness rushed in. Pinpoints of light danced in her vision.

"I told you not to move. You okay?" There was concern in his voice.

"I'm fine," she managed to whisper, even though she thought she might actually pass out.

"You need some water." He produced a canister from somewhere. "Here." He slipped a hand under her neck and held her up enough so she could drink. She sipped at the drinking tube, annoyed that he had to help her. Water had never tasted so good and the dizziness gradually abated.

"You still feel hot," he said.

"Really, I wonder why?" She pushed the empty canister away. "Let go." She put an elbow underneath herself and propped herself up a bit. She was beginning to feel better, the aches in her limbs subsiding. If it was because of his blood, it was acting fast.

"Do you have enough for them?" She looked at the bubble and her dad and her aunt so still and silent within it.

"No time." He checked the nearly empty blood bag. "We have to get out of here. The vision I made for the surveillance won't fool them forever."

"I'm not leaving Dad and Aunt Essie here to die." Rosie sat up and swung her legs off the bed.

"You can't help them right now," he said. "Don't you remember why you came to Mars in the first place?"

"You're not seriously asking me that?" Her outrage at what he'd done was coming back, now she was beginning to feel better.

"Yuang has to be stopped first," he said. "Before anything else."

"So you're switching sides, just like that?

"It's finished." He pinched the tube to the blood bag and yanked the needle from her arm.

"Ow!" She folded her hand up to her shoulder.

"Listen." Pip shoved the bag and syringe into a side pocket of his pants. "The only way you can help them, is by helping me stop Yuang. Besides, even if we did have the time to get my blood into them, we'd never get them out of here. There are grunts all over – you've got no idea how secure this place is. We've only got about eight hours until this whole place is nothing but a big hole in the ground, Rosie. Yuang has already started deciding who gets to go and who stays. And guess who's on the list to stay?"

She felt cold. Her family and hundreds of others.

"The only way to save them," Pip pointed to her aunt and dad, "and anyone else, is to get the info Riley is after and unlock the labs before Yuang pushes the button."

"Yes, but I don't have the code key any more, remember – you stole it!"

"And I can get it back but we have to go now." He reached out a hand to pull her off the cot.

"Don't." She gave him a warning look and slid off on her own. "Why should I trust you? It's your fault my aunt's lying there."

"I just saved your life!"

"Oh, did you? And how do–" She stopped as she heard the thud of boots outside in the corridor.

Pip went very still and she saw fear in his eyes and wondered if it was an act or real. The sound of the footsteps receded but they both remained tense, staring at each other.

She wasn't sure what to do. She didn't want to trust him but there didn't seem to be much choice. Pip knew his way around the Enclave, maybe knew where the labs were. God only knew where Riley was and she couldn't wait for him. She went to the bubble of pyloglass and stared at her aunt and dad lying so still inside. "You can't go in there, Rosie," Pip said.

"I know." She cut him a fierce look. "But I can't just leave them here."

"I promise we'll come back – if we can."

Promise. How much were his promises worth?

"Rosie ..." He jerked a thumb urgently at the door.

If only she didn't have these feelings about him. They messed with her judgement – *he* messed with her judgement. Stupid as it was, she wanted to believe him. And she was out of options.

With a last look at her dad and aunt, she followed him out the door.

The corridors were strangely empty and they met no one as they ventured deeper into the complex.

"Where is everybody?" she whispered.

"This section doesn't get used by many people. Only the scientists and subjects."

The Ferals being tested on, thought Rosie, sickened. "Which way is it?"

"Down this–" He stopped. "Someone's coming."

He grabbed her arm and they raced back the way they'd come. Rosie spied a narrow door. "Here." She reached for the metal doorhandle.

"No!" Pip tried to stop her and too late, she saw the security keypad on the wall. A high-pitched alarm split the air. He dragged her away.

Behind them came the sound of men calling and a door slamming. How could she have been so stupid? Heart racing, Rosie followed Pip back down the corridors, past the room she'd been in. He ran fast and she struggled to keep up. "Wait." He paused in front of a door and punched in a code with shaking fingers. The door opened but instead of going through it, he kept jogging along the corridor.

"What did you do that for?" She could barely speak and felt scarily weak, her legs unsteady. Sweat already covered her forehead. "The doors retain memory of who opened them," he said. "Hopefully the grunts will believe we went that way. Buy us some time." He peered closer at her. "You okay?"

"I'm fine," she avoided his eyes, "let's just go." She started running again, ignoring the pain in her chest.

On their left, narrow windows cast irregular strips of pale sunlight on the floor like stepping stones, and behind them came the sound of heavy footsteps. The corridor was so long that if anyone came behind them, they'd be exposed.

Pip stopped abruptly. "Here." He crouched down in front of a ventilation grate and pulled a pocketknife from his pants. He flicked open the blade and tried to prise the grate away from the wall.

"In there?" Breath coming in gasps, Rosie checked the opening. It was barely wide enough to crawl through.

"We've got to hide, it's the only way," Pip said. But when he glanced at her she realised he knew that she was in too bad shape for them to get away. The worst part was he was right. She was already exhausted. She crouched beside him and pushed her fingers into the grille and pulled as hard as she could as he worked the knife. Her arm muscles shook and ached, but she kept pulling. There was a soft screech of metal and a rivet popped out of the corner and onto the floor.

"Pull harder."

"I can't." Her words were a whispered sob, but right

now she didn't care. Pip pocketed his knife and shoved his fingers into the gap and they heaved together. The other top rivet popped and suddenly they were holding the top of the grille open, the shaft behind exposed.

Rosie went feet first into the narrow opening, shuffling like a caterpillar. It was dusty and smelled sour, but it was wider than she'd thought. Pip slid in beside her and together they grabbed the grille and pulled it back up just in time.

Seconds later, one of the guards walked past. He was talking into a com but too quietly for them to hear.

They lay facing each other, squeezed into the shaft – Pip half on top of her. He had one arm over her head, holding the grille, while the other held it at the bottom. His left leg was hooked over her hip and she could feel his heart beating against her. His skin smelled faintly of dust and sweat.

The guard seemed to take forever to walk down the corridor. Rosie couldn't see him, but she could hear him, his com occasionally emitting static. Rosie prayed he wouldn't notice the tips of their fingers holding the grille in place.

"Not here," the guard said clearly into his com, and Rosie had the urge to fling the grille away and burst out of the vent.

Pip felt her tension and his leg tightened on her hip.

She glanced up at him. He shook his head. No.

Pip's breath was brushing the skin on her neck and she was acutely conscious of how close he was. She tried to distract herself by putting her mind back to the problem of getting out. She thought about the diary codes she'd memorised. The door that had been alarmed, could it have been one of the labs? Or maybe a way into the labs with the Genesis information they needed. It could be worth a try.

After what seemed like forever, Pip finally whispered okay and, with a muffled groan, she let go of the grille. He lowered it outside and she shuffled inelegantly out headfirst, dragging herself past him until she flopped out onto the floor.

He slid out after her, pushing the grille in place and turned back the way the guard had gone. "This way," he said.

"Pip, wait." She gripped his forearm.

"What?"

"That door with the alarm — where does it go?"

"The lower levels, why?" The sun was setting and shadow slanted across his face.

"Is there a way to get to the labs we need through there? One of the codes Riley gave me might open it."

He looked at her for a moment, his expression unreadable. "Maybe," he said.

Frustration filled her. "You work for Helios," she said. "Don't you know your way around?"

"Not all of it." He was tense, almost angry. "I was going to go another way but – okay, it did look kind of familiar." He glanced the way the guards had gone. "But we gotta be quick."

They ran back to the door and Rosie tried punching in one of the codes.

Nothing happened: no alarm went off though, no lights flashed, but the door remained shut.

"How many have you got?" Pip whispered.

"Seven more. But will going through them all set off the alarm?"

"Shouldn't. That alarm's only to stop the kids here getting in."

"Okay." Rosie began punching in the numbers of more codes.

Six codes later the door was still shut.

"We're running out of time," Pip said.

"I know. Last one." Rosie punched in the last code. "6-54-03-Omega."

The door slid open to reveal a dim hallway. The floor was pale blue concrete, the walls a dusty white, and tubular lighting illuminated the narrow space. It dropped away from them on a steady angle to a set of steps, the floor disappearing into darkness.

From far off a soft sound like a distant wail reached them then dissipated. Rosie looked at Pip, but he was staring past her with a strange expression on his face.

"Pip?"

"Come on." He pushed past her.

With a cold scared feeling in her stomach, Rosie followed, the door sweeping shut behind them.

CHAPTER 36

As soon as the door shut, all the lights went out. Rosie froze. "Pip?" She stretched her hands out and shuffled sideways, hoping to find the wall.

She couldn't see a thing. The darkness pressed over her as heavy as lead, as thick as blood. "Pip?" she called again, annoyed at the barely veiled panic in her tone. When was she going to get over this?

"I'm here." His voice was ahead of her.

"Where?"

"Here." His hand bumped against her shoulder.

She resisted the urge to grab onto him. "Do you have a torch or anything?"

"No."

She fought to control her escalating fear. Just

breathe, Rosie. Breathe, she told herself.

"Hey, are you scared of the dark?"

"No!"

"You sure? You sound funny." Was he enjoying this? Her irritation returned.

"I'm okay. It was just a surprise, that's all." She pulled away from his hand, but not so far that she couldn't sense his presence.

Then she remembered she'd put one of the pod's illuminating sticks in her pocket. She shoved her hands into the side pockets of her jeans and, with an intense surge of relief, felt the slim glo-tube under her fingertips.

She twisted the top. A soft yellow glow formed and Pip squinted in the sudden light.

"Lucky," he said. "How long will it last?"

"Maybe an hour or two."

"Great. Let's go then."

Gripping the tube like a lifeline, Rosie held the light aloft and led them towards the stairwell.

It went down three short flights. On the second landing they passed a door that had been welded shut. On the door were the remains of a name: G-5. Rosie wondered if there were unused labs behind it.

"Hey." She played the light over the edge of the door. "This door's been sealed – the metal's all melted."

"Rosie, come on." Pip was two steps further down.

She ignored him. "Do you think this has anything to do with what happened to Riley's parents?"

"No."

"How do you know?"

He paused then said quietly, "I was here."

Rosie turned to him. "But that was ten years ago." Had he been working for Helios since he was eight?

"Yeah, I know." He was strangely still and in his expression she saw reluctance, or guilt, or something else. Shame? "I was born here, Rosie," he said. "I grew up here."

Suddenly, things made more sense. Why he seemed different to other Ferals, why he'd been so loyal to Helios. He was born into it. She took a step backwards.

He watched her move and a bitterness twisted his face.

"I knew you'd think that," he said.

"I didn't say anything."

"You didn't have to." He slouched back against the stair railing.

"Well, what am I supposed to think?"

"I don't know. But I'm not one of them any more, Rosie. It's different now"

"Is it?" Despite everything, she wanted to believe him. "Are your parents really dead?" she said. "Or did you lie about that as well?"

"I didn't lie," he answered fiercely and his voice echoed through the stairwell. "Yuang killed them. He used them as test subjects, just like I don't know how many others. Kids I knew, people–" He stopped his chest working as he tried to control his breath.

"So why did you keep working for him?" Rosie asked.

"You think I knew?" His eyes widened in disbelief. "I had no idea. I thought I was helping. I've known Yuang since I was a kid. He took care of me after my parents–" He took in a sharp breath. He gripped the handrail as if he was going to rip it from the wall. When he spoke again his voice was quieter but tightly controlled. "He told me we were finding a cure for the MalX, Rosie. I didn't know then that Helios was killing people to find a cure." His gaze was intense. "Do you think I would have done all those things if I'd known?"

Rosie couldn't reply. She was shaken by the pain she saw in his eyes, the anger. Not at her but at a man who had lied to him, who'd taken his parents.

"I saved your life, Rosie, and I'm trying to save your family and stop him now. Isn't that enough?"

His gaze was pleading and almost desperate. But she didn't have an answer. She wasn't sure what to think. "I don't know," she said, trying to be honest, but it wasn't what he wanted.

Disappointment filled his eyes and he exhaled and looked down as he said quietly, "Right."

She felt terrible, but really what did he expect? "So what was this?" She gestured at the door.

He paused then said, "It was living quarters, where some of the Ferals they brought up from Earth stayed. They sealed it after the Shore lab blew up."

"What happened to everyone?" Rosie said, but Pip turned away.

"They said they'd been sent back to Earth. Come on, we gotta keep going."

Rosie followed him, a sick feeling in her gut. From his tone it was clear he didn't believe they'd gone back to Earth and she didn't either. But did that mean she could trust him? What would she do if she found out everything she had believed as a kid was a lie?

At the bottom of the stairs was a door with an ordinary handle, no security keypad. Pip put his ear to it and, at her enquiring look, shook his head. "Nothing."

He opened the door a crack and they both peered through.

On the other side was a long, brightly lit hallway intersected by six doors and two more hallways a few metres apart.

"Which way?" Rosie whispered.

He hesitated. "I think it's the second hallway."

They crept along the right wall.

It was very quiet and smelled sharply of cleaning fluid, as if someone had only recently mopped. She turned the glo-tube off and shoved it back into her pocket.

They neared the first door and Rosie thought she heard a soft moan. She froze. Pip had heard it too. Jerking his chin towards the door, he made a dipping and sliding motion with his hand.

There was a square window in the top of the door and he was telling her to duck underneath it. But what if someone in there needed help? She shook her head and mouthed at him, "Let's just take a look."

He frowned and shook his head violently, motioning her to follow him.

Screw that, Rosie thought and peeked through the bottom half of the window as she passed.

The room was deceptively long, much longer than she'd thought it would be; she could barely see the end. Lines of beds filled it, most of them with the humped shape of a person lying on top. Tubes protruded from their arms, running to square machines that hung from the roof above each bed. Moving among them were the buzzing forms of medibots, checking the machines, like farmers checking rows of crops. One of the metallic heads turned and unblinking red lights beamed at her.

Rosie stared, transfixed and shocked.

"Rosie!" Pip dragged her away. "Those robots have a direct link to the surveillance."

"What?"

"Don't you get it?" Pip said. "He'll have seen us now. Run!" He pushed her up the hall.

She ran. They passed a second door and the view of what was inside burned on her retina like the aftermath of a flash. More bodies, more tubes and the unblinking red lights of the medibots.

They sprinted around a corner and down another hallway. This one had doors only on the left side. Pip was a few metres ahead when a door opened right in front of him and a medibot glided out. It extended a metallic arm and unleashed a charge of electricity into him.

"Pip!" Rosie shouted.

He jolted and seemed to just hang in the air, quivering as the charge ripped through him.

Rosie kept running and slammed into him as hard as she could, knocking him away, but the electricity conducted back into her and she screamed in pain as they fell to the floor. Her muscles spasmed and for a second she couldn't breathe. Fighting it, Rosie rolled to her knees. Pip lay beside her, groaning, his eyes closed.

"Pip!" She shook his arm. "Pip, get up!" She could taste blood and behind them, the medibot was whirling and turning back towards them. Beyond it two more emerged steadily from doors at the end of the hall.

"Pip, they're coming!" Rosie pulled at him but he only groaned. The medibot that had zapped him moved towards her, its red eye-lights steady and the arm extended.

She let go of his arm and looked desperately for a weapon, but there was nothing. She tried to remember her robotics studies. The bots were built for working, chores ... The panel at the back. She ran at it, dodging the arm at the last minute and skipping behind. The medibot was not much taller than her, even hovering, and she leaped onto it, using the narrow flare at the base for a foothold. She hooked an arm around its metal head and pulled off the maintenance panel, then grabbed a handful of wires and yanked as hard as she could. The bot's hum increased to a high-pitched wail and it skewed sideways, its hover functions disabled. It crashed to the floor and Rosie leaped clear as it landed.

Not stopping to watch, she ran back to Pip. "Get up!" she shouted, trying to lift him. The two other bots were advancing now and there was no way she could take on them both. They'd be downloaded with enough power to light a small town if they didn't move. "Pip!"

He groaned and rose to his feet. She hooked her arm around his waist and forced him into a run. "Which way?" she said, as he stumbled alongside her. He was so heavy, her shoulders ached from his weight.

"Cage." He pointed ahead with an unsteady hand.

Rosie saw what she'd thought had been a door at the end of the hall was actually a shaft covered by a fine mesh. A cage? Whatever. Dragging him, she ran towards it, the bots humming behind her like a couple of bees.

Thank God they were medibots, not the soldier robots the Senate used for border patrol. They had no guns.

They reached the cage. Pip leaned against the metal casing, watching the medibots, as Rosie fumbled with the latch. "Rosie," he mumbled a warning.

"I know!" She didn't dare turn; she could hear them closing in. The latch sprang open revealing an open-topped cage suspended in a long shaft. She helped Pip over the high lip and then jumped in herself. But as she passed the inner door, something cold and metallic closed around her ankle and pulled.

She screamed and fell facedown. One of the bots had hold of her. It began to drag her backwards. Pip grabbed her arms, but the bot kept pulling. It was cutting into her ankle as it tried to pull her back out. "Shut the door on it!" Rosie yelled.

"It might break your ankle!" Pip was straining to

keep hold of her. His feet were braced against the floor, and she could see the effort it was taking for him to keep her inside. She felt as though her arm was going to pop out of its socket. Tears came to her eyes.

"Do it!" she shrieked. Either way something had to give or the bot was going to wrench the bone out of her flesh.

Pip gave her a worried look then kicked the door control. Immediately, the outer cage door swept shut. It smashed against the metal of the robotic arm and pushed Rosie's foot hard against the cage's inner door. Pain like she'd never felt before pierced her ankle and ran up to her hip. She screamed. The robot let go and Pip hauled her in as the inner door slammed shut. The cage shot upwards, but as it did, the medibot released a bolt of energy that conducted through the metal, hitting them both like a parting kiss. From within a haze of pain, Rosie was almost grateful as the electricity struck her and blackness descended.

CHAPTER 37

Rosie opened her eyes to pain. She was lying on her stomach on the floor of the cage, the metal pressing crosses into her cheek. Hot lances of agony from her ankle throbbed up her calf. She gritted her teeth and rolled over, then dragged herself to the back of the cage. She sat with her back against the cool metal. They seemed to have stopped in the middle of the chute because she couldn't see anything through the mesh of the door other than a blank metal wall. Dim light was falling from above, enough to make out Pip lying on his back next to her, a streak of dried blood on his forehead.

"Pip," she whispered. He didn't move. She reached out and shook his shoulder. "Pip?"

He made a soft noise and encouraged, she shook harder. "Pip, wake up."

"What?" he said, his voice echoing in the chute.

"Sh! Keep it down."

He opened his eyes but didn't attempt to get up.

"How do you feel?" she asked.

"Like I've been electrocuted. How's your foot?"

"I don't think it's broken." She tried to wiggle her toes and almost bit her tongue as pain stabbed her ankle.

Pip rolled over with a grunt and sat up next to her, the cage swaying slightly with his movements. He looked at her foot. "We should strap it."

"With what exactly?" The pain was making her angry.

"I don't know but you're not going to be able to move fast like that."

"Really? Thanks, I wasn't aware of that fact."

"Don't get pissed at me; you told me to shut the door."

"I know." Rosie closed her eyes for a moment. "Wish I had some of Riley's painkillers right now."

"You and me both."

She opened her eyes. "Any idea where we are or why the cage stopped?"

"Yeah. I think I stopped it. Just after the bastard bot zapped us I kicked the controls again before I passed out.

I think I must have hit something. Maybe I broke it."

"So we're stuck here?"

"What, you'd rather be caught by the grunts?"

Rosie tried to breathe through the pain. "I'd rather be just about anywhere than here."

"You should have listened to me. I told you not to look but you had to do it."

"Yeah, well ... okay, you were right. But I saved your life when I pushed you away from the medibot."

He raised an eyebrow. "It was your fault they came out."

"So ..." she faltered, frustrated.

"So I guess that's two to me, one to you."

"It's not a game, Pip."

His eyes were full of weariness. "It's not? You sure? It feels like it and you keep changing the rules."

Rosie kept her temper with difficulty. "What the hell do you mean by that?"

"What do I mean?" He looked at her as if she were dense. "Well, you don't like me, you do like me, you want to hold my hand, you want me to leave you alone. You won't trust me, but you want me to help you. I can't figure you out."

Rosie wanted to slap him. "It's hard to trust someone who lies all the time."

"Not all the time." His look was steady and there

was a something in there she didn't want to deal with right now.

"Did you really not know you were immune to the MalX?" she said, changing the subject.

He stared at her for a moment then looked up at the cage roof. "You still won't believe me."

"What do you expect? You betrayed us. My dad and aunt are dying because of you lying to me." She paused. "You know Riley told me they tortured him."

"Yeah, well, he wouldn't have been the first." Pip avoided her gaze and picked at the hem of his jeans.

"And that makes it okay?"

"I didn't say that, but—" Rosie saw that his fingers were shaking slightly as he pulled at a loose thread. "You have no idea what they can do."

The retort that had been on her lips faded. There was no bravado in his voice. Instead, there was a note that spoke of the experience of things she didn't want to know about. Pain. For the first time she noticed a pale bruise on the side of his head.

"So what are you going to do?" she said. "Kill Yuang?"

He shrugged. "Maybe."

His tone chilled her. It wasn't an empty statement. "Killing him won't bring your parents back."

"I'm not an idiot." His eyes glinted. "But maybe this universe is better off without him."

"Pip ..."

"Don't," he said. "I don't want to talk about it."

She leaned towards him. "Pip," she said. "I'm sorry you had to grow up here and I'm sorry they killed your parents, but they killed my mum too, you know, and I don't want my dad and aunt to die as well. I want to trust you — I just don't know if I can."

His face was impassive. "You said your mum died from the MalX."

"She did. But it's not just some disease that developed on Earth. It was Helios, Pip; they made it up here in a lab. That's what Riley is really after. It's not just about exposing Helios for doing the tests they did on you and your parents; he's after proof that Helios made the MalX and released it on Earth."

He frowned like he didn't believe her.

"Don't you see?" she said. "They sent the disease to Earth by mistake but never tried to fix it. They knew all along and are pretending that they're helping to cure it, while all the time it was their fault."

"Well," he said finally. "I can't say that surprises me."

"Is that all you can say?" she said.

"What do you want me to say?"

"I don't know — something! That you'll help me. That stopping Helios is important, that you won't just run off on some revenge trip to get Yuang and leave me to—" She stopped, suddenly more upset than angry. How could he just sit there? There were tears in her eyes and she blinked them away, annoyed at her weakness.

Pip watched her but she couldn't read what was behind his blue gaze.

"What?" she said angrily.

"I wasn't going to leave you," he said. "Why would I have untied you in the lab if I was going to do that?"

"I don't know ... To get the codes?"

"But I haven't even asked you for them."

No, he hadn't. Rosie looked down at her hands and took a long breath, feeling her emotions subside. Why were they arguing?

"My ankle hurts," she said.

A small smile curved Pip's mouth. "Yeah, so does my head."

They sat silently for a while. All this was getting them nowhere.

"Do you have any idea where that information on the MalX might be?" she said.

He shifted, bending a knee and resting one arm on it. "I'd say most of the really important stuff, including the code key, would be in Yuang's rooms."

"How do we get in?"

"I know his security pass."

"How'd you get that?"

He shrugged. "I'm observant. But we're going to have to strap that." He pointed at her ankle.

"I think we're going to have to get out of the cage first."

"Yeah, well," Pip nodded at the panel, "it's busted."

"Let me look." Rosie got to her knees and tried to shuffle to the controls but a sharp pain stabbed at her ankle. "Ow!" She sat down heavily beneath the panel and closed her eyes for a second. Her ankle felt as if someone was hammering on it.

"Let me see it." Pip reached for her leg and rolled her jeans up.

"No! Don't touch it." She flinched as he lifted her leg up to rest it across his knees.

"Shut up," he said mildly, and inspected the swelling. Through half-closed eyes, Rosie saw her ankle bone had disappeared in a mass of swollen flesh. Please don't let it be broken, she thought.

"Right." Pip pulled his T-shirt off.

"What are you doing?" She tried not to stare. He was slim, but not without muscle, and his pale brown skin stretched smoothly over his well-toned torso.

"It's all we've got to strap it with – unless you want to use yours."

Smart-arse, Rosie thought, and didn't bother replying. Trying not to wince or cry out, she let him tie his shirt tightly around her ankle. The pain was hard to bear and she almost bit her tongue, but after it was strapped, it did feel better. Or at least she felt like she might be able to stand on it without passing out.

"Thanks," she said faintly when he'd finished.

"No worries." He flashed a quick smile and she felt butterflies stir in her stomach.

She looked away and levered herself up to kneel in front of the panel. "I think I can fix the cage," she said, staring intently at it.

He peered over her shoulder. "How?"

"Give me some room, and I'll show you."

"Okay, okay." He backed off to sit back against the wall but she heard the amusement in his voice.

Trying to ignore him, she checked out the simple command buttons. Open and shut for the door, and below it a voice activation slit which looked dead. "Give me that knife you had," she said.

He placed it in her hand. Rosie inserted the blade carefully in the narrow groove and levered the panel off. Surely this couldn't be too complicated.

Luckily, it wasn't. Some parts of the wiring and chips were a mystery, but the voice and movement sectors were easy to spot. And luckily again, Pip's kick had only knocked the connection loose. Rosie easily reconnected it. Now she just hoped their luck would hold out to get the cage moving and themselves out of it.

"Fixed." She turned to Pip, who barely raised an eyebrow. "So now what do we tell it? How many floors up do we go?"

"I think there are four floors to ground level. We were at the bottom but the medibots would have passed our location on to Yuang. As soon as the cage stops, he'll have guards waiting for us on whichever floor we get out at."

"So what's our option? We have to stop the cage to get out."

"Yeah and when we do, we're caught – unless."

Rosie got a bad feeling in her gut. "Unless what?"

He smiled. "What if we get out while it's still moving?"

"Um, translation?"

"We set it for ground level but instead of closing the door, we leave it open and when we pass the first level we jump out."

Rosie stared at him. "Did you not notice how fast this thing goes up?"

"Yeah, but can't you fix that? If you can fix the activator, can't you make it go slower? Slow enough for us to get the outer door of the shaft open and jump out."

Rosie looked at the controls. It was feasible but could she jump with her sore ankle? "I don't know if I can move fast enough to get out."

"That's easy." Pip grinned. "I'll push you."

He looked worryingly pleased by the idea, but really what other option did they have? "Fine." She began to fiddle with the wiring.

It took her less time than she'd thought and in ten minutes it was done. Fingers crossed it would be slow enough. She got Pip to manually push the inner door open, then spoke into the voice slot.

"Ground level," she said quietly, and the cage began to rise. But it was faster than she would have liked. The metal of the chute seemed to fly by. Pip appeared just as apprehensive.

Rosie held onto his waist, trying not to notice the pain that throbbed through her ankle, or that she was leaning against his naked chest. His skin was warm and the muscles hard beneath it as he shifted.

"Ready?"

"No." Rosie tensed as he put an arm around her. He grinned.

"Too late now." He reached up for the latch of the mesh door to the next level as the cage rose rapidly towards it and, with a grunt, thrust it open.

"Hold on!" The cage was already level and getting higher as he rolled them both out. Rosie's foot hit the bottom of the cage and she cried out as pain shot up through her ankle. Pip took the brunt of the fall and

Rosie landed half on top of him, her head smacking against his bare chest.

He groaned and they lay there for a second, stunned, then he was rolling her off him and getting up. "Come on." He pulled her upright. Rosie kept hold of his arm as she tentatively put her weight on her right foot. It wasn't too bad; she seemed to be able to stand.

Level one was a giant storehouse. Along the walls on either side, rows of rectangular metallic containers were stacked to the ceiling. They reminded Rosie of coffins, except at the end of each glowed a small green light. There were hundreds of them. They were stacked three rows deep on each side, leaving a walkway between them. Ahead, a robotic lifting machine sat dormant.

It was chilly and a strange smell hung in the air, like the spray her dad used to keep insects out.

"Is this the food storage?" Rosie asked.

Pip shook his head. He stared up at the containers. "That's above ground."

"There must be an exit at the end." She began to limp forward, moving close to the containers in case anyone came in. At least they could hide among the rows.

Pip followed. "Want a hand?"

"No." It hurt like hell every time she put any weight on her right foot, but she didn't want to hang off him like some useless limpet – especially with the naked factor. She moved as quickly as she could, half walking, half hopping, and studied the containers. Next to each light was an electronic panel with letters in it. It took her a while to realise the letters were names. People's names. She stopped at the closest container.

M Creshaw. Male DOD 06-11-2515. Study 5468.

Pip turned back. "What're you doing?"

"They're people," she whispered, "in the containers. It says DOD – date of death."

"What?" Pip came closer and peered at the small screen. In the reflected light, Rosie saw him go pale. "Bastards," he whispered faintly, then suddenly turned and took off, running away from her through the rows coffins, reading the screens.

Rosie was about to call out to stop him when she realised what he was doing. He was looking for his parents.

CHAPTER 38

Rosie limped down the narrow corridor between the stacks.

There were so many of them: shining silver coffins full of people Helios had killed. Gritting her teeth against the pain, she shuffled around the corner of another row and found Pip at the far end, staring at two coffins above his head.

He didn't acknowledge her as she approached.

"Pip ..." she hesitated. She could think of nothing to say. "Sorry" was useless. People had said they were sorry when her mum died, but it hadn't made her feel any better. It had made her angry – people trying to pretend they understood when they didn't.

She stood back in the shadows. It was unnaturally

quiet and sharply cold. Desolate. The place was thick with emptiness and the flat light silvered everything grey, turning Pip into a half-lit statue before her.

Time was ticking away but she didn't hassle him. He had to be allowed to say goodbye. He stood for a while longer, then began to walk down the corridor. She hobbled after him.

There was a lift in the wall at the end of the stacks and in the far corner, a door that looked like it led to a stairwell. Pip strode towards it.

"Pip." Now she did call out. He was going too fast and she had to speed up to a kind of run to catch him. Her ankle throbbed in agony. "Pip, wait."

He didn't turn around. The muscles of his back were rigid, flexed with tension as he paused with his hand on the doorknob.

He let go and turned to her. His breath was sharp, ragged, and his eyes dark with pain and fury as he stood motionless, watching her approach.

"I–" She stepped towards him then stopped. This was a Pip she'd never seen – all his bravado was stripped away, leaving only the ashes of a profound anger, a desolation in his face that made her both afraid of him, and for him all at once. She put a hand tentatively on the smooth skin of his shoulder, intending to comfort him, but it was as if her touch flicked a switch. He flinched and she saw something else come into his eyes and he pulled her suddenly, violently towards him and kissed her.

His lips crushed against hers so hard, she felt his teeth through the membrane of her skin. It was almost painful. He clutched at her, one hand gripping the back of her neck, the other circling her waist and dragging her up almost off her feet.

She didn't fight him. Couldn't. Didn't want to. She kissed him back. Heat filled her skin and she pressed herself against him, touching him the way she'd been wanting to. She ran a hand over the perfect curve of his skull, the muscles of his back and at her response, his kiss softened. For a moment there was only Pip – his breath in her mouth, his lips on hers and she wanted him closer, but he pulled away abruptly and dropped her back to her feet. Pain spiked through her ankle.

"Ow!" she hissed.

He steadied her. He didn't speak, only stared, breathless also. Her heart beat crazily. His gaze was intense but he looked vulnerable and closed off at the same time.

"We have to go," he said. "Time. You know."

"Yeah, right." She swallowed, trying to slow her heart. "You okay?" It was weird to be talking like this. She could taste the salty warmth of him on her lips, as though some part of him had slipped in under her skin.

"Yeah." He looked like he was going to say something else, but instead he turned to the door. "Come on."

They climbed the stairs and barely spoke. The kiss lay between them like a dripping tap, the faucet half turned to relieve some pressure, but not enough. Rosie felt completely confused, but there was too much at stake to even try to work it out.

It took them nearly an hour to reach the top of the stairs and by that time her ankle felt on fire. She leaned on the wall. Pip rested beside her, breathing heavily, having half carried her up the final flight.

"Do you think he's cleared everything out of the labs yet?" she asked.

"Who, Yuang?" Pip said and shook his head. "No, it'll take him longer than that. There are a lot of labs."

"Maybe he doesn't care. Maybe he'll just leave it all here to be blown up."

"Not likely. Besides, he wouldn't risk anything being found."

Not that much would be left after the explosion. "Open the door," she said.

The corridor on the other side was empty, white and

partly submerged below the soil; high slitted windows looked out to garden and sky. They crept towards a set of doors at the end that reminded Rosie of an airlock.

Pip pressed his thumb to the panel and the door contracted into the frame, opening the way into a circular area with four corridors. A tall bookcase filled the wall between two corridors and in front of it three young boys were lounging on a sofa, reading. They looked up as Rosie and Pip came through and for a moment they all stared at each other in surprise, then a thin boy with a fuzz of red hair pointed at them and shouted, "It's them, it's them!" He dropped his book and ran towards a com in the far wall, yelling for the guards.

Pip swore and grabbed Rosie's hand and they ran down the closest corridor on the left.

Pain shot up Rosie's calf, slowing her down. From behind came the sound of booted feet. They'd never outrun them with her injury.

"You go on ahead," she panted. "I can't run."

"No."

"Pip."

"Keep going, Rosie." He tugged her forward.

The corridor was short, angling right just ahead. The sound of heavy footsteps seemed to be coming from everywhere.

"Stop!"

Rosie looked back and saw two guards. Big men with weapons drawn.

"In here." Pip pushed open a door and they ran through, slamming it behind as the guards reached them. Pip turned the lock, but it was flimsy and the men kicked it, rocking it in its frame.

They were in a dorm. Three bunks lined the walls on either side.

"The bathroom." Pip ran to a door. The white tiled room connected to another dorm, exactly like the first, and Rosie hobbled after him. He wrenched open the door to the corridor, but the guards were already outside waiting for them.

"Run!" Pip pushed her back towards the bathroom but she got no further than a few steps before big hands yanked her back. She shrieked as her injured ankle twisted.

"Let her go!" Pip shouted and the other guard backhanded him across the face. Pip hit the metal bunk face first. He dropped to the floor, blood running from a split above his eye.

"Pip!" Rosie yelled but her cries were drowned by a sudden enormous boom. The whole room lurched and the guard holding her lost his grip as they were flung to the floor. Rosie sprawled, stunned, facedown as another boom came. The floor shuddered and she rolled out of the way just in time, as a bunk bed toppled over, narrowly missing her.

"Rosie!" Pip was shouting, but she could barely hear him over the sound of a siren.

The ground shook again and the guard who had been getting to his feet fell against the fallen bunk, his face smashing into the metal. He groaned and lay still.

"Rosie, you okay?" Pip crawled towards her, blood streaking his cheek.

"Look out!" she cried as a guard lunged for him.

Pip turned, lashed out, and got the guard in the groin. The man fell to his knees with an agonised howl. Pip grabbed the gun from his hip holster and released a bolt of energy into his shoulder. The guard was flung backwards to the floor.

"Get up!" Pip reached over the bunk to help Rosie to her feet. The siren was still screaming and white dust from the now half-collapsed ceiling filled the air. The guard Pip had shot was lying on the floor moaning.

They stepped over him and stumbled into the corridor. Children and scientists in lab uniforms ran past in ragged groups, all heading one way. No one paid them any attention.

"Was that the selfdestruct?" Rosie shouted over the alarm.

"Can't be – we'd be dead. Take this." Pip shoved a

com into her hand, and she saw he had another one and was listening to it. He must have stolen them from the guards.

"What channel?" Rosie activated it but Pip wasn't listening.

"There was a bomb on level three," he said. "The medibots are evacuating the testing labs."

"Riley?" Relief filled her. "It's got to be him."

"Crazy bastard must have reset the bots by remote." Pip grinned. "Come on." He turned to go down the corridor, heading the opposite way to the crowd.

"Wait," she grabbed his arm, "is that the way back to the lab?"

"No, it goes to Yuang's office."

"Are you nuts?" Rosie held on harder as he tried to turn again. "We have to get my dad and aunt and get out of here."

"After we get those files on Helios." He took her hand but she pulled away.

"Pip, the place is falling down and we don't even have the code key."

"So maybe it's in his office, we—" They flattened themselves against the wall as part of the ceiling came down. Dust filled the air and people were shouting and calling to each other. A group of kids herded by two adults ran around the corner and past them, not even seeing them in the haze of debris.

How many bombs did Riley have? Rosie coughed and swiped at the air trying to clear it.

"I know you're worried about your aunt and dad," Pip said, "but we've got this far and his office is only just along there."

Rosie was torn. Helios had done terrible things — killed so many — but they might not have time to get out. Should she risk sacrificing her own life and her family's for files they might not even find?

"We can't stop them if we're dead, Pip," she said, but she could see in his face that he didn't want to give up the chance to take Helios down.

"I promise we'll go back for them," he said. "But, Rosie, this is our only chance. Remember why your mum died — and my parents?"

That was low.

"Please." He slipped his hand in hers, his grip warm and firm.

He gave her a steadfast look that was supposed to make her trust him but his need for revenge was barely concealed. He wanted to get back at Yuang more than anything else — for lying, for killing his parents. And she understood that — she wanted to punish someone too for what her family had been through — but she didn't think she would go as far as he might. There was no getting around the fact that she needed his help. The Enclave was like a maze, and she wasn't sure how to reach her family or, when she did, how she could get two unconscious people out on her own. Then there was the MalX cure in his blood. Both her dad and aunt were as good as dead without him.

"All right," she said, "but if it goes bad, I'm getting my family — and you're coming with me."

"No problem."

He tightened his grip on her hand. Together they went back into the belly of the Enclave.

The corridors and labs in this section appeared deserted but they kept to service accessways and out of the main corridors in case any grunts were around. They had no idea where Yuang was and Rosie just hoped he'd forgotten about them. Listening to the coms didn't help. The grunts weren't talking much and some of it was in a kind of code. Rosie wished desperately there was some way she could contact Riley — if it was him bombing the Enclave. Wait. The coms. She swore under her breath and Pip glanced at her.

"What?"

"I can't believe I didn't think of it," she said. "Riley has a com."

She began trying to tune in the frequency with one hand as they headed up another corridor.

"The grunts might pick it up," Pip said.

"What else can we do? If Riley doesn't know we're still here, he might just go straight on to blowing this part up."

"I thought he wanted to stop the place exploding."

"Yeah, well, maybe he can't get to the selfdestruct, or – I don't know."

Rosie was too distracted trying to find the frequency to worry about that. "Here." She got it and spoke urgently into the com. "Riley, it's me. Are you there?"

For a moment there was nothing but fuzzing air then a grainy image of Riley flickered on. "Rosie?" He looked like hell.

"Yes!" She threw a triumphant look at Pip.

"You're alive," Riley said.

"Yes, and so are Dad and Aunt Essie. Is it you setting off the bombs?"

"Three of them I–" Riley suddenly cut off to look behind him. Rosie heard a series of sharp thuds. "Keep ... com ... open!" Riley shouted, and abruptly the screen went blank.

CHAPTER 39

Riley ran for his life. The guards who'd been tracking him thundered down the corridor firing pulse blasts. Luckily, the small grenade he'd planted went off just in time to intercept them. The explosion threw the guards backwards, smashing down a wall and blocking him from view. All of the guards were crack shots, courtesy of their bio implants, and he'd already caught a blast across his arm. Without the nano cell replicators he'd shot himself full of in one of the labs, he'd most likely be dead. He could still feel the remnants of his injury from the crash in the pod and it was slowing him down more than he liked. But at least Rosie was alive – and apparently free. She was one tough kid, he had to give her that. He crashed through a door into a stairwell and took the stairs three at a time. He reached a landing, then switched the com back on. Thank God she was still there.

"Rosie." He waited a second then saw her face, bruised and definitely scared, but stubborn.

"Riley, are you okay?"

"Don't worry about me. Where are you?" She hesitated and he quickly added, "Just tell me, the guards are too busy with me to waste time going after you."

"We're on our way to find those files," she said.

We. She had to mean Pip, and his suspicion was confirmed as the boy's face came into view beside hers. But there wasn't time to argue the point.

"And your dad and Essie, you said they're alive?"

"Yes, but they're not in a good way." Her face pinched fractionally. "Yuang infected them with the MalX."

Riley was shocked that even Yuang would go that far.

"But I think Pip can cure them," she said.

"What?" Had he heard that right?

"Turns out I'm immune, boss," Pip said, pressing close to Rosie to see him. "I can cure them with an infusion." Pip's gaze held a challenge and for a moment he felt a crack of sympathy for the boy slide in through his anger at him. What had Helios done to the kid? But time was way too short to explore this.

"Forget the files, Rosie," he said. "I can go after those. Just get your family and get out."

"But we're right here." Pip's tone was angry. "Yuang's office is just down the hall."

"The selfdestruct is already set." Riley struggled not to raise his voice. He could hear footsteps below.

Rosie looked scared. "How long?"

"It's an hour," Pip said before he could. "Maybe less. How long has it been on?"

"Five minutes or so," Riley said.

"Can you stop it?" Rosie asked.

He didn't want to lie to her. "I don't know," he said reluctantly.

"Where are you?" Pip said.

"Near level one." Riley knew what Pip was thinking. He was closer to the control room and Rosie and Pip were definitely much closer to Yuang's office. There wasn't enough time for him to try to turn off the selfdestruct then go to Yuang's office to search for the files – especially if he couldn't turn off the selfdestruct, which was very likely.

"We're wasting time, boss." Pip's use of the term "boss" was far from respectful and Riley had to control his anger. The damn kid was right.

"Rosie," he said. "Five minutes, that's all you spend, okay?"

"What about you?"

"Don't wait for me," he said. "I'll provide as much distraction as I can. You get your family. And Pip," he held the boy's unfriendly stare, "you get her out."

Rosie looked annoyed but he ignored her. If he got out of this, he had a feeling Rosie was going to be the kind of ally he needed – regardless of her age. And right now she needed Pip's help.

"I already promised her I would." Pip's gaze was icy, but the hand he put on Rosie's shoulder made him slightly more confident.

"I'm going to blast a hole in level one then put a call out to Yuang and try to get to the control room," he said. "Make sure he's nowhere near you."

"Be careful, Riley." Rosie's expression was worried and scared.

He switched the com off and slammed the door to level two open, then kept on going up towards level one. Hopefully, the guards would check level two before they followed him. As he went, he pulled an explosive from his pocket. It was the last of the lot he'd pilfered from the Enclave's store. He was sorry for any guards left below that would be trapped when he blew the exits, but if he couldn't shut off the selfdestruct, it wouldn't matter anyway. He reached level one and ran out into the massive cold store of bodies and set the explosive to take out the door and lift, then sprinted away.

Time to entice Yuang to try to stop him.

———◆———

Rosie shoved the com in her pocket and glanced at Pip. Level one was where his parents' bodies were.

"Don't look at me like that. I know what you're thinking."

"Sorry for caring." Rosie winced as she came down too hard on her injured ankle.

"They're dead," he said harshly. "It's just their bodies in there now, not them." He looked angry after seeing Riley. Angry at the world.

"Yuang's office is down here." He turned left towards a plain white door and pulled the gun from his waistband.

"Pip ..." Rosie eyed the weapon.

"It's all right. He won't be in there. He'll be after Riley."

He was probably right, but still Rosie watched anxiously as he punched a set of numbers into the keypad.

The room was empty. A large desk dominated the

area and behind it a floor to ceiling shelf, the contents scattered across the floor by the blasts.

Pip went to the desk and began opening the drawers. "He might have left the code key in here somewhere – if he hasn't destroyed it."

"Why would he do that?"

"Who knows why that bastard does anything."

Rosie tried a cabinet against the wall, aware of the time ticking away. The cupboard wasn't locked. Inside the shelves held only files and assorted boxes. She pulled out one of the boxes and opened it: tags, more files and electronic keys. She read the top of a file – *Dome six, storage*. She kept looking. Most of the boxes were filled with the same sort of things: records, memos, notes on security and other administrative junk.

Pip was rummaging around in the detritus on the floor without success, and anxiety ate away at her as she removed all the files and boxes.

A dull boom echoed, vibrating the floor. They paused and stared at each other. That was level one.

"How much time do we have left?" Rosie began flinging more files on the floor.

"About half an hour. We spend three more minutes here." The muscles across Pip's back flexed with tension as he turned away from her.

Rosie dropped to her knees. At the back of the

cupboard was a small square metal box and on the lid the Helios symbol. It looked similar to the box she'd found by the river. She pulled it out. It was almost the same except that it opened with a simple clasp.

Fingers trembling, she flipped the lock. Her heart sank when she saw what was inside.

Nothing but pendants like the one Riley had given her that she wore around her neck.

She sifted the small green discs through her fingers. All of them had the Helios symbol engraved on one side. She dropped them one by one back into the box.

"Find something?" Pip had come up behind her.

"No," she said, looking at the last green disc.

"They're like the one Riley gave you." He squatted down beside her and picked one up. "You know, now I think of it I might have seen the scientists using one of these in a handheld of some kind."

"What?" She stared at him then back at the pendant, turning it over in her hand.

There was no triangle on the reverse side of the one in her hand. Her breath quickened and she pulled the pendant out from under her shirt, comparing it to the other, running a finger over the sharply etched triangle on her pendant.

"What did you see them using it in?"

"Don't know." He looked around at the clutter.

Stooping, he picked up a small, square palm com. "Something like this." He handed it to her.

Rosie inspected it. There was a screen and keypad on the front and on the side a small slot. Perhaps just the right size for the pendant. She slipped the pendant on its chain over her head and tried to push it in. It went in smoothly and the screen activated.

"It's a storage disc," she said.

Lists of files were scrolling across the screen.

Genesis 1, Lab variation.

Genesis 1, Subjects k to m.

Genesis 1, Shore files.

"Look!" She turned it so Pip could see it. "It's got to be what Riley was looking for. It's here."

Rosie felt elated and then almost immediately angry. All this time, they'd had it. They didn't even need to be here.

"Christ," Pip said quietly. He crouched beside her and took it out of her hands. "There's stuff in here about everything. Check this out." He turned the screen towards her. There was a small capture of two scientists and two children, a girl and a boy. The boy looked familiar.

"Riley and his family," she whispered.

"Come on, we gotta go." Pip helped her to her feet. Rosie put the pendant back around her neck and the com into her pocket. Pip found a white long-sleeved collared shirt in a cupboard.

"Better than nothing," He buttoned it halfway, shoved the guard's weapon into the waistband of his pants and they headed out the door.

CHAPTER 40

The corridors were still empty and the signs of hurried leaving and destruction were everywhere. Tables were overturned in the refectory, files scattered across the floors of offices, and when they reached the dome with the labs, they saw broken glass and medibots toppled over by the force of the blasts. They weren't far from the exits now and from somewhere ahead came the faint sounds of vehicles, raised voices and, less distant, people running and doors slamming.

Rosie tried to raise Riley on the com again to tell him what they'd found but got only static. As they neared the room where Rosie's family was, an insistent low-pitched bell began to ring and a calm mechanical female voice echoed throughout the Enclave.

Evacuation protocol one. Time to detonation: forty minutes.

They looked at each other in panic and began to move faster.

"Guess that answers one question," Pip said.

"But why is that on now?" Rosie spoke through her teeth as every step shot pain through her ankle.

"Yuang probably disabled the announcement when he activated it and Riley's turned it back on."

"It's a message," Rosie said. "To let us know he couldn't stop it. His com must be busted."

"Or something could be interfering with the signal."

Rosie hoped it was the latter but when she tried again to reach him she didn't even get static. Both her legs were aching and starting to become unsteady with fatigue. She thought the blows Pip had caught from the grunts had to be bothering him as well, but they kept going in silence now. Time was not on their side.

They reached the lab where her family had been and Rosie hobbled ahead of Pip.

"Rosie, wait!" he hissed a low warning but she ignored him.

She was afraid they wouldn't be there, her anxiety giving her a burst of energy and robbing her of caution when she needed it most.

She activated the door and rushed in. Relief overwhelmed her as she saw they were still there, but as she reached the sealed bubble and began undoing the flaps, a low voice spoke from behind.

"I was wondering how long I would have to wait."

She spun around. Yuang was sitting on a chair near one of the lab stations, his legs crossed casually, wearing an indigo-coloured suit. His smile held a trace of mockery. "Hello, Miss Black. Where's young Pip?"

Rosie just stared at him, frozen.

"Well?" he prompted.

She didn't answer and tried not to look back at the door. Pip had stopped in the entrance and a slim cupboard was blocking Yuang's view so he hadn't seen him. Oblivious, Yuang shook his head with a playful frown and got up. "You're not very talkative, Miss Black. Is he playing the hero? Gone to help Shore?"

She swallowed. "Yes, he has."

Yuang looked disappointed and moved towards her. "You're a terrible liar, Rosie. You're going to have to learn to do better." He reached into his jacket and drew out a small black pulse gun. He pointed it at her middle and she heard the subtle whine of it powering up. "It's time for you to consider your options, child. Helios has room for smart girls like you but we can't have you telling stories about us. Even without proof."

Rosie stopped breathing. Yuang's dark eyes were calm, regretful even, but there was a terrible hardness there as well. He would pull the trigger – he might not be happy about it, but he would do it.

"I can't–" Fear made her voice a whimper and she coughed, tried again. "You want me to join Helios?"

"If you want to save Riley's life and your own – yes."

Was he saying his grunts had caught Riley, or was he just trying to scare her? She glared at him, terrified but furious as well. How was Yuang always one step ahead of them?

Yuang brandished a com in his other hand. "One word and he's free. It's up to you, Miss Black. Otherwise ..." He lifted the gun until it was aimed at her head.

She wanted to scream. As if he would let Riley go, even if he did have him. There was no way out. They had the information. They had Pip to cure her family and now Yuang was stopping it all. The detonation alarm was ringing louder, almost in time with her pulse.

"You'll never let him go," she said.

Yuang sighed and he looked at her with pity. "Don't make me do this, Rosie."

"I'm not making you!" Her voice rose to a shout and she watched his finger tighten on the trigger.

"One more–" He didn't finish as he suddenly sensed Pip behind him. He whirled around but Pip already had his gun raised. Rosie glimpsed Pip's face; his eyes were dark blue and glittering with contempt and a kind of madness. He didn't speak but, with mouth set and a shaking hand, he shot Yuang point-blank in the chest.

The force of the pulse shuddered through Yuang's body and flung him backwards. He fell to the floor, his gun still clenched in his hand, a smoking hole in his chest. He hadn't made a sound as he died but for a sudden intake of breath.

Pip stood over him, shaking, the gun still held high in his outstretched hand. Yuang's face held an expression of angry surprise and the stench of burnt flesh filled the room. It turned Rosie's stomach. The automated voice echoed through the corridors again.

Time to detonation: twenty-five minutes.

"We have to go." Pip's face was empty, pale.

Rosie could only nod. She turned around and pushed open the plastic bubble that held her aunt and dad. She was moving like she wasn't really in her body, like a bot, not really human. The alarm clanged louder.

She went to her dad first. His eyes were closed and his skin covered in the red rash of the MalX, but he was breathing. And he smelled sweet and that almost knocked her to her knees. It was what happened to people with the MalX not long before they died. It was a reaction in the blood and sweat. Her mum had smelled like that. Memory crashed over her like a wave and Rosie began to shake. Not now, she thought desperately and forced herself to keep it together.

She disconnected the drip and peeled the tiny pods from his head as fast as she could. Pip was doing the same for Aunt Essie.

"We need to get your aunt awake," he said. "She's not as bad as your dad. Look for adrenaline."

He was crashing around in the stationary medi units beside the bed. She turned to the unit by her side.

"Is this it?" She held up a syringe sealed in opaque mediplast.

"Give it here." Pip snatched it from her hand. His movements were jerky, unsteady. He punched the needle into her aunt's neck.

It worked fast.

Aunt Essie stirred and opened her eyes. "Pipsqueak?"

Rosie rushed to her side to help her sit up. "Aunt Essie, we've got to get out. Riley couldn't stop the selfdestruct." She was babbling but her aunt seemed to understand.

Her gaze took in Rosie's dad, then Pip, then the rash on her own bared legs, but all she said was, "How long have we got?"

"About twenty minutes," Rosie said.

She swung her legs off the bed and to the floor, wincing. She was only wearing a singlet and underwear, but didn't seem to notice. Then she saw Yuang's body. Her eyes went from Rosie to Pip and the gun shoved back in his waistband. Her mouth hardened slightly but without comment she stepped towards Rosie's dad.

"Can we wake him as well?"

"No more adrenaline," Pip said. He was already kicking the bed's wheels down, rocking the frame.

"You okay to run?" Aunt Essie looked at Rosie's ankle. Rosie realised she had stopped noticing the pain.

"Yes."

"Come on." Pip pushed the bed towards the opening in the plastic.

"No, you lead," Aunt Essie said and grabbed one side of it, motioning for Rosie to take the other. Pip didn't argue. He jogged ahead and Rosie and her aunt followed, rolling the bed past Yuang's corpse and out into the corridor.

The alarm was louder in the empty hall and they pushed the bed as fast as they could towards the airlocks. Long, frightening creaking sounds were coming up through the structure of the Enclave, like a great metal beast seeking to rise – or fall apart – and every so often a dull crash could be heard and the floor would shake beneath them. Riley's bombs must have caused more damage than he'd thought.

The pain in Rosie's ankle returned with a vengeance.

She gritted her teeth against the pain and leaned as much as she could on the bed without slowing it down. She worried about Riley. Was he still alive?

Pip had pulled the gun out again and a few metres ahead she saw an outer airlock.

She tried the com again.

Her aunt was watching her. "Riley?" she said. Her voice sounded weaker than normal.

"He was in the lower levels." Rosie didn't need to see Aunt Essie's face to know what she thought about his chances of getting out.

The com spat loud static.

"Riley, come in," Rosie spoke into the com, leaving the view screen off for maximum power. "Riley."

Hope surged as a faint voice answered. "Rosie?"

"Riley!" she shouted, catching her aunt's eye. "Where are you?"

"M ... n ... lev ..." The signal was breaking up, but Rosie tried anyway.

"Riley. We're getting out – all of us. We have the files."

She could only pray he'd heard as the com erupted with loud static and then the sound of sharp cracks.

"Gunshots," her aunt said, her voice strained with the effort of pushing the bed.

"Riley!" Rosie yelled into the com.

"Greenhouse. Go." His voice suddenly came through clear then the com went dark.

"Where's the greenhouse?" Rosie called to Pip.

"The other side. Too far. It's above ground though."

Rosie looked at Aunt Essie. There were shadows under her eyes and her skin had a yellow tinge to it. She was fading already, the adrenaline being eaten up by the virus.

"He's on his own, kid," her aunt said.

Pip was at the airlock. He checked a cabinet on the wall beside it.

"No breathers." His expression was bleak and Rosie wanted to scream at the injustice of it. Where the hell would they go?

CHAPTER 41

"Rovers?" She practically spat the word at him.

"Not here," Pip said. "This is a service way. I thought there'd be less chance of grunts ..." he trailed off, his dismay at his decision plain.

Time to detonation: fifteen minutes. The calm mechanical voice spoke again.

"We gotta take our chances." Aunt Essie pushed the bed towards the airlock. "Open–"

"Wait," Rosie grabbed the bed and said to Pip, "How about Yuang's ship?"

"It's probably gone."

"Without Yuang?"

He held her gaze for a heartbeat.

"If it's there, I can fly it," Aunt Essie said.

Pip opened the lock. Rosie couldn't even have guessed what time it was, but it was dark and very cold and almost immediately her muscles tensed up against the chill. They shoved the bed out as fast as they could. Rosie kept a hand on her dad's arm and felt the thinness of the air as she took a breath. Not enough oxygen. The alarm was spiking loudly and the bed jerked and rattled over the edge of a slab of crete. The wheels dug in as it hit a dirt path but her dad didn't move. He was so still.

"Which way?" she asked Pip. A garden surrounded the Enclave and the looming mass of the Tharsis Mountains rose behind, cutting a shadow across the starred sky.

"This way." Pip threw Rosie's dad over his shoulder and led them up the path towards a light tower on a hill.

It took them nearly ten minutes to reach the landing platform. It was on the top of a hill surrounded by garden and the *Cosmic Mariner* sat, dark and closed up, above them. They were all suffering badly from the lack of oxygen, as well as fatigue. Pip was sweating and making an awful wheezing sound and Rosie had to support Aunt Essie up the last steep incline to the doors of the launch pad lift. Pip punched it open and they crowded inside. There was a blessed blast of regulated air as the lift sealed and shot them up to the hatch.

The ship came to life around them as they entered the cargo hold. Lights flickered on as automatic sensors picked up their movement. The *Cosmic Mariner* was enormous. Seven decks, ion core, solar flare shielded, a long-distance cruiser. Strapped in web locks on either side of the hold were cases of supplies and a central runway led to a deck access lift at the far end.

The pilot and crew were nowhere to be seen. Maybe they were stuck inside. Maybe they were dead. Rosie didn't care; she was already beginning to worry that Aunt Essie wasn't going to be able to fly the ship. She was way too pale and Rosie had to help her onto a nearby crate. She groaned softly and slumped back against the hull, her eyelids fluttering closed.

"Aunt Essie?" She didn't respond and Rosie looked with fear at Pip as he laid her dad down on the floor next to her. Her dad looked even worse and despair began to work its way up her throat.

"He's breathing," Pip said, but the expression on his face wasn't hopeful. Rosie began to bargain with the universe. *Please, just let them live, get us out of here. I'll do anything.* She kneeled down by her dad and gently touched his cheek. He was so feverish. So still.

"Rosie!" Pip's voice was sharp enough to jolt her out of her misery. He grabbed her aunt's shoulders as she slipped downwards. "Can you fly the ship?"

Rosie tore her gaze away from her dad's face.

"I don't think so. We've got to—"

"You've got to what?" a voice said. They both started as a tall black woman emerged from the launch pad lift.

"Nerita," Pip said under his breath. "Ship's pilot."

"What you doing here, Feral?" she said to Pip and strode towards them. "I'm surprised you're still alive." She had a large gun in her hand.

"Just trying to get off this rock, same as you," Pip answered.

"Uh-huh." She eyed Rosie with her aunt and dad. "And who are your new friends? Haven't I seen them before?"

"We need to get out of here," Rosie said quickly. "The Enclave's going to explode in about five minutes."

Nerita seemed almost amused. "I'd say it's more like three." She went to a panel on the hull and swiped her hand over a bio reader. "And it's lucky for you I'm here. You'd be going nowhere without these." She waggled her fingers with a smile like a shark's grin. Bio dent ignition. Rosie got a sick feeling in her gut. If she'd tried to start the ship, she would have been fried in the chair.

Nerita looked like she knew what Rosie was thinking.

"Let's get one thing straight," she said. "The way I see it, Yuang's gone missing and that means the ship's mine." She tapped the gun.

"Yuang's dead," Pip said in a low voice.

"Really?" She gave him a speculative look. "Didn't think you had it in you, Pip."

Pip tensed and moved as if to step towards her.

Rosie jumped to her feet and grabbed his arm before he did something stupid. "It doesn't matter now," she said quickly. "We've got to go."

"Agreed," Nerita said. "Pip, toss the weapon."

His mouth thinned, but he pulled the gun from his waistband and threw it towards her. She caught it and looked at Rosie. "I saw you fly that pod – you're coming to the bridge with me. Pip, close the airlock, then stay here and do what I say. Move it." She motioned for Rosie to go ahead of her to the lift.

"You sit there." Nerita tossed the guns down on a console and pushed Rosie towards a podium beside her pilot's chair on the bridge.

"You know your charts?" she snapped.

"Sure." Rosie climbed into the copilot chair and placed her palm on the bio interface on the armrest. Immediately, an opaque holo screen rose from the centre of the podium and a slim panel unpacked itself like an elegant spider stretching out two legs on either side of her. It lit up with touch-sensitive controls for navigation and ship functions. Rosie stared in apprehension. She barely knew what half of the controls did.

Nerita already had her bio link helmet on and an orb of amber-coloured holo controls sprang up around her.

"Good, we'll–" Nerita stopped as a deep boom came from outside and the ship rocked hard. Rosie stifled a scream and gripped the armrests of her chair.

"View screen up," Nerita said calmly. The front panel of the bridge became transparent revealing the Enclave slowly breaking apart from beneath. God, Riley. Rosie hoped desperately that he'd got out.

"Disengage the pad lift," Nerita said.

Rosie swiped a trembling finger across the holo image of the lift on her screen, detaching it, and the ship rumbled as Nerita powered it up.

"Strap in, this could be bumpy." She spoke through the ship-wide com so Pip would hear it. "Lift-off in ten seconds."

A massive boom sounded again. The ship shuddered and the patch of trees they'd come through a few minutes ago suddenly disappeared as a hole opened up beneath them. But the abyss in the planet's crust didn't stop there. It kept caving in and the *Cosmic Mariner* began leaning towards it as the ground became unstable.

"Fire the ion thrusters," Nerita said.

Panicking, Rosie stared at the panel. Where were they? Lights and control options were everywhere. The ship was oscillating with its gathering power then it suddenly pitched forward almost twenty degrees. The blackness of the massive hole rushed towards them.

"Rosie, top left!" Nerita shouted.

She found them and punched the control harder than necessary. A savage roaring came and she saw the fierce blue flare of the thrusters burn across the ground outside. The ship pulled back from the hole.

"Lift-off," Nerita said and the *Cosmic Mariner* rose into the air just as the ground crumbled beneath them.

Rosie held tight to her seat as the ship clawed its way out of the atmosphere at full power, leaving a blast ring behind.

"Good job, kid." Nerita grinned at her through the amber light.

Rosie couldn't smile back. She activated the ground scanner so she could see Mars as they left. One by one the domes of the Enclave fell into the crater. The selfdestruct system had done its work well, destroying the complex in a thunder of dust and explosion. Streaming away from it in trails of light were the rovers filled with the test subjects the medibots had herded out. She hoped Riley was one of those tiny dots of life running to the Genesis colony.

CHAPTER 42

"Still not awake?" Aunt Essie looked over Rosie's shoulder.

She stared at her dad's pale sleeping face. Pip had injected Aunt Essie with his blood not long after they'd left Mars and then her dad as well. Twelve hours later, her aunt had been recovering quickly, her rash almost gone, and her dad ... the rash was receding but he still lay so still, as if he'd never open his eyes again.

"Don't worry," Aunt Essie said. "He'll come round. Look at me. Good as new."

Rosie studied her aunt's pale skin and the dark circles under her eyes. "You walk like an old lady."

"I am an old lady. Not everything can be fixed as fast as your ankle." Aunt Essie gently prodded Rosie's recently nano-repaired foot. "I'm hungry. Let's find some food."

Aunt Essie drew her towards the door of the medilab and Rosie put an arm around her waist, feeling how frail she was. Her aunt had always been small but she had never thought of her as weak. But at least she was alive. Almost losing everyone she cared for had made Rosie more than grateful for having them in any kind of shape. She just wished she knew if Riley had made it too.

They entered the galley and she felt a flutter of nerves as she saw Pip leaning against the food lockers eating fruit out of a plaspak. Since coming on the ship he'd barely spoken to anyone and spent most his time holed up in one of the cabins. He wasn't the same boy she'd met. There was no swagger, no jokes. Instead, there was silence and a look on his face that warned her not to even try to ask him if he was okay.

"Pipsqueak," her aunt said, "think you can spare some food for us?"

"There's plenty there." He brushed past them, heading for the door.

"Pip, wait," Rosie said.

He paused at the doorway, half turning to her.

"We have to figure out how we're going to get these files onto the news waves." She pulled the pendant out of her shirt.

"I don't know any news wavers." He leaned against the doorframe.

"We don't need a waver; we just need a comnet that Helios can't track," Aunt Essie said. "Did Riley have any or know of one?"

Pip poked the fork into his fruit. "The Game Pit."

"What's that?" Rosie frowned.

He shrugged. "A place I used to go. They're under the radar, zero surveillance zone."

"Is that possible?" Rosie looked at her aunt.

"With blocking tech – I guess."

Pip pushed off the doorway and started walking away. "I'll take you there when we land," he said over his shoulder.

Rosie tried to follow but Aunt Essie stopped her. "Leave him." She drew her to one of the tables. Rosie wanted to ignore her aunt's advice but nothing in Pip's expression had invited her to follow. She sat down feeling depressed.

"Let it go, kid." Aunt Essie hobbled to the lockers and opened the cold store. "If he wants to talk, he'll talk."

"Guess I don't have a choice."

Her aunt sighed. "He killed someone, hon. That's not an easy thing to deal with – especially not the first time."

Rosie stared at her hands remembering the dreadful

look of pain and anger on Pip's face when he'd pulled the trigger. "I'm just—" She let out a short breath. "He did it because of me, to stop Yuang. I feel like he's blaming me or something."

"He might be, or maybe he's numb, or scared. Killing does strange things to people." Her aunt sat next to her with a bowl of soy protein chilli.

"You want some?"

Rosie shook her head. "How did it affect you?" she said.

Aunt Essie paused and didn't answer right away. "I was a soldier, Rosie. It was my job. And mostly it was from a distance."

"But when it wasn't?"

She dipped the spoon in her bowl, watching it. "It's terrible and you never forget it, just like you'll always carry seeing Yuang die with you. But that's how it should be. It shouldn't be easy."

"Perhaps you should talk to him," Rosie said.

Aunt Essie shook her head. "I don't think so. I'm not good at that sort of thing. And I doubt he'd want to hear anything from me. He might have helped me out before but we're not exactly buddies."

"What do you mean, helped you out?" Rosie said.

"Here on the ship. He convinced Yuang not to kill me, then helped me get loose so I could stop the weapons from locking onto the pod when you were getting away." She half smiled. "The dumb ass took on one of those guards he calls grunts and almost got buzzed as well when I shot the guy with his own pulse gun."

Rosie slowly said, "That's why we weren't hit."

"Yeah, well. Yuang wasn't too impressed with him for that."

So that was where the bruises on Pip's face had come from. Had he helped out of guilt or something else? And did it really matter now? She wanted to talk to him but he was avoiding her. Since they'd left the Enclave he'd been acting like there was nothing between them, like he hadn't kissed her. She'd gone to the bridge last night to help Nerita and he'd been there asking, for what must have been the hundredth time by Nerita's expression, if the sensors had picked up anyone following them. He'd left the bridge as soon as he saw Rosie. That had hurt. Clearly, he didn't want to talk to her.

Her aunt sighed and said softly, "Don't hold out your hopes for that one, Rosie. He's messed up. A boy like that ... he'll break your heart."

Rosie didn't reply. She wasn't sure how she felt about Pip but there were bigger things to worry about. Nerita had picked up a news wave an hour ago. It had called the explosion of the Enclave an accident. Helios must still be pulling strings. Rosie didn't know if Helios knew she had the Shore files, but she had to assume that someone would be sent to ensure they wouldn't be talking about anything that happened. The sooner they got the files out in the open, the safer it was going to be for all of them.

A few minutes later the galley com buzzed and Pip's voice came over the speaker. "Rosie, your dad's awake," he said, and the com switched off.

Her aunt looked at her. "Well, at least he told you that," she said.

Pip left the medilab as soon as they arrived, with barely a glance in her direction. Rosie tried to shrug off his coldness and went to her dad's side.

"Rosie." He smiled weakly at her.

"How are you feeling, Dad?" She took the shaking hand he lifted and tried not to show how his frailty scared her.

"I'm okay." He blinked and looked behind her at her aunt. "Ess?"

"Yeah, it's me," said Aunt Essie and took a step closer. "We're on our way back."

"Back?" He frowned.

"Yeah, but don't worry about it. You look like crap.

Do you want some water? Or maybe you should get some more sleep."

He looked confused and Rosie felt her chest tightening up. Didn't he remember anything? She suddenly felt like she had to leave.

"I'll get the water," she said quickly and, avoiding her aunt's gaze, headed out the door again.

Once out in the corridor she walked fast, not even sure which way she was going. She forgot that she was supposed to be getting water. There was a hard ball in her chest. Everything was suddenly too much, too hard, and she felt her control slipping. She stopped and put her hands against the hull, but it didn't help. Her legs felt weak, like they wouldn't support her. She began to shake and sat on the floor against the cold metal wall, trying to suck in air. It didn't help – the tears came anyway. They burst out with a moan of pain that shocked and frightened her. But she couldn't stop. She put her head in her hands and gave in, her whole body trembling as she sobbed so hard she thought she might break apart. It was Nerita who found her there in what felt like an hour later.

The pilot walked up the corridor and stopped nearby. Her expression was bland as she said, "Bad day?"

Rosie wiped her nose with the back of her hand. "Bad week." The storm of tears had abated, leaving her feeling drained and exhausted so she could barely lift her head.

Nerita was silent for a minute then surprised her by squatting down beside her. "I had a bad day once," she said.

Rosie studied her profile. Was Nerita going to tell her that her problems were minuscule compared with other people's?

The pilot turned to her. Her dark eyes skimmed over Rosie's face, giving nothing away.

"Only once?" Rosie said.

Nerita's expression didn't change. "No one only has one." She settled closer to the wall. "I used to have my own ship – a crew of three, a contract with the UEC out on Gliese transporting the exploratory scientists, providing earth to planet support." She brushed a speck of dirt off the knee of her pants. "A trip went sour. A few UEC guard personnel took a dislike to each other and we had a hull breach between Gliese D and E. Too far to make it to the atmo and too much damage. She broke up. I managed to get into one of the spacewalk units and so did one of my crew, but the others didn't make it." Nerita eyed Rosie. "One of them was my lover, the other my friend. I didn't give a damn about the UEC lot – they brought it on themselves – but the other one, who I got into a suit, was my sister and it didn't have a full tank of air. We were stuck in the black for five hours before they got to us and by then it was too late. I watched her die. Never have forgotten how scared she looked. That was a bad day and my first scar, the one you get on your heart that never heals because someone you loved died due to your actions — or lack of." Her voice was low, almost emotionless, but not quite. "But you go on, don't you?"

"How long ago did it happen?" Rosie said.

"Twelve years." She rose. "I'm going to see if your aunt wants to view the bridge, maybe copilot."

She walked off. Rosie sat for a while longer thinking about what she'd said. It was a terrible story and it made her think of Juli. She didn't like to think about her, or imagine what her last minutes might have been like, but Nerita's words about watching her sister die brought an awful image to her mind of Juli being engulfed in the fire of the explosion at her house. What had she thought of in those last moments? It made Rosie sad all over again for her friend. She couldn't face going back to see her dad — yet another person she loved who was suffering because of this mess.

She got up and went back to the galley instead.

Pip was there, sitting at a table staring at an empty cup. She stopped in the doorway.

"Need something?" he said without turning around.

She almost went out again, but where else was there

to go? She pulled out a chair and sat down opposite him. He didn't move, just kept staring at the cup.

"Pip," she said.

"What?"

"Are you okay?"

His lips twisted in a sardonic smile and he watched his thumb tapping on the tabletop. "Yeah, sure, just perfect, how about you?"

"You look like you haven't slept since we got on the ship."

He stopped tapping and said in a low voice, "Rosie, I don't want to talk about it."

She hesitated. "It might help."

"There's nothing to help."

"Pip—"

"I don't feel anything, Rosie," he interrupted her.

His gaze was so bleak, so empty it frightened her. "Nothing?" she said.

He shook his head. "I'm glad he's dead."

She reached for his hand but he pulled away.

"Don't." He pushed back his chair. "Just leave it, Rosie." He walked out without looking back.

CHAPTER 43

They made planetfall forty hours later, just after midnight Earth time. Nerita uploaded a virus to the Senate's surveillance system to scramble their whereabouts and landed at a derelict spaceport at the edge of the Old City.

"That virus should last about twenty minutes." Nerita glanced at Rosie in the copilot chair. "Should be enough time for you and me to get clear."

"I hope so." Rosie pushed off the chair restraints. "Thanks for helping us."

"Hey, you did me a favour with the copiloting, but if you feel that way," she slid a finger over a halo control, with a half smile on her face, "maybe I'll see you in the skies one day and you can repay me then.

Now hurry up, time's wasting."

Rosie ran to the lift.

"Good luck," Nerita called. Rosie looked back but she was already deep into programming her navigation to leave.

Aunt Essie was waiting for her at the airlock in the cargo bay with Pip and her dad. Her dad was leaning on her aunt and didn't look too great. He barely seemed aware of where they were, as if he was sleepwalking, but he smiled when he saw her. Together they got him off the ship and took shelter behind the crumbling wall of an old building as the *Cosmic Mariner* took off in a wave of heat and ion flare. Rosie watched as the brightness of it faded, leaving them with only faint moonlight to illuminate the surroundings.

"This way," Pip said and headed towards a path through the trees.

Rosie could only just make him out by the white shirt. She put an arm around her dad and followed, Aunt Essie close behind. Everything smelled damp and the trees were grey shadows, the ground patterned with moonlight. The scrub was sparse and she could hear something rustling in the low bushes. Rats probably. She prayed there were no mosquitoes, but then wondered: had Pip's blood made her immune to the MalX?

"How far is it to the Game Pit?" Aunt Essie asked Pip.

"It's on the edge of the Western Rim, through the Banks."

"How long will it take to get there?" Rosie said.

Pip glanced back at her struggling along with her dad. "Too long if he doesn't move faster." He went to her dad's other side and put his arm around him. "Lean on me," he said, and her dad obeyed, staring vacantly ahead at the ground.

"Thanks," Rosie said softly, but Pip didn't reply. Her aunt took her hand and gave it a squeeze and they followed them along the narrow path.

They reached the back streets of the Banks and moved through the quiet apartment blocks, keeping to the darker shadows. The shouts of drunks and the thump of music from the riverside bars and gaming hubs carried in the warm humid air. Occasionally, they passed a street humpy with refugees inside, high on euphorics or worse, but they were too wasted to notice them.

It was slow going as they had to check around every corner, but their caution paid off when, just inside the boundary of the Rim, they spotted a grunt.

Tall, muscular and dressed all in black, he was skulking around a row of closed shops.

"Get back," Pip whispered. He drew back from the corner of the alley and flattened himself and her dad as best he could against the wall next to Rosie.

She took her dad's arm, keeping him close as he glanced vaguely down at her, his eyes half closed. Thank goodness he wasn't speaking.

Her heart thudding, she asked Pip, "How far is it to the Game Pit now?"

"A few blocks." His blue eyes seemed almost black in the dim light. "But the best way is across this street."

"We need a distraction," Aunt Essie said.

With a leap of fear, Rosie gripped her arm. "You can't."

"Don't worry." Aunt Essie smiled. "I'm not up to tackling him."

Pip staggered as Rosie's dad suddenly drooped, his eyes fluttering and closing, his knees bowing.

"Dad," Rosie whispered, shaking his arm. "Dad, wake up."

He swung his head towards her, his eyes opening a little. "Rosie?" he said softly.

Pip was straining to keep him upright, staring at her to do something.

"Yeah, Dad, it's me," she whispered, terrified the grunt would hear them. "Stand up, can you?"

He smiled at her, one hand lifting to brush her face. "Okay." With obvious effort he shuffled upwards, leaning on Pip who was breathing hard.

"We'll have to go back," Aunt Essie said.

"But don't we need to get across this street?" Rosie asked Pip.

"We'll just have to double back. What's the grunt doing?"

Rosie peeped out around the corner. "I can't see him," she said.

Pip swore softly and then they all froze as the sound of a booted footstep echoed in the silent street. It was way too close for comfort.

Pip got a tight hold on her dad and pushed Rosie ahead of him back down the alley, gesturing wildly to her to get moving. As quietly as they could, they all sped back the way they had come, keeping close to the wall. Rosie prayed the grunt didn't look down the alley; there was no way he could miss them.

"Left," Pip whispered at the end of the alley and they headed along the back of the building, moving parallel to the street where the grunt had been.

Rosie wondered if he had any idea where they were or if Helios had just sent out a heap of scouts all over the city looking for them.

They walked in fearful silence for another ten minutes before they risked heading back towards the main street. Rosie went ahead and checked the corner. "Looks clear," she said, but Pip didn't look confident.

"He's probably lying low. They've got heat sensor

equipment. Short range but he could have clocked us already and is just waiting for the right place to jump us." Getting her aunt to hold onto her dad, Pip leaned in close and looked out into the street. The collar of his shirt brushed her face and Rosie felt his warmth and smelled his faint dusty scent. It seemed like he stayed there longer than he needed to.

"Guess we got no choice," he said, looking at her.

For a moment it felt like it had back at the Enclave, like they were in this together. But she was wrong; there was still a vast distance in his eyes. She turned away.

"Is Dad okay?" she whispered to her aunt.

"I think so but it'd be better if he was lying down."

"Let's go then." Pip put an arm around his waist and they moved across the street as quickly as they could. Rosie kept thinking she heard soft footsteps behind them but whenever she turned around could see nothing. She hoped it was just her imagination.

The Game Pit's entrance was almost hidden by the jutting wall of a building, and the only people in there were the barman and a drunk who glanced at them through bleary eyes then went back to his drink.

The Pit was dark, dirty and smelled like rancid oil. The barman gave Pip a curt nod as they came in the door. Rosie watched Pip lower her dad onto a grubby lounge in an alcove and noticed the dark circles under his eyes and the weary slope of his shoulders; he was exhausted.

"Thanks," she said as Pip straightened, wincing slightly.

"No worries," he said and went over to talk to the barman, gesturing at the ancient-looking comnet in the far corner.

Aunt Essie went to the bathroom while Rosie checked on her dad. He didn't look good; he was much too pale and although the rash was fading, he was still feverish.

Pip came back. "Mack said you can use the com whenever you want."

"He a friend of yours?"

"Not particularly, but he hates Helios."

Well that was something. Rosie took the pendant from her shirt and took a step towards the com but Pip grabbed her arm.

"Rosie, wait. Your dad …"

She spun around. His eyes were closed and he'd become even paler. Fear shot through her. "Dad?" He was barely breathing. "Dad?" she repeated, her voice rising in panic.

"Rosie." Pip was behind her. "I think …"

But he didn't have time to finish. The door suddenly opened and the grunt appeared at the top of the stairs.

"Hey, Feral." He called to Pip. "Long time no see." He rested one large hand on the butt of a gun at his waist and from the corner of her eye, Rosie saw the barman reach below the counter. Faster than she could track, the grunt had the gun out and aimed at him.

"Don't be stupid, barfly," he said. "I don't like cleaning messes."

The barman froze and backed away, his hands up.

Rosie stared at the enormous man. Pip had been right; he'd just been waiting to corner them. She scanned the room, wondering if there was another way out.

The grunt chuckled as he came down the stairs. The drunk didn't appear to have even noticed he was there.

"Got yourself a girlfriend," the grunt said. "Help you escape, did she? Poor little Pippie can't get away on his own."

"At least I can get girls," Pip said. "What was your last girlfriend, a nice little pleasure bot?"

The grunt grinned nastily at him. "Always the smart-arse. Don't you remember what that got you?"

"Yeah, I remember. Real brave, aren't you?"

Rosie saw the fear in Pip's eyes. But there was also something else: a desperation to do something stupid.

"Don't," she whispered, but his attention was only on the grunt. "Good dog, come to take me back, eh?" he said and the man lost his smile. "Yuang's dead, you know," Pip continued. "Whose leg you going to hump now?"

Rosie's heart plummeted and at the same moment, Aunt Essie came out of the bathroom. The door banged behind her and Pip ran towards the grunt.

"No!" Rosie screamed as the grunt raised his weapon but the barman shot first. A loud concussive boom hit the grunt full in the chest and knocked him to the floor.

"Rosie!" Her aunt lunged for her, pushing her to the floor as Pip picked up the grunt's weapon and ran for the door.

But the grunt wasn't dead. He was getting up and Rosie watched in terrified amazement as he stumbled to his knees, then to his feet and took off after Pip. Within moments the door had slammed shut behind them. Trembling, she got to her feet.

The barman was still holding his gun. "Goddamn Helios maggots," he said. "You okay?"

She nodded. "How did he get up?"

Her aunt answered. "Body armour and enhancers, not much stops those."

Rosie felt sick with fear for Pip. Could he outrun the grunt? Would he?

Aunt Essie was the first to get herself together. "Where there's one, there's more. We've got to get those files into that com. Pip can only buy us so much time."

Yes, the files. Rosie went to the comnet and pulled the pendant off. Pushing the disc into the slot, she dialled in to find the news agency addresses. She found five and just hoped someone would believe her. She uploaded the files along with a note that it was not a hoax and to check the real story behind the Enclave explosion.

"Done?" Aunt Essie was crouched next to her dad, worry clear on her face.

"Done."

"Good," her aunt said. "Now call the medivacs. Your dad's unconscious."

The hoppers arrived within ten minutes and within twenty Rosie's dad was on life support. He'd stopped breathing in the hopper and the only thing keeping him alive was a machine. The MalX was back in his veins.

Rosie stared at him through the clear glass of the intensive care MalX unit at the hospital. She was too shocked to cry and barely felt her aunt's hand on her shoulder. She pressed a hand to the glass, listening to the muffled beeps of the monitors. It felt like everything, all of their sacrifices, Juli's death, Riley, Pip — had been for nothing. She was going to lose him anyway.

"Come on," Aunt Essie said gently. "Let's get something to eat."

Rosie let herself be guided to a seat in the small waiting room. She watched listlessly while her aunt swiped a card through the credit reader of a food dispenser.

"No drinks," her aunt said.

"I saw a machine down the hall." She got up. "I'll go."

It was very quiet on the MalX floor. You had to give the parasite that, Rosie thought; it didn't make a fuss, just got on with it. Knock them out, suck them dry. There was no one around as she approached the drink dispenser and pushed the buttons for two waters. She was crouching down to retrieve them when a pair of grubby boots appeared in her vision.

"Rosie?"

She looked up and slowly got to her feet. Pip. Her pulse sped up, relief flooding her. His shirt was ripped and covered in dirt and there were scratches on his face, but he was alive. She wanted to fling her arms around him, and he took a step back from her as if sensing her intention.

"What happened?" she said.

His eyes were huge and he looked down at his hand. She saw a smear of blood on his knuckle. "I couldn't go back, Rosie." His voice cracked. "I couldn't let him take me."

He'd killed the grunt. She felt cold. What was Helios turning him into? She wanted to tell him it was all right but the words wouldn't come.

"It's not your fault," she said. But he shook his head and met her eyes and she was shocked to see tears and such a depth of pain, of desperation. He was broken. She stepped forward and threw her arms around his neck, clutching him tight. After a second's hesitation he hugged her back, lifting her off the floor and holding on so tight, she could barely breathe. He buried his face in her shoulder and she held him while he cried. She wasn't sure how long they stayed like that, but eventually he loosened his grip. No one passed them while they were locked together. Maybe they saw their grief and went another way, Rosie wasn't sure, but for that at least, she was glad. She knew he hated her seeing him break down like that, much less anyone else.

They shared her water when he'd recovered enough and Rosie said, "How did you know we were here?"

"I saw the hoppers." He looked incredibly weary now and he reached into the side pocket of his pants. "I came to give you this." It was a full bag of blood. "Maybe he didn't get enough last time."

Rosie hesitated. "I can't just hand them a bag of blood. The doctors will want to know why and where it came from. And then *they* might find out."

"It's worth the risk."

She felt torn. She didn't want to put Pip at risk, but he was right and it might be her dad's only chance. She took the bag.

"Anyway, I won't be hanging around," he said.

Her heart twisted but she didn't argue. It wasn't safe for him to stay. "So this is it?" she said softly. She hated Helios so much for doing this to them. She was close to tears and an echo of the abandonment she'd felt when her mum died came back to her, like a fist to her stomach.

"Where are you going?" she said.

"It's better if you don't know. And … I'm sorry, about everything, you know."

"Yeah," Rosie said.

They stared at each other. Pip swayed away from her as if to leave, but then he leaned forward and took her face between his hands and kissed her gently. "Bye, Rosie," he whispered against her lips and ran down the corridor.

In the end, Rosie put Pip's blood into her dad herself.

She waited until the night nurses had gone, until there was no one else around, then she hooked up the bag of blood to her dad's drip and her aunt kept watch while it leaked into him.

She didn't know what the doctors would think if he got better but she couldn't think that far ahead. Pip was gone. It felt as though some part of her had been chopped out. Was this what love was? If it was, she didn't know how people survived it. The weariness of the loss felt like it might consume her.

EPILOGUE

For weeks the news waves had been full of reports of a secret lab on Mars. They talked about genetic experiments, the missing Ferals who had been taken as subjects and the most explosive claim of all: that the MalX was no natural disease and had been released by a powerful corporation named Helios. After one webnet picked it up, the rest had followed and it had gone global.

Rosie struggled to find any satisfaction in the victory. The real perpetrators, those unseen puppeteers Yuang had answered to, were nowhere to be found. They were ghosts, too powerful to touch. When she and Riley took down the Enclave, they had only touched a skein of the Helios web and she was sure they were off somewhere, repairing it, making it stronger.

The Genesis colony was closed now, restricted access only. All they'd been left with was news vision of the United Earth Commission and the Senate sending the Elite in to raid offices long since devoid of any connections to those who had vanished. She wondered what Riley would think – if he was still alive. Would he consider it enough that the world now knew his parents had died trying to expose Helios's terrible work? Was it enough that he had managed to save at least some of those people who had been in there?

Rosie knew it was selfish but sometimes she felt it was too high a price to pay.

Had it really been worth Juli's life? Had it been worth Pip disappearing? Had it been worth this?

She stood outside the glass walls of her dad's room looking in, watching the doctors.

"You okay?" Aunt Essie put her arms loosely around her neck and rested her head against hers.

"Not really," she said.

"Yeah, I know," her aunt whispered, and they both fell silent.

In the room the doctor was trying to talk to her dad but Rosie could see that he wasn't making much sense. The hospital staff wanted answers he just couldn't give. This had never happened before in the MalX floor; people were brought here to die, not to recover.

Rosie held tight to Aunt Essie's forearm while they checked and re-checked his vitals. Every so often he'd look at her and she tried to smile, but inside she felt a great gaping hole in her chest.

When he'd finally woken in the early hours of the day before, he'd looked at her and smiled a faint slow smile. It was the first time she'd seen him smile for so long and she almost cried, but then he'd spoken. "Rosie, love, where's your mother?" he'd said.

Then she *had* cried. He thought her mum was still alive. He didn't know what day it was, what year. He didn't remember where they'd been.

The doctor said his mind had fractured, like a switch in his brain had been flipped. Whether it was because of the disease or the stress of everything that had happened, they couldn't say, but they were sending him to a psychiatric care unit. She was going to live with Aunt Essie, permanently, until he recovered. If he recovered.

"Time to go," her aunt said and hugged her briefly. "He needs some sleep." Rosie nodded and wiped a tear from her cheek. "We can come back tomorrow."

"Okay." Rosie waved at her dad and he nodded and raised his hand.

Aunt Essie put an arm around her and led her out.

She'd found them a new apartment on the edge of

Central West. There hadn't been enough room at her old one at Orbitcorp. "A new start," her aunt had said. But Rosie wasn't sure if it was. It felt more like hiding. They weren't sure if Helios would be looking for them or not. It seemed unlikely now they'd put the files out and the Enclave was finished, but even so, few people knew where they lived. They would still be looking for Pip, of that she was certain, and if anyone figured out it was his blood that had cured her dad, they would be coming for her and anyone else who had any connection to him.

"I don't know about you but I could handle the biggest, greasiest bowl of noodles ever," Aunt Essie said as she opened the door of their apartment. "And maybe a glass of vodka. How about you?"

Rosie cast her a sideways glance and put the bag of groceries they'd bought on the way home on the kitchen bench. "I don't think vodka is good for my growth," she said.

"What growth?" Essie locked the door and dumped her bag on the lounge.

But Rosie had stopped listening. On the far side of the bench, just in front of an empty vase, was a smooth green pendant – exactly like the one she wore around her neck – except this one had a set of letters carved roughly into it.

"Aunt Essie," she whispered.

They both just looked at it for a moment.

"Is that from who I think it's from?" her aunt said.

"It has to be." Slowly, Rosie picked it up and traced the R and S with her fingertip. Riley Shore.

"Son of a bitch," Aunt Essie said, "he broke into our apartment."

Rosie almost laughed. Only her aunt would look at it that way. "It's a message," she said. "He made it out."

"God knows how."

For the first time in weeks Rosie felt something that she thought might be hope. Riley was alive.

"This calls for a celebration," Aunt Essie said and got out two glasses and her bottle of vodka. She poured a shot into her glass and filled Rosie's with cordial then raised hers high.

"To the man with more lives than a mangy sewer cat." She grinned.

Later, after her aunt had gone to bed, Rosie took the pendant and strung it on her necklace beside the other one. She stood out on their tiny balcony, holding them both in her hand. The air was cooler fifteen storeys up but she could still feel the waft of heat from the streets below. The lights from Central, the towers and shuttle lines, were like dimming stars, bright but shrouded with humidity. The sounds of the streets rose up to become a hum that penetrated walls and kept going up into space. She looked up at the stars, barely visible against the glow of the city.

The new school year would start soon. She thought about Juli and how she wouldn't be going, how she would never see the constellations again or know how it felt to turn seventeen, never kiss a boy again. Never do anything again. Rosie felt the little ache near her heart that she thought would always be there now; the first scar, Nerita had called it, the scar that never heals.

She tightened her hand around the pendants and thought about Pip and about Riley and all those people he had managed to get out from Helios's clutching greedy hands. Perhaps something good had come from it; some people had lived and, miraculously, Riley was one of them. She hoped then that he didn't want to give up fighting yet, because she felt like she wasn't done with Helios. They had killed her mother, her friend and made Pip into a murderer and an exile – they deserved to pay for it. No, she wasn't ready to give up, not by a long shot.

ABOUT THE AUTHOR

Lara Morgan grew up in the hills outside of Perth, Western Australia but has spent the years since then roaming the world and investigating other hills. She has worked in the arts, at a newspaper and, once, a car wash, but all pale in comparison to being a writer which allows her to work in her pyjamas. She is also the author of a fantasy trilogy called The Twins of Saranthium. The Rosie Black Chronicles is her first series for young adults. She now lives in Geraldton, Western Australia – most of the time. You can visit her online at: www.lara-morgan.com.

ACKNOWLEDGEMENTS

Rosie Black's story has had a bit of help in its journey to the page, and if it wasn't for the following people, it might never have made it.

Isobelle Carmody who was my mentor at the very beginning – in fact even before the story had a proper ending – and who gave me invaluable advice on writing for young adults which I have never forgotten. Amanda Lines, Kathleen Wheeldon and Jackie Gill for reading my manuscript, enthusiasm and unfailing support. Dr Stacy Mader who patiently answered my many and random questions about Mars, space and astrophysics and especially about black holes – although one never appears in the book. To Tim Flannery, whom I have never met, but who wrote a fabulous book on climate change called *The Weather Makers* which partly inspired this story. It must be remembered that any errors in the science are entirely mine and were caused by a glitch in the space–time continuum – or by the fact that I don't have an astrophysics or climatology degree. Thanks also to my fabulous agent Clare Forster as always, to Sarah Foster for loving Rosie and her world, and to Virginia Grant for being such a wonderful editor. And also to Writing WA which partnered me with Isobelle in the first place.

And last, but always first, my husband Grant who makes everything possible.

COMING SOON ...

**THE
ROSIE
BLACK
CHRONICLES**

EQUINOX